Shattered Amethyst

JANE BLYTHE

Acknowledgments

I'd like to thank everyone who played a part in bringing this story to life. Particularly my mom who is always there to share her thoughts and opinions with me. My wonderful cover designer Amy who did an amazing job with this stunning cover. My fabulous editor Lisa for all the hard work she puts into polishing my work. My awesome team, Sophie, Robyn, and Clayr, without your help I'd never be able to run my street team. And my fantastic street team members who help share my books with every share, comment, and like!

And of course a big thank you to all of you, my readers! Without you I wouldn't be living my dreams of sharing the stories in my head with the world!

CHAPTER One

July 28th
3:33 A.M.

Amethyst Hatcher struggled against the man holding her.

Tears blurred her vision, and her pulse thundered in her ears, making all other sounds fade into the background.

As she was dragged up a flight of stairs, she lost her footing and stumbled, crashing hard into the wooden steps and sending pain zinging up through her knees. Her captor didn't pause, didn't ask if she was okay—she knew it was because he didn't care—he just yanked her back to her feet and continued on.

They zigzagged down so many hallways that Amethyst started to feel dizzy.

She wanted out of this house.

She wanted to go ...

Her mind wanted to finish that sentence as she wanted to go home, but given what had happened tonight, she never wanted to set foot in that place again.

She felt so lost.

So out of control.

Like she was spinning wildly in a tornado, being thrown left and right, over and over again, until she no longer knew which way was up.

What was going to happen to her?

Well, she knew what was going to happen to her, she just didn't know the specifics, and that was driving her crazy. The more questions her mind conjured up the more she started to panic.

Her parents had sold her and her four sisters.

Sold them.

Sold.

That just seemed so crazy.

People didn't sell other people.

Parents didn't sell their kids because they wanted some quick cash.

Except they did.

"This one is going to be moved quickly, so get her showered, dressed, hair and makeup done, and then ready and waiting downstairs."

The words jarred her out of her own head, and she immediately panicked. She didn't want to take a shower and get dressed up for some evil creep. She wasn't. She just flat out wasn't.

"Get off me," she screeched and flung her entire body weight sideways.

Since she hadn't done anything so far to give him an indication that she was going to do anything but exactly what he wanted, he was surprised by her sudden outburst and lost his hold on her.

Amethyst didn't hesitate.

She ran.

She had no idea where she was going, and she didn't care, she just wanted out of here. She wanted to find Diamond, Ruby, Sapphire, and Emerald, and she wanted all of them to get away, start new lives somewhere where no one would ever find them. They were teenagers, they had their whole lives ahead of them, she wasn't going to spend it as some sicko's sex slave.

Just as she found the stairs, they found her.

With a growl, she was grabbed from behind and shoved against the wall. "That was not amusing." The man shook her so hard her neck snapped painfully, then began to drag her back the way they had come.

It was no use.

She was never getting away from this place.

There were too many men here, and they were all armed on top of being more than twice her size.

This was her life now, she had to find a way to accept it.

Only she didn't want to.

How on earth was she supposed to accept something this big? This horrific? Instead of enjoying her summer vacation and being excited to start her senior year of high school like most seventeen-year-old girls, now she had to find a way to deal with being thrown to the wolves, she would be beaten, raped, tortured.

The more she thought, the more she began to cry until she was sobbing hysterically.

She couldn't so this.

She couldn't.

She couldn't.

She couldn't.

She would rather her parents had killed her and her sisters than do this to them. How much must they hate her? They had made the conscious decision to hunt down human traffickers, contact them, make a deal with them, and bring them to the house where they had dragged them out of their beds in the middle of the night. While those men had touched her and her sisters, her parents had just sat there and done nothing to stop it. All they cared about was the money. Even if they thought they could go through with this, surely the reality of watching their daughters be restrained and taken away would have been enough to snap them back to reality.

But it hadn't.

She was shoved into a bathroom, and without even speaking to her, the man who had been leading her through the house began to strip her clothes off her.

Amethyst squealed and tried to move away from him, but he shoved her up against a wall, yanked the t-shirt she had put on when she went to bed last night over her head, then snapped the metal collar that had been clamped around her neck to a hook on the wall.

"Stop it," she screamed as his hands reached for her shorts. With one hand she tried to cover her breasts while her other shoved at his.

The man didn't even bother to respond to her.

He just grabbed her hand and snapped it into another metal cuff, then did the same to her other hand, leaving her locked in place and unable to fight back.

Tears streamed down her face.

She was standing here half-naked in front of a stranger. She was mortified, terrified, and wished the earth would just open up and swallow her.

But it didn't.

Because life didn't work that way.

Sometimes life just didn't care if it was being unfair to you and messing with you, it just laughed in your face and threw a whole load of awful at you.

The man removed her shorts, then turned the shower on, sending freezing water splashing down on her. Amethyst shivered and tried to cringe away from the cold, but there was nowhere for her to go. Slowly the water warmed up, and the man grabbed a bottle of shampoo and proceeded to wash her hair and then her body.

She squeezed her eyes closed and tried to pretend she wasn't really here.

She failed.

The whole time she kept expecting him to take things from simply bathing her to something sexual, but it never happened.

He just cleaned her.

When he was done, he shut off the water and grabbed a towel, drying her off, then finally he addressed her. "Can you behave yourself or do we need to go with the chains?"

Amethyst just stared.

She was falling quickly into a foggy state of shock.

Her brain couldn't comprehend what was happening, so it was just checking out.

Taking her silence as consent, the man released her from all of the metal cuffs, including the one around her neck that had been put on her back at her house. He led her into a bedroom and gestured to a woman who was waiting there. The woman came over to her and Amethyst just stared wide-eyed at her. She didn't know what to expect. Her life had been turned upside down in just a couple of hours, and she could feel herself starting to shut down. It seemed to be the only way to cope. Her life was never going to be the same, and she had to start finding a way to deal with it. Maybe that way was just to hide away inside her own head.

The woman put her in a blue dress that matched her eyes, and then put a little makeup on her and blow-dried her hair.

"You look beautiful," the woman told her when she was done. "He's going to be so pleased with you. You know your job is to make him happy. To do whatever he tells you to do, no matter whether you want to or not." The woman—who when Amethyst looked closer was really barely older than she was—leaned in closer and lowered her voice so that no one else would overhear. "It's easier just to give in. Do what they want, try to let your mind go blank, block it out. Fighting back only makes it worse."

Those words lit a spark inside her.

The fire grew quickly.

She wasn't going to sit back and let these men own her.

They might have bought her body, but there wasn't enough money in the world to buy her mind.

It was hers, and it was the only thing she had left.

She was a seventeen-year-old girl, she couldn't physically do anything to change her fate—at least not yet. But that didn't mean she had to accept it.

And she wouldn't.

She would *never* accept that this was going to be how she spent the rest of her life.

She was going to fight whoever had bought her every single day, at every single opportunity. She was going to be angry because it was so much better than being afraid. She was going to focus all her energy on hating this man because she would rather die trying to escape than submit like this girl had.

They thought they had all the power, but they were wrong.

As long as she was still in control of her mind and how she chose to react to this hell she had been thrown into, then *she* held the real power.

~

6:42 A.M.

She was hot.

And uncomfortable.

Amethyst squirmed, trying to find a spot on the leather armchair she had been told to sit in that wasn't already hot and damp with her sweat.

They'd been sitting here for over an hour. She knew that because there was a grandfather clock over in the corner of the parlor that ticked loudly, and with nothing else to do, she was sitting there watching the minutes tick by.

That fire that had ignited inside her was still there, and it was still burning brightly. She didn't know who the man who was coming here to collect her—buy her—was, and she didn't know exactly what he was going to do, both of those things should have her quaking in fear, sobbing, and hysterical.

But it turned out she wasn't a normal girl.

Because she wasn't afraid, she was just angry.

A kind of burning, flaming anger that consumed her. Amethyst wanted to take it out on the men who were standing guard at the door, talking to each other, casting her only the occasional glance, but she also wanted to save it up for the man who was coming for her.

As far as she was concerned, he was the real villain. These men here, this was just a business to them, they didn't care about hurting people because they loved the money, but the man who was going to buy her, he was pure evil. He was buying her because he wanted to have someone who was completely at his mercy. Someone that he could hurt and abuse because it was fun for him. That had to be the very definition of evil.

She was going to go and live with the devil, but he had no idea what he was getting. He probably thought he was going to be given some meek and terrified into submission little girl who would do what he told her to do because she was too scared to do otherwise.

But he wasn't.

He was getting a tornado of a teen who was going to fight him at every turn, and if she could, then one day she would kill him.

"It's time, let's go," one of the men said as he came over to her, nudging her bare shoulder with his gun.

Waiting to stage her first attack, Amethyst stood and followed where she was led. The dress she had been given to wear was blue cotton with lace, it was short, barely covering her backside. Her hair had been left to flow freely down her back and was way too hot on the back of her neck. Although she liked her hair long, in the summer she usually kept it up in a ponytail or braided, or even in a bun, basically anything to stop her thick blonde locks from overheating her, but today her hairstyle wasn't up to her.

She was led through the foyer and then out into the sunshine. It wasn't even seven in the morning, but already it was sticky and hot, and she wanted to head right back into the house just for the air conditioning. A limousine was parked in front of her, but Amethyst turned around and surveyed the house.

Were her sisters still here, or had they already been sold?

Were they still alive?

What was happening to them right now?

Part of her wanted to go running off through the house, opening every door and checking every room until she found them. But she knew that if she tried she wouldn't get very far, there were armed men swarming all over the place, she wouldn't even make it up the staircase before one of them was on her.

Amethyst was about to decide if it was worth the risk, even just to know that her sisters were still alive when a shadow fell over her.

She turned around and saw a bulky man looking down at her. He was dressed in an expensive-looking suit that he surely must be sweltering in, his hair was slicked down with way too much gel, and he had thick glasses that made his eyes look enormous. She met his gaze squarely and glared, letting her hatred shine through.

"She's untrained," the man said to the guards.

"She was only brought in a couple of hours ago," one of the guards explained. "But she's seventeen, and she meets your appearance criteria. You need a replacement for your collection quickly, here she is, ready and waiting to be taken."

"She *is* a virgin?" the man in the suit asked.

"She is."

"Stop talking about me like I'm not here," Amethyst snapped. She had only spent seconds in this man's company, and she already loathed him.

"She is unruly and disrespectful." The man frowned at her disapprovingly like she was a recalcitrant child.

"You'll be able to train her just the way you want to," one of the guards countered. "Sometimes, that's half the fun."

"I suppose it is," suit man agreed.

Anger bubbled inside her. She wasn't some puppy that needed to be trained, she was a human being, she wasn't anyone's property, she didn't belong to him. He might have paid money for her, but that didn't make her his. She was never going to be his, even if he took her away today and made her do things she didn't want to do, he could never get his wicked claws into her mind.

"So is the deal on or off, because I'm sure people will be jumping out of their chairs to bid on this one," the guard said.

"She *is* beautiful, and she *does* fit my requirements, and I suppose I am in a pinch, beggars can't be choosers, so fine, the deal is still on."

"As soon as the money shows up in the account, you can take her."

Sick of them talking about her like she was some piece of real estate, Amethyst swung her leg out and rammed it into the shin of the man who was closest to her.

For a second no one knew what to do.

They hadn't been expecting her to do that and she couldn't help but give them a smug smile.

Slowly the suit man's surprised face morphed into a smile. It wasn't a pretty smile, but instead of scaring her she took it as a challenge and once again met his gaze.

"You think you've got it made don't you?" he smirked. "You think that they aren't going to lay a hand on you because you're the merchandise and they can't tarnish it before selling it. But, guess what, little lady, you're sold now. You're mine, and I don't have a problem with blemishes, in fact, I love them."

With that, he wrapped a hand around her wrist and yanked her forward, then locking his gaze onto hers, he snapped her thumb backward. Amethyst didn't need to be a doctor to know that he had both broken the bones and yanked the joint out of place.

The pain was intense, and she had to battle not to faint, but she didn't break their staring competition. He could break her bones all he wanted, but he would never break her spirit. He could break every bone in her body if he wanted to and all it would do would make her hate him more.

"I like you," the suited man said, reaching out to touch her cheek.

Amethyst turned her head, snapping her teeth at him, but he apparently anticipated her reaction and quickly snatched his hand back before she could make contact.

"You're a tough one, I'll give you that. What's your name?"

She could refuse to tell him, but he no doubt knew anyway, and she didn't want him to interpret her silence as intimidation. "Amethyst."

"That's pretty, almost as pretty as you are. We're going to have a lot of fun together, you and I, already I know that every day with you is going to be a challenge and I have to say, I'm intrigued by the prospect. You're different than the other girls in my collection."

He kept talking about his collection, but she didn't really know what that meant. What kind of collection? That it was girls like her was a given. That he liked blonde seventeen-year-olds also seemed to be a part of it, but she wondered what more there was to it.

"What's your name?" she asked. If she was going to have to go off with this man then she deserved to know his name.

"It's Nikos," he replied, and she had to admit she was a little surprised, she hadn't really expected him to answer.

"Money is in the account," one of the guards announced.

"Which means our journey together has just begun," Nikos told her. He still held her wrist, and he began to lead her toward the limo.

The reality of her situation should be settling heavily on her shoulders.

Instead, she had found a weird sort of freedom.

Amethyst realized that she no longer cared if she lived or died. She may be only seventeen, with her whole life ahead of her, the world at her feet, but her universe had just spun into a whole different solar system, and in this place she felt no fear. She would taunt the beast, she would gamble with her life, she would throw caution to the wind.

She was walking into battle knowing that she might not survive.

∼

7:03 A.M.

This was it.

From here on out she was on her own.

Amethyst had watched the mansion through the back of the limousine until it disappeared from sight. She might never see her sisters again, never know their fate. For all she knew they might already be gone, or even dead.

She hated that she didn't know.

Just because she knew that their futures held the same torment that her own did, didn't make this any easier. She wanted them to be okay, she wanted them to be safe, she wanted them to be free.

But she didn't have the power to change their fate.

She didn't even have the power to change her own.

What she did have was the power to make sure that Nikos regretted every day that he had bought her.

She would teach him a lesson.

With the mansion faded out of sight, Amethyst focused her attention on Nikos. Her thumb still throbbed with a burning pulsing beat, her head swam a little, and her stomach was still nauseous, but she didn't have time to worry about that. She was sure this wasn't going to be the first time he put his hands on her, and she was sure that there was a lot worse to come.

"You have questions, child? Then ask them," Nikos said, setting down his newspaper to look at her.

"How rich are you?" Amethyst asked.

"Wealthier than you can imagine."

"Why do you use your money to buy people? I'm not a possession, why do you think you can own me?"

"I'm rich. I can do whatever I want, and I like to spend my money on my collections."

"You keep saying that, but I don't know what your collection is," she said, frustrated.

"You'll see what my collection is when we get to my house."

Amethyst sighed in annoyance. "Why say I can ask you questions if you're not really going to give me any answers?"

"Watch your mouth, child," he warned. "I'm tolerating your impetuousness because it amuses me, but don't push too hard or you won't like the outcome."

"I'm not afraid of you," she shot back, glaring at the man. She had been surprised that he had brought her into the limo with him, she'd thought that he would have her bound and put in the trunk or something, but she was going to make the most of this time with him because she didn't know when she would get another opportunity to ask him questions.

"I know, it's very intriguing, I've never met a girl like you before," he smiled at her, and although it wasn't a warm smile it did convey that he was being honest, he really was intrigued with her.

"Is there any way I can convince you to let me go?"

"I think you know the answer to that."

"I had to ask," she said, shrugging. She had known the answer, but it seemed stupid not to ask. You never got what you wanted if you never asked for it.

"Well, you've had your one pass at asking, and now I don't want to hear any more about it. This is your life now, and while I know you think that you're this tough, strong fighter, I *am* your owner now, and you *will* do whatever I want, I *will* have my fun with you, and there's nothing you can do to stop it from happening."

He said like his word was God's.

Just because he was rich didn't mean that he was above the law.

"I hate you," she said, not angrily, not in the heat of passion, not brimming with emotion, but simply as the fact that it was. "You are an evil, despicable, deplorable, horrid—"

His hand darted out and wrapped around her throat, shoving her back against the leather seat and squeezing so tightly it cut off her air supply.

He wanted her to be afraid.

He wanted her to claw at his hand, silently begging for her next breath of air.

But she didn't care about her next breath of air.

She didn't care if he killed her, it was how this was all going to end anyway, so there was no point in fighting it.

If it ended right here and now, then she would save herself a whole boatload of pain and misery.

Ending things really didn't seem so bad in comparison.

Amethyst closed her eyes and let her mind go blank. She prayed that her sisters were given such a mercifully quick release of their suffering. Either they were rescued and went home to live out the rest of their lives, or they would die before anyone hurt them too badly.

Abruptly, the pressure around her neck disappeared.

Woozy, she opened her eyes to find him watching her, his head cocked to the side, a quizzical and yet irritated look on his face. He was annoyed that she wasn't quivering in her boots, terrified of him. Nikos got off on her fear, and she wasn't giving him his personal drug of choice.

Smugly, she curved her lips up into a smile, it seemed he wasn't the one in control despite the obvious imbalance of power.

"You'll crack, child," he huffed. "You think because you withstood one broken bone that you're invincible, you haven't seen nothing yet."

"I guess we'll see," Amethyst said. She already knew how this was going to work out, he had nothing to lose. If he ended up pushing too far and killing her then he would simply go and buy another girl. But she had everything to lose. This wasn't about her physical life, she knew that she didn't have many days left on this earth, this was about her soul, this was about her maintaining control of the only part of herself that was left—her mind. She wasn't going to submit to him no matter what he did.

"Oh, we'll see," he said ominously.

She just rolled her eyes and turned her attention to the window. They drove for a long time, through the city where she watched people starting their days, happy and content that their lives were their own. They didn't know how good they had it.

She hadn't known how good she'd had it before today.

If she had known that yesterday was going to be the last day she would ever get to live a normal life then there were so many things she would have done differently. She would have worried less about her grades and the girls at school who liked to exclude her. She would have spent more time hanging out with her sisters, and when Peter Grady had asked her to the junior prom, she would have gone all the way with him when he'd snuck her into his parents' restaurant after it closed.

Amethyst had a lot of regrets about the first seventeen years of her life, but she wasn't going to have any regrets about the future. She was going to fight, she was going to accept every broken bone, and every bruise and cut, as a badge of honor. A sign that she was a fighter, that she was stronger than she had ever realized.

The limousine turned into a long, tree-lined driveway, a large gothic mansion appeared in the distance.

This was it.

They were here.

There was no going back, there was no use reminiscing about the past or dreaming about the future.

This was her life now, and she had to do what she had to do.

"Home sweet home," Nikos said as the limo came to a stop in front of the house.

While she didn't have the same sentiments about the house as Nikos did, Amethyst was glad to be here. She wanted to know what she was up against.

The limo door was opened, and Nikos climbed out, and reluctantly she followed, as much as she wanted to know exactly what her future held, she couldn't deny the ominous feeling that covered the house. This was a place of evil, of pain and suffering, and misery.

"Let's go, child," Nikos said, taking her hand—her injured hand— and squeezing it tightly.

Since she knew he was only doing it to punish her, to try to break her, she sucked her bottom lip in and clamped her teeth down, determined not to cry or groan, or do anything that let him know how badly it hurt.

Nikos led her through the front door and into a foyer that was every bit as large and grand as the one in the house where she had been taken just a few hours ago.

Had it really only been a few hours?

How could your life change so dramatically in just a few hours?

Her old life felt like it was a million years ago.

The house appeared to be even bigger than the human traffickers' one, and by the time they weaved through several corridors and stopped outside a closed door Amethyst was lost, she didn't think she could find her way back to the front door even if she had the opportunity.

"Without further ado," Nikos said as he swung the door open, revealing the room where he kept his collection.

His *collection* was girls.

All blondes.

She didn't have to ask to know that each of the girls was a different age. *Every* age all the way up to seventeen. This was why he had needed a seventeen-year-old because otherwise, his collection wasn't complete. There were seventeen cages, braced from the ceiling and hanging a good four or five feet off the floor, inside each was a girl, the youngest was to her left, seven cages ran along that wall, then another three against the far wall, then seven along the right wall, the closest on her right was empty.

That one was hers.

"Still think you're a tough girl?" Nikos asked.

Amethyst just shrugged. "So you collect girls. I knew that already. I just didn't know that you were so sick that you have babies here." Her anger burned strongly. It was a fire inside her that she knew was never going to be doused.

"I'm not sick," the man said, shoving her up against the wall.

"You rape little girls, that makes you sick," she shot back. Amethyst was surprised there was no little voice screaming in her head to keep her mouth shut, that he was going to hurt her worse if she kept provoking him. But her little voice was as furious as she was and was in full agreement.

"I get what I want. Money is power, and despite what you think, child, *I'm* the one with the power. A broken thumb is nothing compared to this." With that, he unzipped his pants, letting his thing spring free, and then shoved her panties down her hips.

She knew what he wanted.

He wanted her to fight.

To scream and cry and try her best to get away from him, to stop him from doing what he was about to do.

So Amethyst did the opposite.

She didn't resist as he fumbled in his pathetic excitement to do this, she just waited for the perfect opportunity.

As he tried to push himself inside her body, he crushed his mouth against hers, and she sunk her teeth down into his lip, satisfied when she tasted blood.

Nikos growled angrily.

His cheeks went bright red, and Amethyst couldn't help but smile.

That was a win for her as far as she was concerned. She knew that sooner or later he was going to end up raping her, but not today. Today she had her very first victory.

A fist swung toward her.

Connected with the side of the head.

And knocked her out.

CHAPTER *Two*

Seven Months Later

February 17th
1:27 P.M.

Today was the day.

Her eighteenth birthday.

It should be a fun day. She was an adult now, old enough to vote, and she should be just a couple of months away from graduating high school. But instead of having a party with her friends, or a date with a boyfriend, or even dinner with her family, there would be none of that —no presents, no balloons, no happy birthday wishes, instead today was the day of her death.

Nikos hadn't been shy about telling her what would happen today. He had taunted her with it several times over the last seven months. That was the way his collection worked, he didn't want adults. He kept the girls for as long as he could, either until they died from malnutrition, an infection, or just from the trauma of what Nikos inflicted on them.

But if they did survive all the way to adulthood, then he killed them on their eighteenth birthdays.

Amethyst suspected that he was going to kill her at the exact second that she had been born, eighteen years ago today. He surely knew what time that was because it was her parents that had sold her, and the human traffickers had obviously intended to send her straight here, being that she wasn't even in that house for more than a couple of hours.

So she was sitting in her cage waiting.

That had been her life for the last seven months.

Sitting in her cage waiting.

Occasionally she would talk to one of the other girls, offer any comfort she could to one of the little ones who regularly broke down, but other than that, it was just waiting for Nikos to make his daily visits. He liked to come in and look at them, walking up and down the room gazing at each of them in turn as though they really were just a collection. Then there were the days when he would open up their cages, pull them out, and have his way with them.

Had he raped her?

Yes, he had.

Did she hate that it had happened?

Yes, she did.

Had it been hard to deal with and process?

Yes, it had.

Did it make her hate him more?

Absolutely.

Amethyst hadn't known that it was possible to hate another human being this intensely. She'd never really hated anyone before. Her sisters drove her crazy, but she loved them, she fought with her friends sometimes, but they remained her friends. She'd broken up with boyfriends, including one who had cheated, and she'd thought that she hated him, but she had been wrong.

This was hatred.

What she felt for Nikos outweighed even her anger at what her parents had done to her and her sisters.

Her sisters who might very well already be dead.

She guessed she would find out in just a little over an hour.

Eighteen years ago today, she had been born at two forty-two in the afternoon. She had come out first, her twin sister, Ruby, thirteen minutes later. Now Ruby might already be dead, Diamond, Sapphire, and Emerald too.

That had been the hardest thing these last few months, not knowing about her sisters. She didn't care about herself, she didn't care what happened to her, every broken bone, every burn, every time he had cut her because he enjoyed watching her bleed, she would gladly live through it all over and over again if it meant that her sisters were some-place safe.

But she had no way of finding out, and no way to make it happen.

She was getting edgy. She knew what was coming and she just wanted to get it over and done with. She wasn't afraid of dying, it was surely better than being stuck in this cage until she was old, but she was a little nervous about how he was going to do it. She would never admit it to Nikos, and when he came in here to get her she wouldn't let him see, but she *was* anxious. There were a lot of horrible ways to die, and she already knew that Nikos liked to hurt people, her in particular.

As if on cue, the door to the huge room opened, and Nikos strode inside.

She knew immediately that she'd been right, and that this was it because he had two armed men with him. Usually, the only people who came in here were Nikos, and the woman whose job it was to feed and change the little ones, and bring them their meals.

"Happy birthday," Nikos beamed as he walked right up to her cage.

"Thank you," she shot back, determined that she would die and Nikos would never even know that she was a little scared. No, not scared, just apprehensive.

"A brat to the very end," he said, unlocking the cage. "But as hard as you've fought me these last few months, the ending is still going to be the same. It was *always* going to be the same. You think that you're beating me by fighting me at every turn, but I still get what I want."

"Not really," she said as she swung her legs over the edge of the cage and jumped down, ignoring the hand he held out to help her. "You want me quivering and shaking, you want me to fear you, but I don't. I know that you're going to kill me and I'm not afraid. So really, I win."

From the way he grabbed her arm, his fingers digging into her muscles, she knew that she had gotten to him again.

Another point in her favor.

"Let's go," he growled, dragging her along with him.

The two armed men walked with them through the house, and all the way out to the very same limousine that had brought her here seven months ago. Again, he guided her inside, and again she was surprised that he hadn't tied her up and thrown her in the trunk.

This time they didn't talk as they drove. She had nothing left to say, and she assumed Nikos didn't either. Despite what he said, they both knew that even though he was going to end her life, he hadn't gotten from her what he wanted.

Proud of herself, Amethyst let herself relax. She had fought so hard these last few months, she had been constantly on edge, constantly fighting against Nikos, and it was nice to know that soon she would find peace.

Soon it would all be over.

This wasn't how she had expected her life to turn out. She'd thought she would graduate high school, go to college, find a job that she loved, maybe fall in love and get married, or travel the world, or care for abandoned animals, or something that would give her life a meaning and a purpose. Instead, she was going to die on her eighteenth birthday.

The limo pulled to a stop in a large abandoned lot. As the door opened and Nikos shoved her out, she could see the highway, but it was too far away for anyone to notice what was happening to her.

There would be no savior, no knight in shining armor riding in on a white horse, no police officers swooping in to save her.

She was going to die, right here, surrounded by other discarded trash, because that was what Nikos thought of her. She was merely a possession that had outlived its use-by date, so he was throwing her away.

He stood before her, a knife in his hand, and she lifted her gaze so that she met his eyes. If he was going to kill her, then he was going to look her in the eye while he did it.

Briefly, she considered making a run for it, try to make it to the road, but she knew she would get no more than a couple of steps before one of Nikos' men shot her. This battle she had been fighting since Nikos bought her was between the two of them, and this is the way it should end.

Nikos looked down at her, opened his mouth as though he were going to say something, but then apparently thought better of it and snapped it closed.

Lifting his hand, in one smooth motion, he sliced the knife across her neck.

Immediately her blood began to gush out.

Amethyst wobbled and fell to her knees, before quickly collapsing onto her stomach.

Her hands pressed to the wound, but it was instinct rather than any real attempt to save herself.

Footsteps indicated that Nikos and his men were leaving, and a moment later she heard the limo's engine rev to life, and the car drove off.

Leaving her alone.

Alone to die.

The world began to dim, go a little gray around the edges.

Her blood pooled beneath her, it was warm, and warmed her a little as she started to get cold.

She let her eyes fall closed as she waited for the end to come.

Just as the blackness closed in on her, she felt hands touching her.

Was Nikos back?

Why would he come back for her?

Had he decided she was going to be the one piece of his collection he couldn't let go of?

As she was rolled over onto her back, Amethyst blinked open her heavy eyelids and was surprised when she saw that the face above her belonged to a stranger.

Someone had found her.

Something was pressed to her neck in what she knew was a vain attempt to stem the flow of blood.

Someone might have found her, but it was already too late.

She was dying.

~

6:48 P.M.

Someone was crying.

That was the first thing that registered in Amethyst's mind.

She felt groggy, not altogether sure where she was.

Pain.

She was in pain.

Her neck ached badly, but she couldn't seem to remember why.

The weeping continued, and she wondered who it was and why they were crying.

Although part of her wanted to float away back into the peaceful slumber from which she had awakened, there was another part of her that felt it was important that she wake up and find out who was crying.

Gathering her strength, Amethyst ever so slowly cracked her eyes open. She found herself in a crisp white hospital room, she was tucked into the bed, a needle in her arm was attached to a clear plastic tube that led to a bag that was filled with fluid. Lifting one of her hands, she touched it to her neck and found that it was heavily bandaged.

Her neck.

The knife.

Nikos.

Nikos had slashed her neck and left her for dead in an abandoned lot near the highway, but someone had somehow stumbled upon her. She had thought that it was too late, but obviously, she had been wrong.

Somehow she had survived.

Somehow she was still alive.

It defied all the odds, but it was what it was.

The crying.

Her sister.

Amethyst snapped her head to the side, barely noticing the resulting tearing pain in her wound. Her little sister, Sapphire, was curled up in a chair beside her bed, her arms were folded, and her forehead rested on them, she was weeping quietly.

"Sapphire," she croaked, reaching out to touch her sister's arm.

Sapphire's head snapped up, her green eyes growing wide when she saw that she was awake.

"Amethyst," she said on a sob, launching herself off the chair and onto the bed, wrapping her arms around her. Sapphire held onto her so tightly that it made the ache in her neck spread throughout her body, but she didn't care. Seven long months of not knowing what had become of her sisters, and now she was lying here holding one of them.

"Are you okay?" she asked Sapphire, she knew what she had just lived through and she knew that her sisters wouldn't have fared any better.

"I'm okay," came the sniffled reply.

She knew that was a lie.

They had just lived through hell, there was no way her little sister could possibly be okay. No way.

"Sapphire," she said gently, taking hold of her sister's shoulders and easing her up so that she was sitting instead of plastered all over her. "Diamond, Ruby, Emerald?"

Fresh tears brimmed in Sapphire's eyes, and she shook her head.

Amethyst's heart dropped.

Her other sisters were all still out there somewhere. At the mercy of a monster much like the one she had somehow managed to escape.

Or they were already dead.

She wasn't really sure which was the better option.

"I thought that you were all dead," Sapphire whispered.

Her sister's eyes were haunted, not like the tough, sassy little sister that she had always known. Is that what she looked like? When people looked at her did she have that dead look in her eyes? It wasn't that she was surprised to see that her sister had changed, that she was no longer the person she had been before, of course it was inevitable, you didn't live through something like they had and come out of it unscathed, but she hated that her little sister was hurting.

"I thought that I was never going to see any of you again, I thought I was going to be the only one who survived," Sapphire added, as tears trickled down her cheeks. That believing she was the only one of them who had walked away alive had clearly been hard on Sapphire.

"Mom and Dad?" Amethyst asked. She hated calling them that because they were hardly her parents. Real parents protected their children, they sacrificed for them, they made tough choices sometimes and did things that their kids may not like or appreciate in the moment, but that was out of love. Her parents had sold her and her four sisters for cold, hard cash. In her mind that revoked their status as parents.

"Are in prison," Sapphire replied. "They lied. They said that armed men broke into our house that night and abducted us. They said that they tried to save us but they couldn't. After I was rescued, I told the cops what really happened, and they arrested them."

"Did it go to court?"

Sapphire nodded.

"Did you have to testify?" The more she learned about what had happened, the more that anger that had been planted inside her seven months ago grew. When she had allowed herself to consider the possibility of being rescued or escaping and returning home, she had thought that the anger would dissipate, but she'd been wrong. It was still there, and while she knew it was early days yet, she didn't think it was ever going to go away.

Sapphire nodded again. With her watery eyes, her pale cheeks, and her long brown hair hanging loose around her shoulders, she looked much younger than her sixteen years. All five of them had birthdays in the same month, Diamond's was the fourth, she and Ruby had been born nearly two months premature on the seventeenth, Sapphire's was the twenty-eighth, and baby of the family Emerald's was the tenth. She couldn't have been lying in this hospital bed for more than a few hours, so it had to still be her birthday, but Sapphire wouldn't turn seventeen for another eleven days. Her sister was so young, and on top of everything that they'd been through, she'd had to testify against their own parents, and she'd had to do it on her own.

Her anger burned.

So brightly that Sapphire actually shrunk away from her.

Deliberately calming herself, Amethyst reached out and brushed a stray lock of hair off her sister's wet cheek. "I'm sorry you had to go through that on your own. Who's been looking after you?"

"Foster care at first," Sapphire told her. "After I was rescued and I told the cops what happened, they arrested Mom and Dad, and there was no one else to look after me. Since I'm only sixteen, they wouldn't let me live on my own, so I had to go into foster care. Aunt Liza and Uncle Tim, when they heard what happened they moved here, and I've been living with them for the last couple of months."

That her beautiful, sweet, headstrong sister had gone into foster care on top of everything else spurred her anger along. She'd always been protective of her family, particularly her younger sisters, and right now those protective instincts were firing into overdrive.

Her parents deserved a whole lot worse than prison.

She wished they could be locked up in a cage for seven months, being raped and tortured just because some guy was rich enough to actually live out his sick, perverted fantasies.

As much as she wanted to rant and rail about the injustices that they had suffered, she knew that wasn't what Sapphire needed right now. Her little sister needed reassurances, she needed to feel like she wasn't alone anymore, that there was someone with her now, someone that actually understood what she had been through. While Amethyst knew that Aunt Liza and Uncle Tim would have taken good care of Sapphire, it wouldn't have been the same.

"Come here," she said, holding out her arms.

"I don't want to hurt you," Sapphire said, pointing to her bandaged neck.

"I don't care, come here," she said again.

Sapphire relented and came into her arms, resting her head on the pillow beside her own. For a long time the two of them just lay there like that, their heads together, their arms around one another.

She was free.

She was alive.

Her life was her own again.

But it didn't feel real.

Too long living like she had for the past several months had changed her. It had twisted her into someone she barely recognized. She was different now, she was angry, at her parents, at Nikos, at whoever had hurt Sapphire, at whoever was holding her sisters prisoner right now. She was angry at the whole world.

Would that anger ever fade?

Amethyst didn't know.

She wasn't sure how she could go back to living her life like she had before because her life had taken a sharp turn in a completely different direction.

She didn't know who she was now.

She was eighteen, an adult, she had been rescued, at least in theory she had her whole life ahead of her and could do whatever she wanted with it, but she didn't know what she wanted, and she didn't know what the future held for her.

Right now, she was a girl who was consumed with anger.

Would she ever be anything else?

CHAPTER

Three

Eleven Years Later

August 21st
12:12 P.M.

It was a gorgeous day.

The kind of lazy summer day that made you wish that summer would never end, and that the blue skies, sunshine, and warmth would last forever.

But it wouldn't.

In just a couple of weeks, summer vacation would be over, and she would be heading back to college.

It wasn't that she didn't want to go, she loved college, she loved her friends and her classes, and she couldn't wait to graduate in a few years and get a job and move on to the next stage of her life, but this summer had been amazing, and she wasn't ready for it to end.

"Hey, babe." She was scooped up into a strong pair of arms and swung around in a circle before lips pressed against her own.

Nineteen-year-old Kayla McTierney curled her arms around her boyfriend's neck and kissed him back. She and David had been spending every day of the summer together, they worked nights, and they were both living with their parents, so they spent their days together, hanging out in the pool at her parents' house.

"You wearing your ring?" David asked when he set her down on her feet.

"I put it on as soon as mom and dad left for work," she said, holding up her finger. The diamond engagement ring caught the sunlight and sparkled like someone had taken a piece of a rainbow and attached it to a gold band.

"I can't wait until we can tell everyone."

"Me either," Kayla agreed, a little of her good mood evaporating. She and David had been engaged since the beginning of summer, but they had to keep it a secret because neither of their families approved of the relationship. Her parents believed that David was a motorcycle-riding, tattoo-covered, high school dropout who couldn't give her the life they thought she should live. His parents thought she was a stuck-up, spoiled brat, rich kid who only cared about possessions.

Both were wrong.

David might ride a motorbike, and he did have tattoos, although only a couple, and while he had dropped out of high school, he was smart and talented, and had the biggest heart she had ever seen in a person. He cared about people, he cared about the earth, he cared about animals, and he wanted to build a tiny house and travel the country working with wildlife rescue. While she had come from a wealthy family, and she was used to having the benefit of all that money could buy, she wasn't stuck-up, she wanted to live with David in the tiny house he was building himself and travel the country. Her dream was to start and run a charity that cared for injured wildlife and run it together with her fiancé.

They were in love, and they were a great team, and Kayla fully intended to spend the rest of her life with David, one day, when they were ready, adding children to their little family. But today wasn't that day. For now, they were keeping their relationship a secret until she graduated from college.

Well, it wasn't completely a secret.

Both sets of parents knew that they were dating, they just didn't know how serious things had become. The only people who knew they were engaged were a couple of their closest friends.

Friends who should be here soon, which meant they didn't have long to spend together, just the two of them.

"I missed you," Kayla said, wrapping her arms around David's waist and kissing him again. When she was away at college he often came and spent the night at the house she rented with some of her friends. Since she had been home, they'd had to make do with a few stolen moments here and there, and it wasn't enough.

Maybe it wasn't so bad after all that summer was coming to an end.

"I missed you too, but you know we do have a little time before the others show up." David waggled his eyebrows at her, then picked her up and tossed her into the pool.

She landed with a splash and the water bubbled around her as she went under. It was cool on her hot skin, and she took her time swimming back up to the surface. She loved to swim and had been a total water baby ever since she learned to swim when she was two. Growing up, she had always spent her summers by the pool, but this summer she had a new favorite water activity.

Making out with her fiancé.

David jumped into the pool, sending water splashing all over her and he swam underneath her then somehow managed to scoop her into his arms as he came up. His lips found hers again, and he swam them to the side of the pool where he pressed her against the tiled wall so he could get busy with his hands.

As his fingers curled around her buttocks, kneading while they kissed, her hands found their way inside his board shorts, and she began to stroke him, slowly at first, then speeding up as he grew hard at her touch.

"My turn," he whispered in her ear as he gently uncurled her fingers from around himself.

They kissed some more, her hands moving to twirl his messy brown locks around her fingers, while he began to touch her. David slid a finger inside of her, stroking deep, then pulling it out and sliding it back in again. He added another finger, stretching her, teasing her, making her wet for him, driving her crazy until she couldn't take it any longer.

"Please," she half begged, half moaned.

"You're so impatient," he teased, inserting another finger inside her and making her stomach clench in delightful anticipation. While she loved foreplay, right now she had reached her limit and wanted him inside her.

When they had gotten engaged they had both had blood work done to check for STDs, and since she couldn't get pregnant thanks to a rare genetic condition, they never had to worry about a condom, so David withdrew his hand and freed himself from his board shorts, sliding them down his legs and letting them float away across the pool.

A shadow fell over them, and Kayla looked up, expecting to see one of their friends standing above them.

But it wasn't.

It was a stranger.

He was dressed all in black, and despite the hot day, he was wearing sweatpants and a hoodie that was pulled down low, mostly covering his face.

"David," she said, pushing on his shoulders to draw his attention to the man.

"Hey, man, we don't want any trouble," David said, quickly swimming them away from the intruder and into the middle of the pool where he couldn't reach them.

The man just stood there.

Kayla wrapped herself around David, she had been mugged once before a couple of years ago, and she had a major fear about it happening again.

"If you came to rob us, you won't get a fight," David said. "Take whatever you want. We'll just stay here, we won't try to stop you."

The man didn't respond.

In his hand he held a can of something, and he unscrewed it and began to slosh whatever liquid that was inside into the pool.

"Hey man, what are you doing?" David asked, starting to swim them towards the other side of the pool.

The man ignored him and also began to circle the pool, throwing the liquid as he went.

"Get out of here," David whispered in her ear, then pushed her towards the steps.

"I'm not leaving you," she whispered back. There was no way she was getting out of the pool and running away leaving David here alone with the creepy man in black.

Curling an arm around her, David held her close. "Get out of here," he said to the man.

The man stopped, dropped his can, and pulled a box of matches from his pocket.

Immediately Kayla understood.

She hadn't noticed before, but now the air was heavy with the smell of kerosene, the man had doused the pool with it, and now he was about to set it on fire. Oil was lighter than water, it would have settled on the top of the pool, and as soon as he threw that match in it would ignite, trapping them in here.

"Swim," David screamed, apparently jumping to the same conclusions she had.

They were too late.

The man in black lit the match and tossed it.

It seemed to fly through the air in slow motion.

The second it made contact with the kerosene fire sprang up everywhere.

It surrounded them.

David dived down, dragging her down with him, and hand in hand they tried to search for a break in the flames through which they could escape.

There wasn't one.

They were trapped.

If they stayed down here, under the water, they would drown.

If they went up to the surface, they would burn.

Drown or burn.

Two horrendous ways to die.

She and David clung to each other and did the only thing they could do; wait for the inevitable.

~

12:36 P.M.

Adrenalin buzzed through her system.

No matter how many times she did this, the rush never seemed to dim.

Amethyst Hatcher and her squad were on the way to a fire. She was twenty-nine-years-old now, had been a firefighter for going on seven years, and she still loved the job every bit as much as she had when the idea to become a firefighter had first come to her.

The adrenalin rush that she got whenever they got a callout wasn't anything to do with the people who might be in danger, she felt for them, the loss of their home or business was a harsh one she didn't want anyone to endure, and the ones who lost their lives, she couldn't think of a worse way to die. The rush was to do with herself, living life on the edge was the only time she really felt alive.

The fire they were speeding to this afternoon—lights flashing and sirens blaring—sounded like it was going to be a bad one.

"Just up there," someone announced, and a moment later the truck was pulling over beside a large colonial. The yard was neatly trimmed lawn with a couple of large trees and several flower beds overflowing with a mass of colorful flowers. The house was painted a crisp, bright white, the large porch had rocking chairs and a swing, if it wasn't for the strong smell of smoke the place would have been picture perfect.

No one wasted a second, they grabbed what they needed and circled through the yard and around to the back of the property with the well-oiled practice of a team that was used to working together.

Although she had known what they were walking into, the scene still caught her by surprise.

The backyard was as pretty and well maintained as the front, there was a fire pit and a pergola with a picnic table, there was a basketball hoop and a small concreted area around it, there were trees, and flowers, and manicured lawns. And there was a pool.

A pool where a fire currently blazed.

She'd been a firefighter long enough to know that the only way to get a fire on a body of water was to throw an accelerant on there and then set it alight, which meant that this was no accident.

As she got closer, she saw them.

The bodies.

Two of them.

They were too late.

That was the worst part about her job. Sometimes they arrived too late to save the victims. Sometimes they got lucky and walked through flames and falling debris to find someone still alive, and were able to carry them out, but today was not going to be one of those days.

Blocking out the bodies and the natural imaginings of what must have happened to them and what their final moments had been like, Amethyst and her team went to work. Setting the hose up, they aimed it at the base of the flames. Slowly they died down until eventually they were extinguished altogether.

It was over.

Just like that.

The fire was out, but it wasn't in time to save the couple in the pool.

Although their blackened bodies were unrecognizable, Amethyst knew that the victims were nineteen-year-old Kayla McTierney, whose family owned the property, and her boyfriend, David Buffy. Neighbors had been alerted to the fire by the sounds of screams and had immediately called 911. Only ten minutes had passed between the time the call had come in and their arrival, but that had been enough. Now, looking at the scene, Amethyst wasn't sure that they could have saved the couple even if they had been here quicker.

"You okay?"

She turned her attention away from the pool and the two bodies that were floating there. She really wanted to grab them and pull them out, cover them up, give them some protection from the myriad of people who were milling about, but the bodies had to remain where they were until the crime scene unit arrived and photographed them, then the medical examiner would come along and finally take them away.

"Amethyst?"

Right.

Theo had asked her if she was okay.

How did she even go about answering a question like that?

As much as she loved her job, the high-pressure situations, walking through buildings consumed with flames to save people, the satisfaction of putting out a fire before it could destroy an entire block of buildings, all of that spoke to the daredevil side of her. But this ... you never got used to this.

And if you did, then you shouldn't be doing this job.

"Yeah, I'm okay," she told her friend and colleague. Theo was about the same age as her and they were good friends, she knew that he found her attractive, and while he was certainly attractive himself, she didn't feel anything beyond friendship for him. In reality, she didn't really see herself having anything with anyone beyond friendship. She wasn't interested in getting married and having her own family, she was perfectly happy with her life the way it was.

"Liar," Theo said.

"All right," she sighed. "I hate this. They're so young, and they were just enjoying a gorgeous summer day. What kind of monster would do something like this?" She had been closer to a monster than most people ever got and lived to tell about it—not that she ever did talk about it—and yet she still got shocked at some of the things she had witnessed on her job.

"The sickest kind," Theo spat out, clearly as upset as she was about this whole thing.

"They weren't already dead when he set the fire, imagine how scared they must have been trapped in there with no place to go." She didn't want to think about the couple's final moments, and yet her mind couldn't seem to switch off.

"Try not to think about it."

"How can I not?"

"Because otherwise, it's going to eat you up inside."

He was right.

Amethyst knew that he was, and yet she really didn't think she would ever stop thinking about it.

"We need to pack up," Theo said, trying to draw her attention away from the pool.

Since she knew there was nothing productive to be gained by obsessing over this, Amethyst forced herself to move, to start packing up. It wasn't her job to find out who had set fire to this pool while Kayla McTierney and David Buffy were in it. That was a job for the cops, they were the ones who would have to figure this out, find someone who hated one or both of the pair enough to kill them. She was glad she didn't have to do that, walk inside a burning building she could do without blinking an eye, but interview a victim or a witness of a crime and she got freaked out. She kept remembering her little sister's haunted eyes that day in the hospital after she had been found close to death. That was something she never wanted to see in another person's eyes.

"You want to hang out tonight?" Theo asked as they put their things back in the truck.

Usually, she loved hanging out with the guys from the firehouse, but tonight was a big night for her family. "I can't. Sapphire and Gideon are bringing the baby home from the hospital, and we're all going to be there to welcome him home."

"I forgot you're an aunty now," Theo said.

"I am." She beamed proudly. She didn't see herself having kids of her own in the future, but she was going to be the best aunty that she could be. She already loved Sapphire's little boy, and Diamond's stepson Archie, she was going to spoil them rotten.

"Maybe we can hang out tomorrow," he suggested.

"Sure," she agreed. Now that she was the only one of her sisters left in the house they had shared for the last few years, she found herself spending more and more time with her friends. Diamond was married with a toddler, Ruby was married and expecting her first child, and Sapphire had a new baby, they had all moved on with their lives, found a way to leave the past in the past, and look to the future.

She was the only one who had remained a prisoner of the past.

As she headed back to the truck, ready to be far away from this yard and the horror that had occurred here, she caught sight of her brother-in-law Judah. Judah was married to her twin sister, and he was obviously one of the cops working this case along with his partner Zebadiah Tuck.

They were standing with a couple of shell-shocked people that she assumed were the neighbors that had called in the fire.

Amethyst was glad to hand this over to them, and go back to the station, and wait for another call.

As she climbed up into the truck, she looked over at Zeb and found him looking right at her. Their eyes met, and she got a weird feeling in her stomach. An unsettled feeling like something was about to happen, and she wasn't sure she could stop it.

Shaking it off, she sat down and closed her eyes, she was ready for today to be over.

∾

12:53 P.M.

Detective Zeb Tuck watched Amethyst Hatcher as she walked back to the fire truck.

Even dressed in the heavy gear she wore for her job, she was a beautiful woman. Her long blonde hair was pulled into a ponytail, she wasn't wearing any makeup, and her shoulders were hunched over as though she were carrying a heavy burden. Given what they had all witnessed here this afternoon, he couldn't blame her.

Just as she climbed up into the fire truck, she turned around and looked right across the yard.

Their eyes met.

Her blue eyes bore into his brown ones.

It felt like the world stopped spinning for a few seconds.

He was attracted to her, he had been since the first time he met her. His partner was married to Amethyst's twin sister Ruby, so they'd hung out together plenty of times, but he had never approached Amethyst and asked her out because to be honest, he was pretty sure that he would be turned down.

But in this moment, he wondered if he had been wrong.

Was she really as standoffish as she appeared to be?

The moment ended, and Amethyst got into the fire truck, the

doors closed, and the truck drove off down the street. He stood staring after it, unsettled by the feelings that had just ignited inside him. He wasn't on the lookout for a girlfriend, he occasionally hooked up with a girl, but it was never anything serious, and given who Amethyst was and what he knew about her past, he couldn't just treat her like he was using her to pass the time and meet his personal needs.

"Zeb."

"Yeah?" He turned around and found that both his partner and the couple they had been speaking with were staring at him.

Judah narrowed his eyes, silently asking him what was going on. They were interviewing the couple who lived behind the McTierney house, his focus should be on that, not on the beautiful but remote firefighter. He gave a small nod to his partner, and although Judah's blue eyes remained unconvinced, he turned back to the neighbors.

"Did you notice anyone hanging around the house this morning?" Judah asked.

"No," Tricia André said softly, her eyes still wide and shell-shocked. If he was in the middle-aged couple's place, he would have been feeling the exact same way. Even as a seasoned detective, he was feeling a little queasy about what he had witnessed in that swimming pool.

"What about the last few days?" Zeb asked. "Has anything unusual happened? Any cars hanging around, anyone loitering in the street?"

"Nothing that stood out," Tricia's husband said, looking just as shocked as his wife.

"What first alerted you to the fire?" he asked. The fire had been reported quickly, and the fire truck had been on the scene in less than ten minutes, he and Judah had been only a couple of minutes behind it, but none of them had been here in time to save Kayla McTierney and David Buffy.

"Screams. We heard screams," Nick André replied.

"It's summer, and there are always kids having pool parties, and playing ball, and having fun, it's not that we're not used to hearing screaming, but this was something different, this was ..." Tricia trailed off, but she didn't need to finish her sentence. They had all seen the swimming pool and the two bodies floating in it, they could all imagine the horror that had been the last few minutes of the young couple's lives.

"What did you do when you heard the screams?" he asked. They knew that the couple had called 911, but they needed specifics, especially whether or not either Tricia or Nick André had seen the killer.

"We were sitting in the backyard reading, when we heard the screams we ran down to the fence. We saw the pool, the flames, and we called 911," Tricia replied.

"Did you see anyone in the yard?" Judah asked.

"There was a figure in black running away," Nick replied.

A figure in black. Could there be a more stereotypical description of a killer than that? "Did you see a face?"

"His back was to us," Nick replied.

"Were you able to see skin color or any other distinguishing features?" Judah asked.

Tricia shook her head. "All I saw was a figure in black."

That narrowed down their suspect list not one iota. They knew someone had started the fire, Kayla McTierney and David Buffy didn't douse the pool with fuel themselves and then set it on fire. If they were going to find out who had set that fire, then they needed something concrete to move forward with.

"What do you know about Kayla and David, and Kayla's family?" Zeb asked.

"We haven't lived here very long so we don't know the McTierney family very well," Nick explained. "But from what we've overheard, just from sitting in the yard when Kayla and David have their friends over in the afternoons, neither Kayla nor David's families are supportive of their relationship."

That perked him up a little.

That was an actual direction they could move in.

Could the killer be an angry family member who was determined to destroy Kayla and David no matter what the cost, even if that meant ending their lives to do it?

Casting a glance at his partner to see whether Judah thought the same thing he did, that there wasn't anything else that the Andrés could give them, they needed to start speaking with the McTierney and Buffy families, getting alibis for this afternoon, and interviewing them to figure out which one was the most likely to have done this. The look on his partner's face said that he agreed they needed to get moving, get this man in custody in case there was anyone else on his hit list. For all they knew, it was someone from Kayla's family who intended to take out the entire Buffy family as well, or vice versa.

"Here's a card, it has our numbers on it, call us if you think of anything else," Zeb told the couple, handing over the card.

"We will," Nick said, taking the card and looking enormously relieved that he and his wife could leave now. They probably thought that going back to their home, back to their lives, would erase what had happened today from their minds, but that wasn't the way it worked.

Neither Nick nor Tricia André would ever forget this.

Those screams, the flames, the couple trapped with no hope of saving their own lives, would be seared into their minds until their dying day.

This case would be one that would no doubt be seared into his mind until his dying day as well. While being a homicide detective didn't desensitize him to death and the pain and suffering of the victims, it did kind of take the edge off. There weren't a lot of cases that touched him the way this one had, and he knew he wasn't going to be able to think of anything else until they had this guy in custody. Cases involving fire always touched him a little deeper than others.

Once the couple had scurried off, he turned to Judah. "Crime scene and the medical examiner just showed up, but I don't think there's anything they can tell us at this point that we need to know right now. We know how they died, and if he left anything behind CSU will find it. We should focus on doing the notifications, seeing if anyone gives anything away."

"Since we know that neither family was supportive of the relationship we can't count anyone out. There's also the chance that someone hired a hitman to kill the couple."

Zeb hadn't thought of that, but they couldn't discount it as a possibility. "The McTierney family is wealthy," he said, waving a hand at the house just behind them. "I'm sure they could afford to pay someone, but do they have a reason to do so?"

"The only way to find out is to talk to them," Judah said.

"McTierney or Buffy family first?" he asked. They had to move quickly if they wanted to notify the families before they heard from anyone else, or anywhere else, there were already news crews filling the street. Given that the families were currently their top suspects, being able to be there when they found out about the fire and the murders, and witness their reactions, could help them narrow down who they should be looking at more closely.

"McTierney family," Judah replied. "They're more likely to find out first since the fire was at their house."

As they walked down to where they'd parked the car, ready to head to the business the McTierney's owned, Zeb couldn't help but think of Amethyst. Physical attraction aside, he really didn't see a future for the two of them so it was probably for the best that he keep his distance from her for the time being. At least until that attraction dimmed.

It wasn't like he didn't have plenty to keep him busy in the meantime, between this case and the others piling up on his desk, he doubted he would have a spare second to think of the sexy firefighter.

And yet as he climbed into the car, Amethyst remained stuck firmly in his mind.

∼

5:58 P.M.

"Do you think we should have stayed in the hospital a couple more days?" Sapphire Hatcher-Barlow asked her husband as she twisted in her seat to look into the backseat of their car.

"We can't stay in the hospital forever," Gideon reminded her.

"I know that but he's only four days old, and we've never cared for a baby before," she contradicted. As enraptured as she was with her new baby son, she was equal parts terrified of him.

"They showed us at the hospital how to give him a bath, and change his diaper, and you know how to breastfeed him, we'll be fine."

"How can you say that?" Sapphire demanded. "We don't know

anything about caring for a newborn, and we're on our own now. There aren't any nurses there to help us out. What if he stops eating? Or what if he starts crying and we can't get him to stop? What if he won't go to sleep?"

"Whoa, whoa, whoa." Gideon reached over and took her hand. "You're creating problems that aren't there. We'll be fine."

"You keep saying that, but how are we going to be fine? We're on our own now, and I don't know anything about kids. I never even held a baby this small before Leo was born."

"Stop stressing yourself out, everything is going to be fine. We're going to figure things out as we go along, together, we're a team, you're not doing this on your own."

"Why are you always so calm?" she snapped. Gideon had no right to be so calm and practical about their parenting skills when she was a freaked out mess. She was so scared that she wasn't cut out to be a mother, and she was going to make too many mistakes and mess up her son's life. "You're always so calm about everything, you never get worked up about anything, do you have any idea how infuriating that is?"

Gideon just chuckled, which only made her so much more annoyed. "Sapphire, I know you're stressed, and I know it's scary being responsible for another human being, but I promise you that everything is going to be okay. We're going to learn as we go along, sure we don't know everything right now, but by the time we have baby number two we're going to be experts."

She just harrumphed, she was stressed enough with one baby she didn't even want to think about having two. "You really think we can do this?" Sapphire knew she sounded neurotic, but her hormones were in a mess, and she was legitimately concerned about her abilities as a mother.

A mother.

It still hadn't really sunk in that she was a mom now.

She had a son.

A tiny, beautiful, perfect baby boy.

She already loved Leo more than she could express, and she didn't want to do anything to jeopardize his happiness. She didn't want to do anything that would mess him up for life.

"We can do this," Gideon assured her, squeezing her hand.

Just as she was about to calm down a little, convince herself that Gideon was right and that the three of them would be fine, Leo began to wail.

"He's crying."

"Babies cry, honey," her husband reminded her.

"I know that. But is he hungry? Does he need to be changed? Is he sleepy?" She wished that babies could talk, she had no idea how to figure out what they wanted when they cried, at least with older kids you could ask them questions and they could tell you what they needed, but newborns, you had to trust your instincts, only she didn't have motherly instincts yet.

"He's probably hungry, you can feed him when we get home," Gideon said calmly.

As much as she sometimes complained that he was always so calm, she was so glad to have that calming presence in her life. After everything that had happened to her when she was a teenager, she had changed. She'd become angry. She'd focused all her energy on her job because she needed to save people. Gideon said it was because she suffered from survivor's guilt over being rescued so quickly while her sisters suffered for so much longer, and while she supposed that made sense, she didn't really care why she was messed up, she just didn't want to pass it along to her little boy.

She had to pull it together.

This should be one of the happiest times of her life, and it wasn't that she wasn't happy, it was just that she was so afraid of making a mistake.

But she had to set those fears aside.

Dragging in a deep breath through her nose, she let it out through her mouth, Gideon was right, the two of them would figure things out as they went along like all first-time parents did, there was nothing to panic about.

"Do you think I should get in the backseat with him?" she asked.

"We're only a couple of minutes from home, I think he'll be okay."

"You're probably right; I just hate to hear him cry." His tears hurt her heart. Sapphire knew he was just a tiny baby and that he was just crying because he was hungry or needed to be changed, or both, but when he hurt she hurt. "Do you think we should move his crib into our room for these first few nights, just until he gets settled?"

"We can if you want to."

She and Gideon had spent months working on the nursery. They'd painted the room, including stenciling on a safari motif that went around all four walls. They had picked gorgeous furniture, and the room was filled with more stuffed animals than a store had, and more cute little onesies than he could wear before he outgrew them. She had wanted everything to be just perfect for when they brought him home, she wanted him to have the perfect room, but now that it was time to bring him home she wanted to keep him close.

"I think I want him to stay in our room, especially for these first nights, then maybe in a couple of weeks we can put him in his own room."

"Okay, I'll move his crib when we get home. You sound a little calmer," he said, casting a quick glance her way before returning his eyes to the road.

"I love him so much already, and I'm scared I won't be the mom he deserves." Although she had wanted to have a baby—both she and Gideon had—and had suffered two miscarriages before getting pregnant with Leo, she hadn't realized she would have all these doubts and insecurities. She just wanted to have fun with her new son, and Gideon, who was taking a month off work as they settled into their new family life.

"What was one of the first things I told you when we met?"

"That you thought I was pretty," she smirked.

"Touché," he laughed. "I told you that you are one of the kindest, most compassionate people I've ever met. The way you throw yourself into your job, working yourself into the ground because you want to save as many people as you can, you have such a big heart, and you hate to see anyone suffering. *That's* what you're going to give to our son. We're a team, we're here to support one another, and any time you start having doubts I want you to tell me, okay?"

Sapphire smiled. Gideon was a psychiatrist, and there was no way he could turn off that side of himself even if he tried. "Okay," she agreed.

They pulled into their driveway and her resolve to not panic wavered.

This was it.

They were home, and that meant they were on their own with Leo from here on out.

As much as it scared her to be completely in control of caring for Leo without the backup of the nurses in the hospital, it was kind of nice to be just the three of them. They were a little family, and given how messed up her own family had become, it was nice to have a chance to have a family that was how she wished her own had been.

"I'm going to get him out of the car seat," she said as she climbed out of the car. She wanted to hold him in her arms, rather than bringing the baby capsule inside, he was still crying, and once they got inside, she was going to feed him. As soon as she reached into the car and scooped him up, he stopped crying. Her confidence in this whole motherhood thing skyrocketed. "Gideon, did you see that? He stopped crying when I picked him up."

"He loves his mommy," Gideon said, grabbing the baby bag and then slipping an arm around her shoulders.

"Do you think he loves us already?" Leo was only four days old, she knew he wasn't capable of even understanding that they were his parents, but she wondered whether that love was implanted in him as he'd been growing inside of her.

"I believe that he does."

"I think so too," she said as she looked down at him. He was so tiny, his little eyes were closed, his little mouth was so cute, and she was in love with his tiny little fingers and toes. This itty bitty little baby had stolen her heart, and Sapphire felt extremely lucky to have the best husband and now the best baby in the world.

~

6:19 P.M.

. . .

"We have enough baby things to stock an entire store." Amethyst laughed as she set another brightly wrapped box of baby gifts on the dining room table.

"And that's on top of all the things Sapphire got at the baby shower," Ruby added.

"*And* all the things she bought on her five dozen trips to the store." Diamond chuckled.

"Five dozen? More like five million," Ruby said with a grin.

"Like you're one to talk." Diamond rolled her eyes. "How many shopping trips have *you* made?"

"I may have made a few." Ruby poked her tongue out at Diamond.

"A few?" Diamond scoffed. "You're three and a half months pregnant, and you already have clothes for when the baby is a year old."

"Baby clothes are cute, it's so hard to resist buying them all." Ruby shrugged. "And remind me again just how many toys and clothes and things Archie has."

Diamond giggled. "Toddler clothes are just as cute as baby clothes."

Amethyst watched her sisters joke about their families. Ruby and her husband Judah would be welcoming their first child into their family in less than six months, and Diamond had become stepmother to her husband Elijah's two-year-old when they'd married last month. She was the only one without kids and a husband. She didn't even have a boyfriend. As much as she didn't envision herself ever having a family of her own, it didn't mean that sometimes she didn't get a little lonely.

Just a little.

"Balloons and streamers are all up," Judah said as he, Elijah, and Archie came into the room.

"There are streamers on every wall, and balloons covering every inch of every ceiling of every room in the house. We went through almost three containers of helium blowing them all up," Elijah added.

"Dad, I want balloons," Archie said, tugging on the hem of his dad's t-shirt.

"I'm sure Aunt Sapphire and Uncle Gideon will let us take a bunch home," Diamond told the little boy who beamed in delight.

She had never thought of herself as a kid person, she liked teenagers and older kids because you could talk to them, but little kids and babies made her uncomfortable, maybe because they were so demonstrative with their emotions and affections and that was unsettling for someone like her. But having spent time around Archie these last few months, she was starting to have second thoughts. Now there was a new little member of the family, and she was looking forward to being Aunty Amethyst, who else would take the kids to do all the fun and crazy things that parents thought were too dangerous?

"I hear a car," Ruby exclaimed, hurrying off down the hall.

Amethyst and the others followed, all excited to see baby Leo come home. They'd all been in the hospital the day he was born, they'd seen him just minutes after he entered the world, and every day since, but this was his very first milestone, and no one wanted to miss it.

"They're getting him out of the car," Diamond said, peeking out the curtains.

"You ready, Arch?" Diamond asked, giving the little boy a party popper, they were all going to send confetti shooting all over the trio when they walked through the front door.

"Ready," Archie said.

"You know how to use it?" Elijah asked his son.

"Yes," the child replied, he was starting to look less like a toddler and more like a little boy, he had grown up a lot in the few months since he had become a part of their family.

"They're coming," Ruby said as they all heard the footsteps on the porch.

A moment later the door swung open. "Welcome home, Leo," they all cheered, firing off their party poppers. Confetti showered down on Sapphire, Gideon, and Leo like colorful rain. With the hundreds of balloons floating up at the ceiling, and the streamers draped everywhere, the house looked like the joyous celebration that it was.

"Aww, you guys," Sapphire gushed, her bright green eyes shiny with unshed tears. Amethyst wasn't used to seeing her sister so emotional, Sapphire wasn't really an emotional woman, or at least she hadn't been, but being with Gideon, and now having Leo, she had really learned that she didn't need to keep such a tight lid on her emotions.

"How is the little guy?" Diamond asked. "Can I hold him?"

"Of course, he might be hungry though, he was crying in the car, but he stopped when I picked him up." Sapphire beamed as she handed the baby to Diamond.

"Judah, you want to help me move the crib into the master?" Gideon asked Ruby's husband.

"Sure."

As the two men went upstairs, the rest of them headed through to the family room. "We have cupcakes," Amethyst told her little sister, they were Sapphire's favorite treats.

"Yum. Oh, they're so cute," she said when she saw them sitting on the kitchen counter. The cupcakes had blue buttercream icing, and little teddy bears made with marshmallow fondant sitting on top. "You missing me yet, partner?" she asked Elijah.

"Can't wait to have you back, when you can tear yourself away from this little guy," Elijah said, putting his finger against the baby's palm and watching the little fingers curl around it. "Did Diamond tell you our news?"

"What news?" Sapphire asked.

"Well, we decided that we want to add another member to our family, we intend to keep fostering, but since I can't have kids we're going to look into adoption," Diamond explained.

"That's great," Sapphire exclaimed. "Ruby's baby is only going to be six months younger than Leo, how awesome would it be if you adopted soon too, then our kids could all grow up together and be close, as we'd get to raise them all together, we'd get even closer too." As if she realized what she had said, Sapphire turned apologetic eyes on her. "Oh, I'm sorry, Amethyst."

Her sister's words had hurt her.

Not because she thought that Sapphire had meant to hurt her, but because she felt left out.

It was silly and immature to feel left out over something that she didn't even want. She didn't want a boyfriend, she didn't want a husband, and she didn't want kids, and yet she couldn't help but feel out in the cold now that her three sisters had their own families.

One by one they were moving on with their lives, and she wasn't moving anywhere.

She was still in the same place she had been this time last year, and this time six years ago, and this time twelve years ago. Her life hadn't changed, she had her job, she worked out, she did her bodybuilding, she liked anything that gave her that adrenalin rush she craved.

But that was it.

That was all she had in her life.

And it was a little depressing that she didn't see anything changing.

"I know what you meant," Amethyst assured Sapphire because she didn't want to ruin this day for her sister. Sapphire was starting a new journey, she'd found everything she wanted, and she wanted her to love every second of being a mom.

"Maybe one day we'll get you married off," Ruby teased.

"Maybe," she agreed with a pasted-on smile. She knew there was no maybe. She wasn't going to get married and have kids. It wasn't what she wanted.

"I wanna hold baby," Archie said, and Amethyst said a silent prayer of thanks to the little boy for interrupting.

"Come sit up here on the couch," Sapphire said, taking Archie's hand and leading him over to the couch.

"You have to be careful, okay, bud?" Elijah said, propping a pillow under his son's arm.

"'Kay," Archie said.

"Here you go," Diamond said as she carefully set the baby in Archie's arms, and Archie beamed proudly.

"He's going to make such a good big brother," Sapphire said.

"Crib is in our room," Gideon announced as he and Judah rejoined them in the family room.

"Thank you," Sapphire said.

"We have gifts for Leo, but how about dinner first?" Diamond suggested.

"I'm starving," Sapphire said. "I think my body still thinks it's eating for two."

"We can cook, you rest," Amethyst offered.

"No, I'm tired of resting, I'll help with dinner, and you can hold Leo. Arch, you want to help cook dinner?" Sapphire asked.

"Okay," the little boy agreed.

Before she could protest that she wasn't really the right one to be holding the baby, he was lying in her arms, and everyone had left her to go to the kitchen.

Amethyst looked down at the little baby in her arms. His eyes were closed, his lashes dark against his pale cheeks, she ran her fingertips across his silky soft head, was she crazy for not wanting to have kids of her own one day?

As much as she didn't want to admit it, she was lonely.

Seeing how happy Diamond, Ruby, and Sapphire were with their husbands and their families was making her think about her own future. She didn't know that she wanted to get married, she had to admit that even as kids, she had been the least likely one to get married. She didn't know that she wanted to have kids, she wasn't sure that she was really mother material.

But now she wasn't sure that she *didn't* want it.

She was so confused.

Her hormones had her all mixed up.

One person kept flitting through her mind.

Zeb Tuck.

Her body wanted him, but her mind knew it was a bad idea. He was her brother-in-law's partner, and she didn't want to make things awkward by sleeping with him and then never taking things any further. Because that was all this was about, she was sure of it, she just wanted to not feel alone for a while.

Loneliness.

Her sudden confusion about her future was just because she was feeling lonely. Nothing more.

Nothing more.

CHAPTER *Four*

August 22nd
8:53 A.M.

Zeb stifled a yawn as he settled into his chair at his desk. He was going to need a lot of coffee to make it through the day.

Even though he'd slept well last night, he hadn't woken up feeling rested. In fact, there had been days where he'd worked through the night on a case and felt less tired than he did today.

It probably had something to do with the subject of his dreams.

They hadn't been bad dreams, on the contrary, they had been great dreams. Amazing dreams in fact, so good that he hadn't wanted to wake up, and when his alarm had gone off he'd had to take a cold shower before he left the house.

It was all Amethyst Hatcher's fault.

He hadn't been able to get her out of his mind since yesterday at the McTierney house.

"Morning," Judah said as he walked up to his desk. "Coffee?"

"Yes, please," he said, taking the cup his partner held out and taking a long drink.

"Rough night?" Judah asked with an arched brow.

He arched one back, silently asking what his partner meant. How could Judah possibly know what he'd dreamed about last night?

"You just drank half a cup of boiling hot coffee, I can still see the steam pouring off it. I'm guessing your need for coffee this morning means you didn't sleep much last night," Judah explained.

"Yeah, something like that," he replied vaguely. He didn't want to get into a discussion on his sudden desire to rip off Amethyst's clothes and have wild passionate sex. Amethyst was Judah's sister-in-law, his wife's twin sister, which would make it one awkward conversation. "You guys have fun last night?" he asked, diverting the attention away from himself.

"We oohed and aahed and passed the baby around until I'm sure he was sick of us all," Judah said with a smile.

"Won't be long until everyone is oohing and aahing over your little bundle of joy."

"No, it won't be," Judah agreed, his smile growing wider. Ever since Ruby had found out she was pregnant, his partner hadn't been able to wipe the smile off his face.

Having kids of his own was only something Zeb had started to think about recently. He liked kids, and he'd stopped by the hospital to visit Sapphire and Gideon's new baby, little Leo was a cutie and holding him had made him think that maybe it would be nice to have a son one day. He and his father used to spend a lot of time together when he was a small boy, they'd go fishing, and his dad coached his little league team, they'd go camping, and bike riding, and Zeb thought it would be nice to do that with his own little boy one day.

"It is weird without Sapphire around here," he said, looking over at her empty desk. In all the years he had worked here, he couldn't remember a single time when Sapphire's desk had been empty. Usually, it was piled high with all her current cases plus a ton of cold ones that she was looking into.

"It is," Judah agreed. "As much as she loves being a mom, I don't think it'll be long until she is itching to get back to work."

That was Sapphire, a workaholic, it was something that he understood on a very personal level. When you had lost everything, then work became your one stable place, it was where you sought meaning, it was what kept you going when there wasn't anything else in your life.

"Speaking of work," Judah said. "We need to figure out what we're focusing on today. We spoke to all immediate family of both Kayla McTierney and David Buffy, did any of them stand out to you as a potential suspect?"

"None immediately. We need to confirm a couple of alibis, but when we did the notifications, both sets of parents appeared genuinely devastated." They had managed to speak with both Kayla and David's families before they heard the news from another source, which meant they had been able to see their reactions to the news.

"They did. If one of them organized the deaths, then they could have practiced their reactions, made sure they seemed genuine."

"Let's say that a family member did decide to end the relationship by killing the couple off, to buy that, we would have to believe that they were disapproving enough of the relationship to decide that killing them was worth it. And then we'd have to buy that the hitman they hired decided that throwing kerosene on a pool and setting it alight was a good way to kill them, and I'm just not sure that I *can* buy that. It's not usually how hitmen do business. Something quick like a bullet to the head, maybe fake a home invasion or robbery, run a car off the road perhaps, but something like this seems too extravagant, it seems more like something a ..." Zeb trailed off because he didn't want to say the words.

He didn't want what he was thinking to be true.

It was so much easier to work a case where the victims knew their killer, and it was an isolated incident.

As awful as death always was, at least it was a relief not to have to worry about more victims.

Only he wasn't so sure that there wouldn't be more victims.

"More like a serial killer," Judah finished for him.

"You've been thinking the same thing?"

"Although we know that there was a potential reason for someone to want our victims dead—even if it is a flimsy reason because I don't know that you'd kill two people like that just because you didn't approve of their relationship—this whole thing just doesn't feel right. I've never in all my years as a cop seen a case where a killer used kerosene on a swimming pool and a fire to kill anyone."

"So, are we seriously looking at this as a serial killer case?" Zeb asked, that was the last thing he wanted. A serial killer meant that there would be more victims, probably a lot of them. It was summer, school and college were out, meaning there were a lot of kids and families hanging around in the middle of the day. A lot of houses had pools, and the weather was still hot, which meant that the victim pool was huge, there was no way they had enough information to narrow down who the killer might target, which meant it could be anyone.

"I don't know that we have enough to come to that conclusion yet. Since we do have a motive, according to both the McTierney and Buffy families they were determined to break the couple up, the McTierney's because they thought David wasn't good enough for their daughter, and the Buffy's because they thought Kayla was a spoilt rich brat, I think we need to keep looking into that."

"If we do go with the theory that someone hired a hitman, then it would be more likely to be the McTierney's as they're the more affluent of the two families."

"We should start looking through their financials, see if anything stands out."

"We interviewed neighbors yesterday, so we already know that no one in the block saw anything useful, and we interviewed the parents, and the siblings of both Kayla and David, we should look into the extended family."

"And we should speak with Kayla and David's friends," Judah added. "Kayla was found with an engagement ring on, neither family knew they were engaged, maybe the friends did and can tell us something helpful. Maybe a family member found out about the engagement and decided they had to move quickly, and that's when they decided to have them killed."

"I think we should start with Kayla's cousin, he has a criminal record, and he's just out of rehab," he suggested. He wasn't sure why the cousin would feel the need to kill Kayla and David, but sometimes people's minds didn't work normally, they saw things that weren't there, and they did things that made no sense.

"As good a place as any to start. We'll speak with the cousin, then move onto the friends, once we find out if they know anything helpful we can decide who to talk to next."

"Sounds like a plan," Zeb said. He hoped that this panned out. He hoped that in their interviews today they found enough to identify and arrest their killer. He wanted this killer in custody, he didn't want anyone else to die the same horrific death that Kayla and David had.

He knew what fire was capable of, he'd watched as fire claimed his family.

He still remembered the feel of the heat on his skin, feeling like it was going to burn right through him.

He still remembered the fierceness of the flames as they lunged towards him, wanting to claim him too.

He still remembered the screams of his parents and little sister.

Fire was the only thing on the face of the planet that truly scared him, and anyone who would use it as a weapon was too dangerous to be at large whether they had been targeting Kayla and David for personal reasons, or because they were a serial killer who could go after anyone in the city next.

10:26 A.M.

Sliding open the box, he pulled out a match.

For a moment he studied the small piece of wood. It was hard to believe that something so simple, something so seemingly innocuous, could cause such disastrous tragedies.

Striking the match, he watched as a tiny flame emerged.

One little flame.

That was all it took to cause devastation.

He lifted his free hand and held it above the flame. The heat seeped into his skin, warming him, even as it started to burn he didn't move his hand.

Fire had fascinated him for as long as he could remember.

As a small boy, he would sneak matches from the top shelf of the laundry room closet as soon as everybody else went to sleep. He would go out into the backyard and pile up dead leaves and then set them on fire. The flames in the dark night were like something out of another world. The way they leaped about like they were alive, it was thrilling, and he had been enamored from that very moment.

The very first time he could recall having ever seen a fire was his third birthday. Sitting at the table, his parents and siblings surrounding him, he was hyped up on ice cream and soda, and then his mom had brought out the cake.

It had been a chocolate cake, covered in chocolate frosting, with little fondant animals sitting on top and millions of colorful sprinkles.

But he hadn't cared about that.

His gaze had zeroed in on the candles.

Three bright blue candles with little flames flickering above them.

He'd been transfixed.

It had awakened a part of himself that he hadn't understood at that young age. But over the last couple of decades, he had slowly, bit by bit, come to understand who he truly was inside.

Now he knew.

This was who he was.

With a single puff of air, he blew out the match and dropped it on the ground.

Yesterday had been amazing. He had been planning it since last summer and to see all his hard work and preparation go off without a hitch, it was exhilarating. It was like all his life he had been searching for something, not quite sure what it was, and now he knew.

He was a killer.

A fire obsessed killer.

That made him an evil person, a person who deserved to be sent straight to Hell, but he didn't care.

He really didn't.

Those screams yesterday hadn't fazed him at all. Not even a little bit.

In fact, the only thing he had been concerned about was the fact that he hadn't been able to hang around and watch until the end. He'd had to flee pretty much as soon as he threw the match into the pool. The couple in the water had started screaming, and he'd known that those shrieks—while music to *his* ears would be like the howls of demons to others—would soon bring people running. He'd been right, just as he had been walking down the street and climbing into his car, the sounds of sirens had filled the air.

Today, he had chosen a house with a pool in a quieter area, hoping that there might not be as many people about and he'd be able to spend a little more time watching. He was interested to see how long it took them to die. Did they stay down under the water until they drowned? Could someone do that, or would the urge to breathe become so overwhelming they couldn't help but swim to the surface even knowing that they would be consumed by flames if they did so? He hoped today he might get some answers.

Strolling confidently across the street, he found the house that he had chosen in his searches. The houses had to have a pool, that was a given of course, but they also needed to have people who would likely be at home during the day. It was summer vacation, and school was still out, although in a couple of weeks the new school year would start, it was still quieter and less risky to strike during the day then at night. At night, people came home from work and day camps, they had friends and family over for barbecues and cookouts, they sat around fire pits well into the evening, enjoying the warm summer nights.

This house was a smaller one than the one he'd hit up yesterday. The neighborhood was mostly filled with couples without kids, so the residences would be empty this time of day. But there was one house that had a couple of teenagers, and that was where he would be going.

There was always the chance that he would walk into the backyard to find that the kids had decided to spend the day someplace else. It was summer, it was hot again today, and kids gravitated to pools on days such as these, but that didn't mean that he would find what he had come here for. If he didn't, he had a whole list of other houses that he could move on to so he wasn't worried about it.

Luck appeared to be on his side though.

As he rounded the house, making sure to keep close to the wall so he wouldn't be noticed, he heard the unmistakable sound of teenager chatter.

They were here.

He wondered how many. If there were too many, then there was a chance that they would try to do something stupid, and although he was sure he could take a bunch of kids, he would be outnumbered so it was possible they might get the upper hand.

He didn't think so though.

He was too prepared, and he wanted this too much to make any silly mistakes that would lead to him being caught and arrested.

Carefully, he edged closer, dressed as he was in black sweatpants and a black hoodie he stood out to anyone who should notice him. While dressing in shorts and a t-shirt would make him blend in, it also gave people the chance to notice distinguishing features that they would rattle off to the cops if they were interviewed. Weighing the pros and cons of both options, he had decided that going with the black sweats that virtually covered him from head to toe was the safer option.

Creeping closer, he moved stealthily from the side of the house to the nearest tree, he wanted to know how many he was up against. He was comfortable with up to maybe three or four, but above that, he didn't know if he could handle it. If there were more than five people would he leave? Slink away with his tail between his legs, or would he forge onward?

Onward and upward.

That had been his father's favorite saying, before he ditched them and disappeared from all their lives anyway.

He didn't really resent the man for leaving, he would have left that hellhole if he could too, so onward and upward it was.

Moving closer, he saw that once again luck appeared to be on his side. He didn't have to worry about whether or not he could handle too many kids at once because there were only three kids swimming in the pool. Two girls and a boy, and from the looks of things both girls were vying for the attention of the boy.

Well aware that his luck could end at any second, he knew he didn't have time to waste. So to that end, with his box of matches in his pocket, and his can of kerosene in his hand, he strode over to the pool.

The kids didn't even notice him until he was standing right above them. It was always so much easier to wait until everyone was in the water so he didn't have to carry a gun on him and order them in. Once they were in there, there wasn't really anything they could do to stop him.

"Hey," the boy said when they finally noticed him. "Who're you?"

"Is that the guy you said was coming to fix the broken window, Gia?" one of the girls asked the other.

"I don't know, maybe," Gia replied. "Are you the glass guy?"

Since he wasn't here to waste time chatting with a bunch of kids, he ignored the question and opened his can then began to slosh the kerosene into the water.

"He's not the glass guy," the other girl said, and for the first time, he saw true fear cross their faces.

"Who are you?" the guy demanded, trying to sound all tough, but he could see that the boy was every bit as afraid as the girls were.

Tipping the last of the kerosene into the pool, he pulled out the box of matches. "I'm the man who's going to kill you," he said as he lit the match and threw it into the pool before they could react in any way.

The flames sprung to life immediately, quickly spreading across the surface. The kids screeched in terror and did exactly what Kayla McTierney and David Buffy had done; dive down under the water as though there was a secret tunnel down there that would lead them to safety.

But there wasn't.

There was no safe place for them.

They would die beneath the water or they would die above it, there was only one way this was ending.

The flames danced about, leaping and roaring as though they were greedy to claim another life, like the souls would feed them, giving them their own sort of immortality.

Thirty seconds had passed, he could see them moving about down there, and he knew their lungs must be burning for oxygen. Were they going to come up now? What would it look like when the fire claimed their bodies? What would it sound like?

Excitement bubbled inside him.

Any second now they would come up, he was sure of it.

"Fire, there's a fire!"

The screeched words came from behind him, and when he turned, he saw a person standing in the yard.

Again.

Once again someone had ruined his fun.

Now he was the one who had no choice about what happened next. If he stayed to see what happened next, then the neighbors would get a good look at him, or since everyone carried a cell phone on them these days, they could get a photo of him as well.

He had to get out of here.

With a frustrated growl of disappointment, he turned and ran.

~

10:48 A.M.

Why was this happening again?

The fire at the pool was supposed to be something about the young couples' families not being supportive of the relationship. It was supposed to be a one-off. So why were she and her team rushing to put out another pool fire?

Amethyst jiggled her foot in impotent frustration as they drove towards the house of Luther and Martha James and their seventeen-year-old daughter, Gia. She knew that there was at least one person in that pool when the killer had set the fire, and she knew that they would be too late to save them.

She hated that.

From the tension practically boiling over inside the fire truck, her team hated it too. Oz's concentration was focused on speeding through the neighborhood as quickly as he could, but she could see the tight way he held his lips pursed, and Greg who was sitting in the passenger seat had the window down and was half hanging out it as though that would spur them on. Theo sat beside her and was fiddling with the hem of his jacket. You became a firefighter because you wanted to help people, you wanted to save them, and knowing that you were going to be too late and that people would die was the worst kind of hell.

This neighborhood, while only a mile away from the one where Kayla McTierney and David Buffy had lost their lives not even twenty-four hours ago, was not quite as upmarket. The houses were newer, this estate had only been built about five years ago, but the lots weren't as large, and the trees lining the streets hadn't quite grown enough yet to provide a lot of leafy shade.

As they pulled up in front of a gray concrete single-story house with a simple lawn front yard, an ambulance pulled up alongside them.

"Did someone survive?" she asked.

"According to dispatch, the 911 call said that there were three people in the pool, didn't mention any of them getting out," Greg replied.

"Maybe someone got out once the caller had already disconnected," she said, jumping out of the truck the second it stopped moving.

"We can only hope," Theo agreed.

While someone—or multiple someone's—surviving was exactly the news she wanted to hear, Amethyst knew that if someone had been able to get through the kerosene-fueled flames and out of the pool that they wouldn't be in good shape.

Grabbing the hose, she and the others ran around the side of the house and out into the backyard. There were a couple of trees between the house and the pool, and the first thing she noticed was the postman standing a few yards away from the pool, a garden hose in his hand, pouring water onto a prone body.

Even from this distance, she could see the seriousness of the burns.

Even with the ambulance arriving so quickly, she doubted that whoever had swum through hell to fight for their life would survive past the next few hours.

If that.

Flames still roared on top of the pool, and she tried not to get distracted by the surviving victim and focused on her job. Her job was to put out the fire, it wasn't to deal with the victim, and it wasn't to find whoever had started it.

Squirting foam onto the flames, it didn't take long to put the fire out. Again, the fire had been called in quickly, and again they had arrived on the scene within minutes of receiving the call, and yet once again it hadn't been quick enough to save the two teens whose bodies floated in the foamy water.

They were so young, they should have been able to enjoy a summer day by the pool, laughing, talking, eating, swimming, instead their lives had been cut short. Way too short.

It wasn't fair.

Life wasn't fair.

She knew that, probably better than a lot of people. It hadn't been fair that her parents had sold her and her sisters to human traffickers, and it hadn't been fair what Nikos had done to her and all those other girls, and yet at least she still had her life. There had been times—quite a few of them—over the last twelve years that she had wished she hadn't been granted her life, but she had come to realize that it was a gift, and one that she shouldn't squander.

Something an outsider looking in might think she did.

She took chances, she lived life on the edge, she went skydiving, bungee jumping, she loved to rock climb, and she didn't care that in doing so she was putting herself in dangerous positions.

Life was full of danger, she had accepted that, and the risks involved in all that she chose to do with her spare time, and in the end, it wasn't like there was anyone who would truly miss her if the worst happened and she died. Her sisters of course would be upset, but they had families of their own now, husbands and kids, they had people who relied on them, but she had no one.

Amethyst lingered a little as she and her team began to pack up their tools ready to head back to the station and await another call. She wanted to know about the kid, not so much the details on who they were and how old they were—there was only so much her heart could take and knowing too much about victims was her limit—but she wanted to know what their chances were of surviving.

Paramedics were hunched over the teenager, and the postman still had the hose running. That quick thinking on the man's part could be the difference between life and death, first aid treatment for burns was to keep the person in cold water until help arrived, and that garden hose might just have increased the odds in the teenager's favor.

She hoped so.

She really did.

Just because she was willing to let her own life hang in the balance with all the risky sports and activities she enjoyed, didn't mean that she treated anyone else's life with that same lackadaisical attitude.

"Amethyst, you ready," Theo asked, nudging her shoulder.

The others had already headed back to the truck, but she was lingering in the backyard, close enough to watch what was happening with the kid, who appeared to be a teenage girl, but not so close that she got in the way. "Yeah, I'm ready," she said with a sigh. She would try to find out later if the kid had survived or not. They weren't supposed to follow up on cases like that, but sometimes you just had to know.

With a last look back, she followed Theo around the house. Coming towards them was their boss, Lieutenant Ewan Oswell, she wondered what he was doing here. He didn't come to every scene they attended, there really wasn't any reason for him to. Maybe, with two fires now, the cops were thinking that this wasn't personal and they were actually looking for a serial killer, one with an affinity for fires.

Walking with the lieutenant were Judah and Zeb.

Zeb.

Why did she have to see him again?

She'd dreamed about him last night, not that she would ever admit that to anyone. Maybe if he wasn't her brother-in-law's partner, then she would just go for it, but causing tension in her family wasn't worth it for one night of awesome sex. And she knew it would be awesome.

What she really needed was someone she knew and felt comfortable around who was amenable to the occasional fun between the sheets with no strings attached. She and Theo had tried the whole friends with benefits thing before, but it had almost destroyed their friendship when he wanted more than she could give.

And that was really the crux of her whole problem.

She didn't have anything to give.

Surviving Nikos had meant shutting a side of herself down, a side that she hadn't been able to find again. She had trained herself to view herself and her own life as though they were immaterial, disposable, focusing her whole being on simply not letting Nikos break her.

And she had succeeded.

Succeeded, but the cost had been high.

It wasn't that she had lost her ability to love, she adored her sisters, and their families, and would gladly die for any one of them. She had pushed all three of them to set aside their fears and the past to find the happiness they deserved, but when it came to herself, she just didn't see things the same way.

What could she possibly offer a great guy like Zeb Tuck?

Nothing.

Nothing except a woman who spent all her spare time working out and finding the most dangerous pursuits she could because that adrenalin rushing through her veins was the only time she felt truly alive.

It wouldn't be fair on Zeb to give him a lifetime of that. There was no way she could give him more, even if he wanted more, and she really had no indication that he did.

Her eyes met Zeb's, and she saw something flick through his. Something she couldn't quite read.

She could read what flickered through her body though.

Heated desire.

Her mind knew that even one night of passion wasn't a good idea, but her body clearly hadn't gotten the memo.

Eager now to get out of here and as far away from Zeb as she could, Amethyst quickened her stride.

Just as she was about to hurry past the lieutenant, Zeb, and Judah, her boss stopped her.

"Amethyst, just the person I was looking for," he said.

"Oh?" she replied, wondering what he wanted her for.

"I don't want you to go back to the station with the others," Lieutenant Oswell told her.

"Why?" she asked suspiciously.

"Because I'm assigning you to work with the cops to find this pyromaniac who is killing teenagers in swimming pools."

Assigned to work with the cops?

With Zeb?

Why did life like to torture her?

~

11:01 A.M.

"You're assigning me to what?" Amethyst asked, looking at her boss in shock.

"To work with the cops to find this guy," Lieutenant Oswell repeated calmly.

"Oh," Amethyst said, dropping her gaze to the ground.

She sounded about as happy with the idea as Zeb had been when the lieutenant had met him and Judah here at the scene of the second swimming pool murders in as many days, to say that he had spoken with their boss and that Amethyst would be working this case with them.

Spending that much time around Amethyst was the last thing Zeb wanted. He was having a hard enough time trying to stop himself from thinking about her and how much he wanted to lick and nip at every part of her body until he had her screaming his name and begging him to let her come, and now he was going to have to spend all day with her.

Great.

He was going to end the day how he'd started it, with another cold shower.

Clearing his throat, he deliberately looked away, aware of the fact that his partner, the lieutenant, and Amethyst were now looking at him quizzically.

"I'll let you guys get back to work, catch Amethyst up on what your theories are at the moment, and she'll be able to give you any information you need from the fire side of things," Lieutenant Oswell said as he headed off to where paramedics were working on a teenage girl who had somehow managed to survive the fiery inferno.

At least for now.

Zeb chanced a glance in Amethyst's direction and found her staring at him, an inscrutable expression on her face. He knew why he wasn't thrilled to be working with her, but why was she so unhappy to be working with him?

Their eyes met, and he got a chill.

A chill.

That was bad, right?

It meant that this was a bad idea. It was the fireworks love at first sight thing that would mean that hooking up with her was something that he should move to the top of his to do list.

But a chill meant back off.

"I'll have to go back to the station to change," Amethyst said, her tone as frosty as that chill he'd just gotten.

"No need, your boss brought your clothes," Judah said, holding up a bag. "Why don't you go change inside the house then meet us back out here."

"Fine," she agreed, snatching the bag and stalking off.

"What's with you two?" Judah asked. "I could cut the tension with a knife."

"Nothing," he muttered, stalking off in the opposite direction to where Amethyst had gone. "Absolutely nothing."

"If you say so," Judah said.

The paramedics had bundled their survivor onto a stretcher and were wheeling it this way. Zeb had no idea how anyone had managed to get through the flames and out of that pool, it was a miracle, and one that he hoped was big enough that the kid wasn't just going to linger on in pain for a few hours or a day or two, and then pass away anyway.

"How is she?" he asked as both he and Judah followed the EMTs toward the ambulance.

"Third-degree burns to seventy-five percent of her body," a medic replied.

He winced at that. He knew how painful burns were. He might have survived the fire that had claimed his family, but he hadn't escaped unscathed. He'd had second and third-degree burns on the backs of his legs as he had wriggled through a small window to escape his burning home.

"Chances of her making it?" Judah asked.

The medic shot them a pained glance, and that told them all they needed to know.

The chances weren't good that Gia James would make it.

"Any chance we can speak with her?" he asked.

"She's sedated, burns to her airway meant we had to tube her," the EMT replied. "We gotta move."

Zeb and Judah stood back as they bundled the stretcher into the back of the ambulance, then took off, lights and sirens screaming.

"Is she still alive?" Amethyst asked, joining them on the sidewalk.

"For now," he replied.

Amethyst sighed, and he could feel her pain. She may like to give off the impression that she was this tough girl, who lifted weights, and ran marathons, and did every crazy, dangerous sport or activity she could find, but he knew that she had a big heart.

"I don't know exactly why I'm here and what I'm supposed to do," she said. "I don't know anything about working a case like this, I'm a firefighter, I put out fires, I don't solve crimes."

"I think that's exactly why you're here," Judah told her. "To give us a different perspective. A unique one. We know how to solve crimes, but you know fire. I'm going to go and interview the postman who gave Gia James a chance at life by being quick thinking enough to use the garden hose on her while he waited for help to arrive. Why don't you two go and track down the 911 caller."

What was his partner doing to him?

Leaving him alone with Amethyst was a definite recipe for disaster.

"The postman didn't call it in?" Amethyst asked.

"No, a man who was supposed to be here to fix a broken window did, only he then split," Judah explained. "I'll catch up with you two at lunchtime, and we'll compare notes."

With that, his partner walked off.

Leaving them alone.

Alone.

While it would be extremely unprofessional to drag Amethyst into his arms and kiss her senseless at a crime scene that was teeming with cops, and crime scene techs, and nosy neighbors, Zeb couldn't deny that the thought crossed his mind.

"So …" he said.

"So …" she echoed.

This was ridiculous, they couldn't stand here staring at each other all day. Or more accurately determinedly looking anywhere but at each other.

Like it or not, they were working together until this case was closed, and he was going to have to find a way to make this work because it wasn't like he could be taking cold showers all day long. He wasn't a teenage boy, surely he could manage to keep his hormones under control for a few hours a day. Okay, so a lot more than a *few* hours a day, but still, he was an adult, he could separate his sexual needs with his need to do his job.

Job.

That was the way to get through the day, he just had to keep things focused on the job.

Hard as it would be to ignore the way her long legs looked in those tight-fitting jeans, and the simple white t-shirt that seemed to draw his attention right to her small round breasts, he was going to have to do it, and keeping his mind glued to the job was probably the only way he could achieve it.

Clearing his throat again, he took a step toward where he'd parked his car a little way down the street. "As Judah said, the 911 call came in from a man who was supposed to be here installing a new window to replace one that had been broken earlier this morning. We then got a second 911 call from the postman who said that there was no one else here but him, and a kid who had just climbed out of the burning pool. Obviously, we thought that was suspicious, why would someone call 911 then disappear before anyone arrived, so we looked into the man and it turns out he has quite an extensive record. He is currently out on parole after serving two years on an assault charge, and there was an outstanding warrant on him for a brawl at a bar earlier in the summer, he ran that night too before cops could arrest him. Maybe he was afraid that this time he would get picked up if he hung around."

"Do you like this guy as the killer?" Amethyst asked as she walked along beside him.

"Too early to tell yet, but we definitely want to look into him more closely."

"So you're going to go and what? Drive to his house, see if he's there? Interview him if he is? And I'm coming with you?"

"Yes, and yes, if you're up for it."

"I've never done anything like that before, but I guess so," Amethyst agreed. Then opened her mouth to say something else, but tripped over a tree root as they crossed the grass verge to get to the car.

Instinct had him reaching out to grab her elbow and steady her before she could fall, but the second his hand curled around her lean but muscled arm, he knew that touching her was a bad idea.

Electricity.

There was definite electricity between them.

From Amethyst's sharp gasp, he knew that she felt it too.

Great.

Their physical attraction was mutual.

Zeb really hoped that Amethyst was going to be able to do a better job at ignoring it than he was doing because that urge to kiss her was back.

So much for focusing on the job, the way things were going, he'd be lucky if he didn't have her naked in his bed by the end of the day.

Lucky, yeah.

Damned if he did and damned if he didn't.

Sex with Amethyst would be amazing, but it would make things awkward with the partner he had to see every day by bedding his sister-in-law, not having sex with her was torture.

2:24 P.M.

Delia Arthur stretched and wiggled her toes.

The sun was warm on her bare skin, making her want to close her eyes and drift off to sleep. But she couldn't because she had to mind the kids. As much as she loved being a mother, there was certainly the odd time where all she wanted was to just lie in the sun, sip iced coffee, and read a book or nap. Today was one of those times.

Setting the book down on her lap, she looked up at the kids. They were splashing about in the pool, laughing and squealing, throwing a ball about, and squirting each other with water pistols. They were having fun and enjoying the last couple of weeks of summer vacation before they had to go back to school, which to them was like being in prison.

Summer vacation was always nice, but Delia had to admit that she was looking forward to her kids being back in school. She ran her own business, designing book covers and teasers, and she found it so hard to get anything done while they were around. The first few weeks of vacation had been fun, she'd enjoyed playing with the kids, and taking them out to do fun things, but now she was ready to get the kids back in school and get back to work.

Still, back to school meant that summer would be nearly over, and she hated when fall arrived. She was definitely not a cold weather kind of girl, the cold weather made her want to just curl up in bed and hibernate.

Today was deliciously hot though, so she was going to banish all thoughts of the coming change in seasons and just drink up the sunshine.

Sipping her iced coffee, she watched the kids and decided that she would probably just order pizza for dinner, she wasn't in the mood to cook. There was plenty of ice cream in the freezer, and a bottle of soda in the fridge left over from her daughter's eleventh birthday party earlier in the week. The kids would probably play in the pool until well after dark, then they'd have dinner, and maybe watch movies before they went to bed. Since it was summer, she let them stay up way past their bedtime since they could sleep in.

They were eleven and nine now, about to be a sixth-grader and a fourth-grader when the new school year started. Both her daughter and her son were excited about school, and she loved that they were still inquisitive and curious learners, she hoped it was something that they never lost. It wouldn't be long until Jessa was a teenager, already she was moving away from being a child and becoming a pre-teen, soon she would completely leave behind the world of dolls and toys, and take the next step toward adulthood.

As much as she sometimes wished she had more time to herself, more time to do her own thing, she would miss her kids being little. She loved being able to wipe away their tears and make all the bad things in the world better just because she was their mom. And she loved when her kids wanted to hold her hand while they were out, or snuggle up beside her on the couch when they hung out watching movies. Soon all of that would be behind them, and they'd be teenagers who would be embarrassed by her just because she existed.

"Mom."

"Yes, honey?" she said as Jessa and Johnny appeared before her, dripping water all over her.

"Can we ride our bikes to the store and then go to Kiki's house?" Johnny asked.

"You guys can't just turn up at Kiki's house," she reminded them. Kiki was Jessa's best friend and lived with her family just two streets over. The kids had hung out a lot together over the summer, but she was trying to make sure they didn't take advantage of the other family and got the kids to spend time on their own some days.

"Kiki texted that it's okay with her mom for us to come over," Jessa told her.

"Then I guess it's okay," she gave permission. If the kids spent the rest of the day at Kiki's, then she could enjoy a little alone time. "But I want you home for dinner tonight, Daddy will pick you up on his way home from work." Delia expected the kids might have complained about that, but they both nodded. "Make sure you mind your manners, listen to Kiki's mom, and put on more sunblock if you're going to be spending the rest of the afternoon outside."

"We will, Mom," Jessa said with a small eye roll like she was too old for these little reminders.

"Be careful on your bikes, watch for traffic." Delia knew that the kids already knew all of the rules, and this wasn't the first time they had ridden their bikes to the store and then over to a friend's house, but they were her babies no matter how old they got, and she didn't want anything to happen to them.

"We'll be fine," Jessa said, already turning to leave.

"Hey, goodbye kisses, please." She stopped her daughter.

With another eye roll, Jessa leaned over and gave her a quick peck on the cheek. Johnny gave her a hug and a kiss, then both kids went running off to grab their bikes and head off to buy snacks and have fun with their friend. As she watched them go, Delia missed the days when she was the most important person in her kids' lives. She was proud of them seeing them growing up, and she did like that they were more independent and she could spend more time on her work, but she really had enjoyed the days when she was the sun of her kids' world.

Standing up, Delia stretched, and took off her sunglasses, setting them on the table beside the lounge where she had been reading. Since the kids had gone, she might take a little dip in the pool. Some days she'd jump in with them, and some weekends and evenings their dad would join all of them, and they'd splash about, dunk each other, toss a ball around, and just have fun.

How many more summers like this would they have?

In just two years, Jessa would be a teen, and she doubted she would want to play with her parents and little brother in the pool. Then two years after that Johnny would be a teenager too. She had to treasure these moments because there wouldn't be too many more of them.

Diving into the pool, Delia started swimming laps. She'd been a swimmer ever since she was a very little girl, even considered swimming professionally for a while, her coach had thought she was good enough to try to make it to the Olympics, but then she'd been in a car accident, hurt her shoulder, and never been able to swim well enough to take it anywhere. So now she just swam for fun, when the kids had been little, she had hoped one of them would have inherited her skill and love for swimming, but neither of them really enjoyed competitive swimming.

Swimming lap after lap relaxed her, and she rethought her decision to have the kids come home for dinner. Maybe she and her husband could enjoy a little alone time, and then they'd ride their bikes over there, grab the kids, and take an after dark bike ride as a family before coming home and watching movies.

It wasn't until fire suddenly sprung up around her that Delia realized there was a man dressed all in black standing in her backyard.

The kids.

Her first thoughts were of her kids, had this man hurt Jessa and Johnny?

Before she could look for her babies, the flames closed in on her and she had nowhere else to go but under the water.

Fear bubbled inside her as she swam about trying to find a place where there was no fire so she could go up and get out of the pool.

But there wasn't any.

The flames were everywhere.

How was he doing this?

How did you set fire to water?

Delia circled the pool over and over again, hoping against hope that the flames would disappear, but they didn't.

She was trapped.

There was no way out of this pool other than to go through the flames, and they would kill her anyway.

As a swimmer, she could hold her breath for a long time, nearly two minutes. Two minutes was an unbearably long time to be swimming about under the water waiting to die.

Die.

She was really going to die down here.

Just a couple of minutes ago she had been planning out the evening like she had the rest of her life to spend time with her husband and kids.

How wrong she had been.

Her lungs screamed at her to take a breath, not knowing that there was no oxygen for them to inhale.

Delia fought against the impulse, which was so innate that eventually it couldn't be denied.

Her mouth opened.

Water rushed in.

It looked like she was out of time.

∾

2:44 P.M.

. . .

So far, all they had done for the last three hours was drive around.

The longer she sat in this car, the harder Amethyst was finding it to not kiss Zeb.

He was sexy, that little dimple an inch above the corner of his mouth kept catching her attention every time he looked at her, and the shirt he was wearing did little to hide the fact that he probably worked out more than she did, and that was saying something because bodybuilding was her hobby. She ran ironwoman competitions, and any extreme marathon she could get her hands on, the latest being the polar circle marathon which she would be running this coming winter.

She wished that her boss hadn't given her this assignment. What was he thinking? What help was she possibly going to be to this investigation? She had no idea about interviewing suspects or looking for clues, she wasn't even any good at the game Clue let alone at solving a real-life crime. So having to sit in a car for hours with someone that she was attracted to and who she knew was attracted to her too, was a special kind of Hell.

Neither she nor Zeb had spoken more than a couple of words in the last three hours. They'd driven out to the house of the glass guy, but he hadn't been there, so they'd driven to his place of business, but he hadn't been there either, so now they were going to the man's mother's house to see if she knew where her son had disappeared to.

"It's Judah," Zeb announced when his phone beeped.

Somewhat reluctantly, Amethyst glanced over at him to see if there was news, specifically news that the killer had been caught and was now sitting in a prison cell where he belonged.

"What is it?" she finally asked when he didn't say anything else.

"Another fire just got called in."

Her heart dropped.

When was this going to end?

It was only a few hours since the last fire, and he had struck again already. How were they going to find this guy if he kept moving this quickly?

"Where is it?"

"Domino Street," he replied.

"That's only around the corner from here," she said. "When was the fire called in? How long ago?"

"911 knows to alert us to any swimming pool fires, so Judah was called as soon as they were called."

"So, like only a minute or so, if we hurry, we might get there in time." She wanted to save someone this time, although Gia James had survived the fire after dragging herself through the flames, according to a phone call Zeb had gotten about an hour ago, she had passed away shortly after arriving at the hospital. Amethyst hated that the girl had fought so hard for her life only to lose it anyway, but at least she had gotten a chance to say goodbye to her parents before passing away.

But this time could be different.

This time if the person—or persons—had been in the water for only a couple of minutes, then if they could put the fire out and get the person out then there was a chance that they could survive.

Zeb turned on his lights and sirens, and thirty seconds later, they were screeching to a stop outside a red brick two-story house. There were no other cop cars, and there was no fire truck, they were the first ones here.

Flinging off her seatbelt, Amethyst jumped from the car and started running, there had to be a way to save whoever was in that pool.

There had to be.

Her heart needed there to be.

As she rounded the house, she saw the flames. Fire was a part of her life, and she wasn't afraid of it, instead of running away from the flames like most people might do, she ran straight for them.

"Check the house for a fire extinguisher," she screamed over her shoulder to Zeb. Since the killer was using kerosene to set the fires they needed a fire extinguisher designed to put out flammable liquid fires. Hopefully, the house had one in the kitchen to be used in case of a cooking emergency.

Leaving Zeb to take care of that, she circled the pool, trying to find a place where the flames were smaller, where she might be able to dive through them to reach the body she could see floating underneath and pull it to safety.

The fire was raging.

She wasn't sure that she could find a safe path through the flames.

Amethyst was about to risk it and jump in any way, sure that she could be quick enough to get the woman out before the fire devoured them both when an arm snapped around her waist yanking her back.

"You can't go in there, it's suicide," a voice hissed in her ear.

"I can save her," she countered, struggling against Zeb's hold, but he only tightened his grip on her and held her pinned against his chest.

"No, you can't," he said simply, but his voice was coated with empathy. He felt the same need to dive into the pool and try to save the woman floating in there that she did, but his brain was able to function logically.

Hers wasn't.

She had to try.

She *had* to.

"It's already too late, I'm sorry, Amethyst, there's nothing you can do."

Too late.

She was always too late.

How many people had she been too late to save in her years as a firefighter? More than she wanted to count.

"I have to try," she said, aware that tears had started to tumble down her cheeks, but she couldn't stop them. The more she tried the faster they came. The fire roared, the body floated amongst the flames like it was one of them now. There was nothing she could do to save the woman, and yet that didn't diminish her need to try. If Zeb wasn't still holding on to her, she may very well have dived into the fire and tried to pull the woman to safety, only to get eaten alive by the flames.

"Shh, it's okay," Zeb whispered soothingly in her ear, and his strong arms gently turned her around so that she was no longer facing the fire but was being cradled against Zeb's chest. It was strong and hard, and even though she wanted to wrench herself free, she didn't. Instead, she leaned into him, resting against him and blocking everything else from her mind.

Sirens sounded in the distance.

Help was coming, but just like her and Zeb it would be too late to do anything to save the poor woman who had done nothing but spend a day in her own back yard by her own swimming pool.

This killer was relentless.

Sadistic.

He was using fire as a weapon to torture innocent people and throw them into a horrific nightmare where they would suffer a long and painful death.

This was too much.

It was one thing to come in with her team and try to put out a fire then walk away. Then she could compartmentalize, not think too much about the victims or the perpetrator, do her job and go home, but today she was forced to change all of that. She had to see the victims as people that were now her responsibility, and there were so many potential victims out there that it was overwhelming to think about. She didn't want to try to get inside the killer's head, she just wanted to go home, cry a little more, and then have a work out so she could let her mind settle and focus on training for her upcoming marathon.

Only she wasn't sure that she would be able to put today out of her head.

She and Zeb had been supposed to find this man who had been at the James house earlier and called in the first fire before disappearing.

They had failed.

That meant that this fire was their fault.

"I don't think I can do this," she murmured into Zeb's chest. Her way of surviving the hell Nikos had put her through was to focus on keeping a tight control on herself and her thoughts, it was making sure she never saw herself as a victim and making sure she always remembered that life was fragile and could be lost in a single moment.

But this case was making her world view shimmer out of her grasp.

She wasn't in control here.

She was so far outside her comfort zone that she felt like her whole world had been rocked off its foundations.

"You *can* do this," Zeb contradicted. Grasping her shoulders, he gently stood her up straight and then touched a finger to the dark red scar that marred her neck.

She never bothered to hide it, it was just a scar, and everyone at the station knew about her past, and that she had been found half dead in a vacant lot on her eighteenth birthday, so there was no point in pretending it didn't happen by covering up the scar.

"This proves you can do anything," he told her. His steady voice, the sincerity in the honey-colored eyes that looked down at her, the way he kept one hand clasped reassuringly around her bicep all touched her in a place deep inside. His words strengthened her, reminded her that she never shirked on any responsibility she was given, and she never backed away from any challenge.

She could do this.

She *would* do this.

She would work this case with Zeb and Judah and help them find this killer.

Brushing at her wet cheeks, Amethyst resolutely straightened her spine. "Let's go do this."

~

7:27 P.M.

Evenings were her favorite time of day.

Diamond looked forward to it all day long. After dinner, she and her family would play a game, and then curl up on the couch together and watch one of Archie's favorite shows. She loved just hanging out together, doing family things, enjoying each other's company, and just being a family.

She had everything she had ever wanted.

As much as she had been worried that her being unable to get pregnant and have biological children would be a stumbling block for her relationship with Elijah, she had been wrong. He hadn't been fazed by it, and now they were happily raising his adopted son, who she hoped to adopt herself in the near future, fostering a teenage girl, and planning to adopt another child.

Everything had moved so quickly. Just four months ago, she and Elijah had started dating, and now they were married with a growing family. She'd thought that Ruby and Judah had moved quickly, but she and Elijah had outdone them by months. At first she had felt like maybe they were taking things too quickly, and that they should wait an appropriate amount of time before marrying, but what was the point of that? She had liked him for over a year before they finally started dating, why wait longer just to say they waited longer? And what was an appropriate amount of time to wait to marry the man you loved anyway?

"Okay, buddy, its bedtime," she told Archie, who was snuggled up on her lap.

"'Kay," the little boy agreed, he was such a sweet little boy, and always so well behaved. He had the occasional tantrum like all toddlers did, but he usually did what he was asked the first time, and he hardly ever complained or whined.

"Brooke, can you go help Archie get into his PJs and get his teeth brushed?" Elijah asked their teenage foster daughter who was curled up in an armchair in the corner with her phone.

"Sure," Brooke said with an eye roll, but Diamond knew that really she already loved her little foster brother. She'd seen the teenager reading him stories, and playing trains with him, and she'd make him breakfast in the mornings, so she knew that Brooke really didn't mind helping out, she just had to give the usual teenage disinterest and complaint.

Brooke was a good girl, and both she and Elijah wanted her to feel like this was her home, they didn't know how long she would be here, the fourteen-year-old's mother was currently in prison, her father in the wind somewhere, but when the mother got out she could petition to regain custody. While Diamond hoped that didn't happen, she believed that she and Elijah could give the girl the stability that she needed, there were no guarantees when it came to fostering.

Being a foster parent had long since been a dream of hers. Ever since her little sister, Sapphire, had spent a short time in the foster system, she had wanted to take in teenage girls and love them. So when she had brought up the idea of fostering to Elijah, she'd said specifically that she would like to take in older kids and not babies like most people wanted.

"Come on, Arch," Brooke said, picking up the little boy and swinging him around, making him giggle.

Once the kids were gone, she turned to Elijah who was sitting beside her. "I hope we get to keep her, she's such a great kid."

"She is," Elijah agreed. "I hope she gets to stay with us as well, but we have to make sure we don't get our hopes up because things could change."

It was such a delicate balancing line between not getting so attached that it broke your heart when a foster kid went back to their family, but also loving them enough that it felt like this was really their home. And she *wanted* Brooke to feel like this was her home. As far as she was concerned, Brooke was a member of this family now, regardless of the fact that she had only been here for two months, and she hoped that Brooke would always feel like she had a home here no matter how old she got and what the future held.

"I know," she assured her husband. "But I do care about her, and I hope she knows that. I hope that she knows that this is her home now and that she's always welcome here."

"She knows. She's settled in well, better than I expected, especially since this is our first time fostering."

"Not our last though," she said. Diamond saw fostering as a permanent part of their future and their family even if they did adopt a child.

"Definitely not."

"I got the paperwork for us to fill out to start the adoption process," she said, settling against Elijah's side. Since everything that had happened a few months ago, she'd felt like she needed to take some time away from work, so she had resigned from her job. Her life had needed an overhaul, and it has got one, she'd married Elijah, she was helping raise his son, they were fostering and planning on adopting, and she was going to be teaching art in a local elementary school when school started back. Every aspect of her life was just perfect.

"Once we put Archie to bed and spend a bit of time with Brooke, we can take a look at it and start filling it out," Elijah said, and she could feel his excitement.

She was excited too, as perfect as her life felt it was only going to get better, she couldn't wait to welcome a new member into their little family. "What time is your mom coming home tonight?" Elijah's mother had moved in with him while he'd been a single dad to help him out with Archie, and even though they hadn't gotten off to the best start, now she loved Marcia Newton and had been the one who suggested that she remain living with them. But now that she was there, it meant that Marcia had more freedom to do her own thing and she had certainly taken advantage of that and taken up several hobbies.

"She won't be home until late, after ten, gives us plenty of time alone together after the kids go to bed," Elijah said with that smile that said he was already thinking of undressing her and having his way with her.

Diamond's mind immediately ran in the same direction, and she was just leaning up to kiss him when Archie yelled out.

"Daddy, Diamond, I'm ready for stories."

"Until later," Elijah said, giving her a quick peck on the lips that was only a drop in the ocean compared to what she wanted, but the kids always came first.

Hand in hand they walked upstairs to Archie's room and found him already snuggled under the covers, Brooke tucking him in and passing him his bunny that he slept with every night. Once she saw them, the teenager immediately headed for the door as though she thought she was intruding if she stayed now that they were here. That wasn't how she wanted Brooke to feel.

"Why don't you read the stories tonight," she said to the girl. "Archie, would you like Brooke to read tonight?"

"Yes," he said, clapping his hands enthusiastically.

"Are you sure?" Brooke asked.

"Of course," Elijah told her. "Why don't you choose two stories from the bookcase, and we'll all squeeze into Arch's bed."

Brooke grabbed two books, and then they all crammed onto the bed. Diamond rested against Elijah's chest and held Archie's little hand as Brooke began to read. She knew all of Archie's books by heart and didn't really listen to the words, she was too busy enjoying the moment. Brooke's mom had another year left on her sentence, by then, the girl would be fifteen, and hopefully her mother would see that she was happy and thriving here.

Who would be the next member of their family?

Their home had five bedrooms, she and Elijah had one, Elijah's mom had one, and Archie and Brooke each had their own room, that only left one spare bedroom, one that the baby they would hopefully be adopting soon would have. They had been discussing building an apartment over the garage for Marcia, she'd been talking about having a bit more privacy but still wanted to stay nearby, so that would give them another spare bedroom. In her mind, that meant they had room to bring in another teenage girl who was in the foster system and needed a home.

Home.

Growing up, that word hadn't been a bad one, but she certainly hadn't had the happiest home in the world.

Then after what had happened to her and her sisters, her home had been the place where she sought refuge, her safe haven.

But now, her home was both a safe haven and the place where she was the happiest.

Home sweet home had never meant so much to her as it did in this house where she lived with her husband and their kids. Blood didn't make a family, none of them in this house besides Elijah and his mother shared biology, but the love that filled this place made them one strong family unit.

CHAPTER
Five

August 23rd
8:23 A.M.

It felt odd walking into the police station in the morning instead of going into the fire station like she was used to.

Amethyst felt much calmer this morning than she had been at the second fire yesterday. Zeb had helped her realize that she could do this because of one simple reason. She had to.

It was as simple as that.

And she liked to keep things simple.

Keeping things simple was how she had survived Nikos. She had kept her focus only on making sure that he never got his disgusting, filthy hands on her mind. That was all she had worried about, all she had thought about, the only thing that had mattered to her in those long months.

So she was going to do the same here.

She was going to do her part. She was going to do whatever it took to find this guy, from here on out, that was the focus of her life.

That meant there would be no more thinking about Zeb.

They were working together, that was it. There would be no more thinking about kissing him. No more thinking about how sexy he was. No more dreaming about what they might do to each other if they both just admitted that they wanted to.

Work.

From now on, she was all about work.

With that resolve, Amethyst parked her car in the parking garage underneath the police precinct, and walked to the elevator. It was already hot, and the temperature was set to soar. That was not good news. Never in her life had she wished so hard for gray skies and rain. Rain would mean that people would head indoors, away from their swimming pools, which would mean the killer would lose his victim pool.

But it didn't look like that was going to be the case.

It would be another hot day, and people would head out into their yards, to sit by their pools, and go for a swim to cool off.

Amethyst hated that there was nothing she could do to stop another fire from happening today.

The lift door opened and she got in, drumming her fingers on her arm as she waited for it to reach the homicide floor. When the lift dinged and the doors opened, she stepped out and immediately felt out of place. She knew she was here to bring a different perspective to this case, but she really didn't know how much she had to contribute, and she wanted to pull her weight, she didn't want to be the weak link that let this guy roam free setting more fires and killing more people.

Since she had been here several times before visiting her sister, Sapphire, she knew where Zeb and Judah's desks were and headed straight there. She saw Judah standing at his desk, gathering his laptop and a pile of papers into his arms. She didn't see Zeb. That was good, she didn't need him to be the first thing she saw this morning because he had certainly been the last thing she had thought about before she went to sleep last night.

Reminding herself of her work first resolution, Amethyst walked over to her brother-in-law. "Morning, Judah."

"Hey, Amethyst, we're set up in the conference room."

"I can carry that," she said, grabbing the second stack of reports off his desk so he didn't have to balance them on top of what he was already carrying.

"Thanks." Judah looked stressed this morning, since she had already texted Ruby, she knew that everything was fine with her sister and the baby, so she assumed that what had him concerned was this case.

Together they walked across the squad room to the conference room, and since she only had one stack of things in her arms, she reached out and opened the door. The first thing she saw as she stepped into the room was Zeb.

He looked over at her, his eyes were smoldering, and her own eyes couldn't help but drop to his lips.

Work, she reminded herself, shoving those thoughts quickly away.

"We have the crime scene report from the latest fire," Judah announced as he brushed past her and set down his things on the table.

"Good, hopefully there's something in it that will help us," Zeb said.

She deliberately kept her gaze focused on the table as she walked up to it and set down her own armful of things. Although she wasn't looking at him, she could feel Zeb's eyes on her, watching her every move. It made a shiver ripple through her, one she hoped no one noticed, and if they did then they didn't know its cause.

"So, what does the report say?" Zeb asked as they all took seats.

Judah rifled through the reports piled up in front of him and pulled one out. Before he could read any of it the door swung open, and a pretty woman in her late thirties came bustling through the door.

"Morning, Elsie," Judah greeted her.

"Morning," the woman returned. "Hi, I'm Elsie, I work with the crime scene unit," she said, holding out a hand.

Amethyst shook it. "I'm Amethyst, Sapphire's sister. I'm a firefighter, and my boss and their boss decided that maybe I can help with this case." She still wasn't sure that she had much to contribute, but she was going to do her best to be as helpful as she could be.

"Nice to meet you, Amethyst." Elsie took a seat. "Judah, I see you guys got my report, have you read it yet?"

"Not yet, we were just about to, but since you're here you may as well give us a rundown."

"Sure." Elsie nodded vigorously. "I definitely have something for you that might actually give you a direction to move in."

Amethyst's ears perked up at that, and she saw both Zeb and Judah straighten in their chairs, they all wanted to hear something that was going to close this case.

"Once we finished up at the second fire, the one at the James house, going through the pool and the yard, we moved onto the street, and we found something just outside the house, on the grass verge. We found a match. It had been lit then put out and dropped on the ground. Since we know he loves fire, he might have been out there, getting in the mood for what was to come."

She was new to this whole working a case like a cop thing but that made sense to her.

"We know he's a pyromaniac so it does make sense that he might have been out there for a while before he went to the backyard and set the fire," Judah agreed.

"But how does that help us find this guy?" Zeb asked. "We already knew the pyromaniac thing, that doesn't help us narrow down our suspect pool and give us a direction to move in."

"But this will," Elsie told him. "Next to the match, we found a boot print. The boot print was a nice clear one, and it had a logo in the center of it. I ran the print through the system, and I got a hit. The print comes from a boot used by the fire department."

All eyes fell on her.

Amethyst felt her mouth fall open.

What was she supposed to do with that information?

Were they suggesting that the killer was a firefighter?

Were they suggesting that *she* was the killer?

"Do you guys think that I did this? That I killed those people?" she demanded shrilly, about ready to launch to her feet to go running out of here to find the nearest bathroom so she could throw up.

"What? No," Zeb said emphatically. "Not at all. You were at the first two fires with your team within minutes of them being called in, there's no way you could have set them. And you were with me when the third fire was started. You are not a suspect, but ..."

She didn't need him to finish the sentence.

She knew what they were all thinking.

They believed that the arsonist was a firefighter.

One of her colleagues.

"Is there anyone you can think of who might have done this?" Judah asked her.

Amethyst glared at him. "No one I know would do this. Firefighters *put out* fires they don't *start* them."

"CSU found a print at the crime scene, right next to a match," Judah told her like she hadn't been sitting right here at the table while Elsie had told them that.

"I heard what she said," she snapped. "But she's wrong. We were all over that scene trying to get in there quickly enough to put out that fire and save those kids. It's probably one of our boot prints."

"It's not," Elsie said. "The print isn't near any of the others we found. Someone must have watered the grass verge not long before the fire because we got a lot of good prints, but these ones were off to the side, toward the neighbor's house, and they were right with the match. I believe that they belonged to the killer, and if he was wearing boots issued to firefighters, then it goes to reason that he *is* a firefighter."

She wanted to argue, she wanted to disprove what the crime scene tech had said, she wanted to find something that would show that they were wrong.

But she had nothing.

Had she been working with a sadistic killer?

The very idea left her nauseous.

∼

9:08 A.M.

Amethyst looked like she was going to be sick.

Zeb got it, he *really* did. He knew what it was like to find out that you had been betrayed in the most hurtful of ways.

Now Amethyst had to deal with the fact that the man they were looking for was most likely someone she knew. And not just someone she knew, but one of her colleagues, someone that she was friends with. He knew how badly she had been taking these deaths, she felt responsible for them because she hadn't been able to put the fires out in time to save them. Yesterday she had cried in his arms, convinced that she couldn't do anything to help them find this guy. He had told her that she was wrong and he believed that, even more so now that they knew they were looking for a firefighter.

He wanted to reach out to her, comfort her, take away some of her pain if he could. Zeb was quickly coming to realize that maybe he felt something for Amethyst beyond the strong physical attraction. He didn't just want sex with her, he wanted something more, maybe a lot more.

It was when he realized that she intended to jump into the flaming pool to try to save Delia Arthur that things had changed. In that brief second, when he had been reaching for her to drag her backward and prevent her from committing suicide in her attempt to save someone who was clearly already gone, that he realized that if she was gone he would miss her.

She wasn't just his partner's wife's sister.

She was a whole lot more.

She was someone that he wanted to get to know better, she was someone who he could see himself caring about.

When he was holding her as she cried, he had felt a stirring in his heart. A stirring that he hadn't felt before. He'd never been in love, never even really had a serious relationship, he'd never had a girlfriend that had lasted more than a couple of months. Usually, once the heat died off and things started to settle into a routine, he bailed because he didn't feel anything. But Amethyst ... well, it was too early to tell, but who knows, maybe something could happen between them.

"You have anything else for us, Elsie?" Judah asked.

"Nope, not really, nothing that's going to help you find this guy."

"Then we should start going through every firefighter that isn't on

Amethyst's team, or the team that went to the third fire yesterday, since we know it can't be any of them, figure out who might be our most likely suspects, or at least who we can rule out," Judah said.

"We also need to track down the glass guy from the James fire yesterday, just because he's probably out as a suspect now that we know we're looking for a firefighter we still need to talk to him, find out what he saw. Since we know that the killer probably only ran off when he realized someone else was there then the glass guy probably saw him," he said.

"How about I go and interview the glass guy—presuming I can find him—and you two start going through the firefighters and make a list of who we need to look into more closely," Judah suggested.

That was exactly what he had been hoping his partner would say. He really wanted to get a little time alone with Amethyst, but he wasn't going to come right out and say that. "Sounds like a plan," he agreed.

"You guys didn't get a chance to go to his mother's house yesterday because of the fire at the Arthur house, so I'll start there. I'll walk you out, Elsie."

"Okay, good luck, guys. I hope you can find him before there's another fire," the crime scene tech said as she stood up and followed Judah out the door.

Leaving Zeb and Amethyst alone.

The first thought he had shouldn't be that all he wanted to do was curl an arm around her waist, draw her close, and kiss her until she forgot all about what she had just learned.

That would be unprofessional.

They had a job to do.

Before they got started going through all of Amethyst's colleagues, he wanted to let her know that he understood what she was going through, and that he was here if she needed to talk.

Reaching over, he lightly touched his fingertips to the back of her hand. Amethyst jumped, her head snapping in his direction as heat flashed through her eyes, she tried to cover it, but he saw it. What got to him more than that was the defeat on her face. Defeat and hurt.

This wasn't the first time she had suffered a betrayal.

What her parents had done to her and her sisters was despicable, and he wasn't sure he could have survived it had he been in their places. But the Hatcher sisters were strong, they had survived, and Amethyst would survive this too.

"You okay?" he asked.

"Of course." Amethyst straightened in her chair like she had to prove to him that she was strong, but she didn't, that wasn't what he wanted.

"I know it's hard to accept that we're looking for one of your colleagues."

"We don't know for sure that we are," she shot back defensively.

It was fine if she wasn't ready to accept it yet, as long as she was able to be objective enough to give them the information they needed. "I know what you're feeling, I understand it completely."

Understanding flashed through Amethyst's eyes. "Because of what happened a couple of years ago?"

While she was right, what happened a couple of years ago had been a major betrayal, and one that still smarted, it wasn't what he'd been referring to. "That was bad, and it was a betrayal, but it wasn't what I was talking about. My dad was a cop, he's the reason that I joined the force. He, and my mother and baby sister, were killed when I was eight. My father's partner was a dirty cop, he was taking money from gangs and drug dealers to turn a blind eye, but IA caught on and started investigating. He decided to try to pin it on my dad. He broke into our house one night, tied us all up, then set fire to the house. My dad was able to get me free and told me to get out of the house, I climbed out through the laundry room window, but the rest of my family died. Since I survived, I was able to testify against my father's partner so my dad's name was cleared, but I lost everything because of that man and what he did to my father."

Tentatively, Amethyst reached out and curled her fingers around his. "I'm so sorry. You know I know all about betrayal."

"I do, and I know that this is hard. I know that you don't want to believe that we're looking for a firefighter, and maybe we're not, but for now it looks like we are, so we have to work that angle until we get the next piece of information. So as much as you wish this wasn't so, and as much as it hurts to think that you might have been working with someone who would do this, we need you. Okay? We need you if we're going to find him before anyone else dies."

Although she looked like she still wanted to argue that it wasn't one of her colleagues they were looking for, Amethyst nodded. "I'll give you everything I can think of to help try to stop this guy, but ..."

"But what?" he prompted when she didn't continue.

"But I don't think we're going to find him before he kills again," she said, the pain in her eyes making him want to do whatever it took to wipe it away. Unfortunately, the only thing that would make her feel better was something he couldn't do. She needed this guy to be off the streets, and she was right, there was no way they had enough evidence to know who they were looking for yet.

"You can't let yourself feel guilty because this guy will probably kill again before we catch him," he warned her. Doing that was a surefire way to destroy yourself emotionally. "What he's doing is not your fault, it's not my fault, it's nobody's fault but his own. So no more beating yourself up, okay?"

"Okay," she agreed with a small smile. "I'm new to all of this cop stuff."

"You're doing great for a beginner," he encouraged with a smile of his own. They were still holding hands, and he felt that change from a simple offer of comfort to something more. Heat passed between them, he glanced at her lips, then lifted his eyes to meet hers. They were so blue, the kind of blue of a summer sky, the kind of blue you could stare into until you lost yourself.

Amethyst's lips parted, and of its own accord his head dipped, he wanted to kiss her, and it looked like she wanted it as well.

At the last second he stopped himself.

They were at the precinct, anyone could come in here at any moment.

"We should start making a list," he said, voice husky.

"Uh-huh," she nodded breathily. Then she shook her head as though to clear it. "Of course. I know most of the people at the other firehouses in the city, so we should start with mine and go from there."

"Sounds like a plan," Zeb said, first they'd get this killer off the streets, and then maybe they could see if there was something between them.

~

1:32 P.M.

This time he was doing things differently.

He was sick of getting interrupted before he was finished, so this time he was choosing a spot where no one was going to even know about the fire before he was finished.

Three times now he had tried this, and all three times he hadn't gotten from the experience what he wanted.

What exactly did he want?

Well, for starters, he wanted to be there to watch the whole thing. He wanted to watch his victims dive under the water, swimming about trying to find a safe passage through the flames, only to realize there wasn't one. He wanted to watch as the fire leaped and danced, entertaining him with its beauty and power. He wanted to watch as his victims gave into the innate need to breathe and opened their mouths, flooding their lungs with water, and sending their dying bodies up to the surface where the flames would consume them. He wanted to watch as the fire raged, reaching its hands up to the sky, showing its might and its majesty.

None of that seemed like it was asking for too much.

And yet, all three of his previous attempts had been foiled. Three times and three interruptions, this time he wasn't going to let anything get in his way.

So he had chosen a secluded location, this house was on the outskirts of the city, the lot was almost two acres, there would be no one who was going to stumble upon him before he was done.

This time he wasn't going to be forced to flee.

This time he was going to enjoy every single second.

This time he was going to get everything that he wanted.

He wasn't really sure why his love for fire had taken him in this direction. He'd never thought that he would use it to kill, he didn't even know when or why the thought had first occurred to him, and he didn't know why it was so important to him, all he did know was that it was.

Fire was everything to him.

He couldn't imagine his life without it.

Pulling out his box of matches—he *always* carried a box of matches with him wherever he went—he lit one and held it up. It glowed brightly in the dull light of the trees. The colors were mesmerizing, the way it seemed to change from red to yellow to orange, and then back to red again.

The flames always lulled him into a sort of trance, and he stared into the fire. He always imagined the flames reflected in his eyes, the way they were in movies and television shows. It made him feel like the fire was inside him.

The phoenix.

That was how he saw himself. *He* was the phoenix, and he was going to rise from the ashes and become every bit as powerful as the thing he loved the most—fire. It was what he would become if it was possible to be anything in the world.

The little flame on the match flickered, and he held his hand above it, letting the heat soak into him. Without even thinking about it his hand moved closer, touching the flame, letting it burn his skin. He relished the tingling pain, it made him feel like he was one with the fire even if it was just for one second.

As much as he would like to stay out here and stare at the flame until it consumed him, he was here for a reason, and if he wasted time hanging around then he might end up with another failure, and that wasn't acceptable.

Extinguishing the flame with his hand, he tossed the match on the ground then picked up his bottle of kerosene and walked from his car to the property he had chosen for the sole reason that it was remote and had a pool. None of this was personal, he had no grudge against any of the people he had killed so far, that wasn't what this was about. This was about him. Nothing more and nothing less. He wasn't specifically out to hurt people, he was just out to do something that he had always wanted to do.

This was his time.

The house was large, and he wasn't completely sure how many people were here, but today he wasn't going to worry about that. He wasn't going to worry about anything, he was just going to have fun.

As he walked through the woodsy yard, he spotted the pool, and as he got closer, he saw that there was a single person lounging on a towel beside it. One person was nothing he had to worry about, he'd killed three at one time just yesterday. Although there had been three people at the second house yesterday, he had waited until the two children left before setting the fire. After all, he wasn't a monster. He didn't kill children, not little ones anyway. Teenagers maybe, any younger was not his thing.

Since the person lying beside the pool looked like a teenage girl, he wasn't concerned about the fact that she wasn't already in the pool. In case there was someone else lurking about somewhere on the property, he didn't hesitate or pause or stop to run through everything he was going to do one last time, he just walked straight over to the girl, picked her up, and threw her into the pool before she even knew that he was there.

She landed with a splash, spraying water all over him. As much as he loved fire, he hated water. It made sense, water was fire's adversary, they clashed, and the winner was usually water. Except in this scenario he had worked out. He had found the one way that fire could beat water.

"Hey," the girl spluttered as she broke the surface. "Who are you and what are you doing here?"

He ignored her.

Just like he had ignored any of the things that his victims had said to him in the moments before he started the fires. He didn't care what they had to say, and he didn't want to engage with them, he didn't want to think of them as anything other than props in his game. He was afraid that if he engaged with them, started to see them as real people, then he wouldn't be able to follow through with this, and he so badly wanted to live out this dream of his.

"Hey, you," the girl growled as she started to swim toward the side of the pool. This one had an attitude, and he didn't like attitude. As a child, it had been drilled into him that attitude was something that got you punished. Life with an obsessive control freak certainly taught you that giving in and going the route of least resistance was sometimes the easiest way to live your life.

Unscrewing the can, he sloshed some kerosene into the pool, although he wanted to enjoy this it was the *fire* that he was here for not to listen to some bratty kid.

"I'm speaking to you," the girl said. "What are you doing? Why are you here? What are you throwing into the pool, what is that?"

That was a lot of questions all shot off in short succession.

None of which he had any interest in entertaining.

Walking around the pool he continued to throw the kerosene into the pool, it landed on the water and shone with that wonderful oily shimmering rainbow that he liked.

"Stop," the girl ordered in a tone that said that she was used to getting her own way. Well not today. Today he was going to get his way.

Since he was moving quickly, the girl kept trying to shy away from him, moving around the pool looking for a way out but unsure about what he was throwing in and not wanting to get too close to it.

Emptying the last of the kerosene out of the can, he dropped it on the ground and pulled out his matches.

The girl's eyes widened, and then she opened her mouth and screamed.

Secluded as the property was, screams could still attract someone. Lighting the match, he tossed it into the pool and immediately the fire ignited, the perfect way to shut the bratty kid up.

As the fire flared to life, he pulled up one of the lounges that were over to the side and set it right next to the pool so he could sit and watch and enjoy. This was exactly what he had missed out on the first three times, but this time it was like his own personal fireworks show.

The kid had darted under the water as soon as the fire started and he could see her swimming about down there, unsure what she should do. Intrigued, he put his elbows on his knees and leaned closer to get a better look. The fire was raging, and it was hot, the heat prickling his skin but he wasn't going to back up. He intended to enjoy every second of this, and he wasn't leaving until the flames finally died out and he was filled with the peace that only came when he was one step closer to being that phoenix.

~

9:40 P.M.

She should be heading home.

It had been a long day, and although Zeb had offered a few times to let her call it quits and go home, Amethyst had insisted that they keep going through every firefighter in the city until they were done. The city was large, and there were several firehouses, so there were some firefighters that she didn't know, or only knew enough to say hi to in passing, but because she was determined to be as helpful as she could, she reached out to all her contacts and tried to as surreptitiously as was possible gather information.

By the time they were done, it was already dark out, and she was exhausted. Although she was used to carrying around the heavy equipment they used every day to put out fires, never in her life had she been this tired. Sitting at a desk, trying to figure out a killer's identity was the most draining thing she had ever done.

But besides being tired, she felt great.

She felt like she'd made a difference, like she had actually managed to be helpful to Zeb and Judah and their investigation.

Then the phone call came.

Another fire, another dead body.

Only this time the fire was already out by the time it was discovered.

For some reason that hurt more than anything else. This poor young girl, who had only just turned sixteen two days before, had been floating in the water, dead and alone, for hours. That shouldn't bother her, it wasn't like them arriving within minutes of the fires had helped any of the other victims, but somehow this just seemed worse.

Parking her car behind Zeb's, she turned off the engine and took a moment to gather herself. She wasn't usually one to be this emotional about things like this. Yes, she always felt bad after they lost someone—

even a beloved family pet—in a fire, and yes, she always gave herself an extra vigorous workout that day, but she had never felt this kind of crushing sense of guilt and responsibility.

"This isn't your fault," she hissed to herself. "Come on, pull it together, they're waiting for you."

With limbs that felt like they had been replaced with concrete, Amethyst dragged herself out of the car and walked over to where Zeb and Judah were waiting for her. She had never felt so out of place in her life. All of that good energy and buzz from feeling like she was contributing was gone. She had no idea what she was doing here, she should have taken Zeb's offer to go home, and they'd brief her in the morning. But she was committed to this now, and she was an all-in or all-out kind of girl.

"We'll take a quick look at the scene, then we'll speak with the father," Zeb told her as they started walking through the leafy yard. Although it was dark, the property had a big entertaining area around the back, and someone had turned on all the lights, so it was bright enough to see pretty well.

The medical examiner was already here, and the body had already been pulled from the pool, lying on the tiled area surrounding the pool, and was thankfully covered with a sheet. She didn't want to see the poor girl's horrifically burned, barely recognizable as human, body. She had definitely seen enough burned bodies in her years as a firefighter, enough survivors too. She had seen the agony they had to endure as their body wanted to give in and die, but their mind and their will to live was too strong. They had a long road of fighting ahead of them, even once the burns healed that road wasn't over, then there were the issues of scarring and contracting skin to deal with. But she had seen people triumph over the flames, and she respected them and the fight they had won.

But that wasn't Cara Trent.

There had been no escape for her, and now instead of enjoying being sixteen, her parents would be choosing her a casket and planning a funeral.

Crime scene people were also here, bustling about looking for enough evidence to nail this guy to the wall—when they found him.

And that was most likely still a long way off. The list she and Zeb, and then Judah when he had joined them, had made had seventeen people of interest that had to be looked into. Some of whom she considered friends. It had been hard to be objective, put people she knew and liked under the microscope, but every time she thought she couldn't do it she pictured Gia James. The girl had swum through the flames in an attempt to hold onto her life, and she wanted to honor that spirit by working this case as hard as she was physically able.

Now that same drive made her scan the area, looking for anything noteworthy. Her gaze fell on a lounge chair that was closer to the pool than the others. "He chose this place because it was more secluded than the others," she said. "He was annoyed that he didn't get to watch until the end the last few times, so this time he was determined not to miss out on a single second. He pulled the chair up to watch like this was a show to him."

"Good catch," Zeb said, nodding appreciatively. His pride in her shouldn't warm her, but it did. It was nice to have someone acknowledge that while you were out of your element, you could still contribute something.

"He left the kerosene can behind again," Judah added.

"It's not hard to find, so he probably doesn't care that we have it," Zeb said.

"And he hasn't left fingerprints on any of them, so he knows we won't get anything useful from them," she added.

"CSU will go over everything, maybe he got sloppy, left a glove off when he touched something, the lounge maybe," Zeb said, but they all knew this guy was too clever to be sloppy like that.

"The father is waiting for us in the house," Judah said.

Talking to Cara's father scared her. Terrified her actually. She had dealt with plenty of terrified people that she and her team had pulled out of burning buildings, but that was different, she knew fire, and she knew first aid, and between the two she could usually calm them down.

But what did she know about dealing with a grieving father?

Back after she had been found and gone to live with her aunt, dealing with Sapphire's emotions about what they'd gone through, and her aunt and uncle's reactions, that had been so much harder than dealing with her own.

"Mr. Trent?" Zeb said as they walked through the back door of the house and into the kitchen.

The man sitting at the table, elbows propped up, head resting in his hands, an untouched cup of coffee sitting beside him, slowly lifted his head and looked up at them, giving a single nod. The kitchen was large, and there were still decorations from Cara's sweet sixteenth birthday party strewn about. Just two days ago the girl had been celebrating life and an important milestone, and now she was dead. Why did life have to be so cruel sometimes?

"I'm Detective Tuck, and this is my partner Detective Willow, and our consultant, Ms. Hatcher, we won't take much of your time, we just have a couple of questions," Zeb said, easing down into a chair beside the man. He made this all seem so simple, his tone was empathetic without sounding fake, and he sounded sure of himself which no doubt made victims and their families feel like they were in good hands. Amethyst was really glad he was here.

"Cara is dead," Mr. Trent said softly, like the words sounded foreign to him, not something he thought he would ever have to say.

"She is," Zeb said. "We're very sorry for your loss."

"It wasn't an accident, someone killed her," Mr. Trent said, a little fire returning to his face and his voice.

"And six others over the last three days, which is why we need to ask you a couple of questions. Cara was alone here today?"

"Her birthday was two days ago, she was so excited to turn sixteen, she'd been planning her party for six months. My mother-in-law keeps poor health, but my wife hadn't wanted to go and visit her until after the party because her mother insisted that Cara's birthday was more important. She flew out yesterday to spend a couple of weeks with her mom. My company has sites in multiple cities, and I flew out early this morning to visit one of them. Cara said she was looking forward to a quiet day to recover from the party. She was just going to hang by the pool, lie in the sun, just relax."

"What time did you get home?" Zeb asked.

"My flight was delayed, I was supposed to be back here by six, and we were going to have dinner together. I was so excited that my sixteen-year-old still wanted to spend time with her dad," he said with a sad smile, tears shimmering in his eyes. "I didn't get back to the house until a little after nine."

"Did you try calling Cara to tell her that you'd be late?" Judah asked.

The man nodded. "I tried calling twice, and I sent a few texts, she didn't reply, I thought she was just taking a nap, or a bubble bath, or lost in a book, I didn't think anything was wrong." Regret and guilt battled on his features, he would likely never forgive himself for that even though Cara would have already been dead by six o'clock, there wasn't anything that her father could have done to save her.

Now they, on the other hand, should have been able to do something to stop this guy. Four fires, seven dead, and they had nothing more substantive than a list of names.

"When you got home, did you notice anything unusual?" Zeb asked.

"No. The place was dark, no lights on, that's when I thought something might be wrong. When I came inside and called out for Cara she didn't answer, I searched the house, thinking maybe she had fallen down the stairs or in the bathtub, then when I couldn't find her I went outside, and she was ... she was in ... her body was floating in the pool," the man finished with a sob.

Tears burned her own eyes.

She couldn't do this.

Helping Zeb and Judah was one thing, but being here in this room, filled so strongly with this father's grief, she couldn't do that for a single second longer.

"I'll see you two tomorrow," she muttered to Zeb and Judah, before making a hasty exit. She knew she was being rude, and she knew she was backing out and leaving everything to the cops, but this was their job after all, she was just a firefighter.

The father's loss made her think of her own loss. While she and Diamond, and Ruby, and Sapphire, had gotten their lives back, Emerald hadn't. Her baby sister was still out there somewhere, alive and suffering, or dead. Although they didn't talk about Emerald much, she was

constantly at the back of all of their minds, and Mr. Trent's grief made
her own come rushing to the surface.

She had made it all the way to her car when a hand suddenly rested
on her shoulder. "You okay?" Zeb asked.

"Fine," she murmured, but she knew her rough voice gave her away.
"You shouldn't have left him, Cara's father, he shouldn't be alone."

"Judah is with him, and we don't really have any other questions
anyway, he didn't see anything, Cara had been dead for hours before he
got home, we just had to make sure, go through the process." Zeb's
other hand landed on her other shoulder, and he turned her around to
face him, his warm brown eyes were full of sympathy. "It's hard to do
that, I know. Over the years you get used to it, but it's never easy."

"I'm fine," she said dismissively, this wasn't about her, this was
about all the families who had lost people they loved because of one
sadistic pyromaniac.

"It's okay to hurt because he's hurting," Zeb said gently. "It means
you care, and that's never a bad thing."

"So many people have died, and I know that more people are going
to die, and we can't stop it from happening," she said, her voice waver-
ing, she hated to be vulnerable around people, but there was something
about Zeb that told her he was a safe space to say what was raging
inside her.

"But we will," he said firmly.

"I don't know how you do this every day, I feel wrecked and I've
only been at this whole cop thing for one day," she admitted.

"Because running into burning buildings to save people is so much
easier," he said, one side of his mouth quirking up into a smile.

"It is," she said quickly.

"Because you don't care as much about your own life as you do
others, to you, risking your life to save people is easy, but having to deal
with their pain is a whole other thing."

Wow.

That was a shockingly close to truthful statement from someone she
barely knew.

Tentatively, Zeb released her shoulder and touched the backs of his
knuckles to her cheeks. Amethyst sucked in a breath, her pulse fluttering

wildly like a mass of butterflies flapping their tiny wings, her heart was hammering in her chest, and it suddenly became quite the ordeal to remain standing because her knees had turned to jelly.

She wasn't used to someone touching her like this, so intimately, so gently, so sweetly. It made her both extremely uncomfortable and stirred something deep down inside her. Something that made her feel like it would be nice to be cared about by someone other than her family.

"You're important, too," Zeb said softly. "The world would be much worse off if you weren't in it."

Years of treating her life like it was an afterthought, nothing of great importance, internally, she raged wildly against Zeb's words. But outwardly, she forced her lips to turn up into a smile, and stepped backward, away from Zeb's touch.

"Thank you," she said, with a sharp nod of her head, then she turned her back on him, opened her car door and got inside. As she drove off she knew he was watching her leave, no doubt bewildered by her sudden change in attitude. That was fine, she didn't care if Zeb was confused by her, she didn't even care if he was attracted to her, as long as he didn't see the tears streaming down her cheeks or hear her gut-wrenching sobs.

He was wrong.

She wasn't important.

The world didn't care if she was in it or not.

Her life was nothing.

She was nothing.

Nothing.

~

11:51 P.M.

Ruby rested her cheek against the cool bathroom tiles.

The cold felt so good against her burning skin.

She felt like she was about to catch fire, and in just seconds, her skin had sapped the refreshing coolness out of the tile, and she had to shuffle backward a little bit to lie against the next tile.

Moving was a bad idea.

A *really* bad idea.

Her stomach protested immediately, and she struggled to sit up, her arms shaking so badly she very nearly crashed back down, and only just managed to get her head above the toilet before she threw up.

Again.

That made the eighth time in the last sixty minutes.

"Come on, little one," she whispered, holding her hand to her stomach and urging her unborn baby to stop torturing her.

It seemed like the baby wanted to prepare her for all the sleepless nights she was going to have after it was born because while she felt fine all day, as soon as night hit and she wanted nothing more than to curl up under the covers and go to sleep, her morning sickness arrived. She knew that unborn babies couldn't tell the time and that morning sickness didn't have to actually be in the morning, but why did the baby have to choose this time of night to make her throw up? Didn't it realize that she needed sleep?

"Of course it doesn't," she admonished herself as she wearily sunk back down to the floor. "It's not even born yet."

She was so tired, she hadn't had a good night's sleep in the last three and a half months. She had been hoping that once she hit the second trimester of her pregnancy, the morning sickness would ease off and she could go back to sleeping regularly, but that obviously wasn't the case. She was fourteen weeks pregnant now, and her morning sickness was every bit as bad as it had been at the beginning.

"Only five and a half months to go," she told herself. That sounded so long, longer than she could survive on virtually no sleep. And then once the baby was born, and they brought him or her home with them, they'd just replace morning sickness with feeding and crying as the reasons for lack of sleep. This whole parenting thing was hard, even this stage when the baby was still living inside her.

Still, despite the crippling morning sickness, and the lack of sleep, and the fears about raising a baby, Ruby couldn't be happier.

Her life had changed so much in the last year that it was hard to believe that she was actually still living the same life. Back then, she had been someone who kept to herself, spending most of her time with her nose buried in a book, afraid to move out from the fictional world and into the real one because she had been plagued by thoughts of suicide.

Then Judah had entered her life.

She had known him before since he was one of her sister's colleagues, but she hadn't been in a place where she was ready to even envision sharing her life with another person.

Taking that first step had been the hardest thing she had ever done, but she was so glad she hadn't let the fear and doubts hold her back. Since late October, she had gone from dating to marrying the man of her dreams, and was now carrying his baby, if that wasn't a miracle then she didn't know what was.

Preparing for this next stage of life was exciting, she couldn't wait to meet this little person growing inside of her, and to know that her baby would only be a few months younger than Sapphire's son, and that soon Diamond might be adding another baby to the quickly growing Hatcher family, made her that much more excited. As kids, she and her sisters had been close, since there were only four years between oldest sister Diamond and youngest Emerald, they had gone through most things together. But they hadn't been close like they were now. Their ordeal had cemented that sister bond, and now it was unbreakable, and she was glad that they got to share motherhood as well.

Her stomach felt like it might finally be settling, but she knew from experience not to rush things. If she got up off the bathroom floor too quickly, she was likely to relapse and spend the entire night in here with her head over the toilet.

Footsteps sounded outside the bathroom, and she lifted her head just as her husband appeared in the doorway. He'd called earlier to tell her that there had been another fire in the case he was working and that he would be home late. In the ten months they'd been a couple, she had gotten used to his crazy schedule, and while she preferred to lie down in bed next to her husband, she was used to him sliding beneath the covers at all hours of the night.

Not that it was something she really had to worry about at the moment since she spent most nights in the bathroom.

"You okay, honey?" he asked, concern crinkling his handsome features.

"More morning sickness," she croaked, her voice hoarse from throwing up for the last hour.

"I hate that you were suffering alone," he said, stepping over her to get to the sink. Judah was thrilled to become a dad in the new year, and he wanted to be involved in everything, she knew he felt bad that sometimes he had to work late and wasn't there for her when she was sick, but he had a job to do, and she would never expect him to miss it just because of a little morning sickness.

"You're here now," she told him as he wet a face washer, then knelt beside her and blotted her sweat coated face before draping it over her forehead.

"I sure am, think you're ready to go back to bed?"

"I think so," she replied. She hadn't felt the urge to throw up in the last few minutes, so hopefully, things had settled down enough that they could both get a little sleep.

"Good, you need your rest." With that he scooped her up into his arms and carried her back into the bedroom, setting her gently down on the bed before fussing about, fluffing pillows and arranging the covers over her.

She liked this, her husband fussing over her, there wasn't a day that had gone by since she and Judah got together that he hadn't made it clear in both his words and his actions that he loved her. He was everything she could have dreamed for in a man to share her life with, and every day she gave thanks that they had found their way to one another.

"Comfortable?" Judah asked, standing beside the bed.

"Almost."

"What do you need? Something to eat? Water? Another blanket? Or pillow?"

"Nope," she smiled up at him. "I need my husband in the bed beside me."

"That I can do," he grinned. Slipping off his clothes he folded them neatly and set the shirt in the hamper, and the pants and shoes back in the closet. His OCD brain couldn't switch off and let him get to sleep at night unless everything was just the way he liked it.

As he joined her in bed, Ruby immediately curled up against his side. His body was warm, and she was still a little flushed, but she didn't care, this was exactly where she wanted to be. His arm came around her and drew her closer, and she nestled her face against his neck.

This had to be what heaven was like.

Being cocooned inside a circle of warmth and love that made you feel all gooey inside because it was so wonderful to be made to feel like you were the center of someone's world.

Soon their world would be changed forever, their little family would be adding a new member, and that soon to be arriving little addition was already loved and cherished. While she knew that she and Judah would make mistakes along the way, they wouldn't—couldn't—be the perfect parents that she wanted to be, but they would always put their child's best interests first, and make sure that their son or daughter, and any other children they had, knew—without a shadow of a doubt—that they were loved.

She never wanted her child to doubt that it was wanted, that it was important, and cared about. While she couldn't shield it from all the bad things in the world, it would experience pain and suffering and heartache, it would know that it always had a safe place to come to, a place that could provide a sheltering rock for the storms of life.

This little baby was already loved by her and its daddy. So long as she loved her husband, and he loved her, and they both loved their children, then their home would always be the perfect environment to raise their family.

Content, Ruby drifted off to sleep.

CHAPTER Six

August 24th
7:49 A.M.

It was chaos.

Amethyst had been on her way to the station to meet up with Zeb and Judah when she'd gotten a call that there was another fire raging in a family pool.

She had been surprised to hear that the killer had gone back to suburban houses, she'd have thought he would have stuck with larger properties on the outskirts of the city so he wouldn't be interrupted since he seemed to have enjoyed the show yesterday. Instead, the killer had gone back to more populated areas, she wasn't sure what that meant, or even if it meant anything at all, she just wanted this guy caught and off the streets, and she was hoping that he wasn't going to turn out to be anyone she was close with.

Sirens sounded, and a moment later the fire truck went screeching past her. Amethyst pressed her foot against the gas and sped up, although she knew that no matter how quickly they got there it would already be too late, she couldn't help but hope.

Sometimes she hated hope.

It was such a double-edged sword, it brought a little piece of brightness to the dark, but it also brought pain when that little light was extinguished.

Pulling in behind the fire truck just as her colleagues jumped out, she tried to stay out of their way as she followed them into the back yard. There was a fire raging on the swimming pool, and she had to quash the urge to go running over to try to do something to help put the flames out and get whoever was stuck in the pool out of there.

But that wasn't what she was here to do.

She wasn't here as a firefighter, she was here as a consultant with the cops.

"Am."

She looked over her shoulder and saw someone coming toward her. She had expected it to be Zeb and Judah as she knew they were on their way here, but it wasn't, it was a friend and colleague of hers, Joaquin Burton. He used to work at her station, but he'd been injured on the job about a year ago and hadn't returned yet. She wondered what he was doing here.

"Hey, Joaquin," she said, returning her gaze to the fire. The team had foam squirting at the flames, which were persistently burning. "What are you doing here?"

"I was the one who called it in, this is my neighborhood, I was out jogging when I saw the flames," he explained.

Immediately her hackles went up.

Joaquin hadn't been on the list of suspects, she hadn't seen any reason for him to be on the list. He was a great guy, and she always had fun when they hung out, he didn't seem like the kind of person who would do this, but ...

Now she was second guessing that decision.

Maybe, she had been spending too much time around Zeb and Judah and too much time playing at being a cop, now she was suspicious about everyone. Joaquin was a firefighter—and they knew that they were looking for a firefighter—and now he was the one who had found one of the fires.

That put him on the suspect list.

They had gone through a profile of the kind of person they were looking for, someone who had a poor home environment, one or both parents missing from the home, or abusive parents, a bad relationship with his father, a controlling or overprotective mother, and he would enjoy attending to fires that he had started himself.

While she had no idea about Joaquin's childhood, this could be his way of inserting himself into the scene, calling in a fire that he himself had set. Since he was on leave, there was no way for him to have responded in an official capacity to this—or any of the other fires—but this still gave him an in.

"Amethyst?" Joaquin said, staring at her quizzically.

All of a sudden she felt anxious, if Joaquin was the killer, then what would he do to her if he realized that she was on to him?

There were lots of people about, but that could actually make her less safe. If he decided to pull a gun on her and dragged her out of here, everyone was so busy and so preoccupied with the fire, that they probably wouldn't even notice until she was already gone.

Before she could panic, she saw Zeb and Judah getting out of their car and let out a relieved breath. "Zeb," she called out.

He looked up and nodded, both he and his partner headed over to where she and Joaquin were standing. "Morning."

"Morning, this is Joaquin," she said quickly, "he's the one who called in the fire. He used to work at the same station as me, but he's on medical leave at the moment." She hoped Zeb got where she was going without her actually having to outright say it.

"You called it in?" Zeb asked, zeroing in on Joaquin.

"I did," Joaquin nodded.

"You live around here?" Judah asked.

"Yes, just two streets over. Like Amethyst said, I was injured on the job almost twelve months ago, and as part of my physical therapy I run every morning, I was running down the street here when I heard a fire, you're not a firefighter for a decade and don't know the sound of flames when you hear them."

"Did you see anyone hanging around? Anyone go running off when you came back here?" Zeb asked.

"I saw a man dressed in black running around the side of the house, over there," Joaquin pointed to the opposite side of the house from where they were standing.

"Did you get a good look at him?" Zeb asked.

"Not really, he was running, and he had a hoodie mostly covering his face. Besides I wanted to get to the pool, I heard about these crimes, and I thought someone could be in there, There was, but I wasn't there quickly enough to do anything for them. I ran inside, got a fire extinguisher from the kitchen, but it was too small, and the fire was too big, it didn't do any good." Joaquin looked and sounded genuinely distressed, but she wasn't trained well enough in reading body language to know whether or not he was telling the truth, or telling them what he thought they wanted to hear.

"Okay, thanks, Joaquin, we might have more questions for you later," Zeb warned.

"No problem. Later, Amethyst," Joaquin said as he headed off toward the team who had just put out the fire.

"Do you think it's him?" she whispered, just in case he was still within earshot.

"Do you?" Zeb asked, studying her closely. She couldn't tell if the way she was being scrutinized was just because of Joaquin, or because of last night and their heated talk before she drove off and left him standing there, staring after her.

"I don't know," she squirmed, uncomfortable, she felt bad for just leaving Zeb hanging when he was being so sweet with her.

"Something made you uncomfortable," Zeb pushed. "When we drove up you looked scared, he had to have said something to you to make you concerned."

"It wasn't really anything specific he said," she admitted, worried now that she had blown things way out of proportion. "He came over, and he told me that he was the one who called in the fire, and I remembered the profile of the man we're looking for and I thought that it was odd that he was the one who found the fire when we're looking for a firefighter. And then I started worrying about letting on what I was thinking, and what he would do if he is the killer, and he knew that we were on to him."

"Once we finish up here, we can take a look into Joaquin, see if there's anything there that indicates he might be the killer we're looking for," Zeb said.

"And we still need to track down the glass guy from the second fire. So far, the only people who we know aren't the killer who have seen this guy and lived, are the elderly couple who didn't see anything, and the glass guy who is still evading us," Judah said. "I'll continue to try to track him down while you guys focus on Joaquin and then work through the list we made yesterday."

"Sounds like a plan," Zeb agreed.

Amethyst wanted to say that maybe it was a better idea if she worked with Judah today. The less time she spent around Zeb the less she had to worry about the crazy mixed up feelings she had for him. Working with Judah was definitely the smart thing to do.

And yet she didn't open her mouth and say anything, she just trailed along behind them as they headed toward the pool.

Looked like she wasn't going to do the smart thing after all.

2:34 P.M.

"So far, we don't have any proof that Joaquin is the killer, maybe he really was just out for a jog, and he happened to notice the fire and call it in, I feel like I maybe just jumped to conclusions this morning, I told you I have no idea what I'm doing," Amethyst said.

She sounded defeated, and while Zeb understood, they had spent the morning looking into Joaquin Burton only to keep coming up empty at every turn, that was the nature of this job. You had to pursue every single line of inquiry that presented itself because you never knew which path was going to be the right one. "You were a massive help yesterday," he reminded her, as he stopped the car at a red light. "It would have taken Judah and me days to go through all the firefighters in the city and narrow it down to a manageable list."

"All I've done to help so far is just tell you what I know about my colleagues. That's it. And that's not because of any skill or anything, it's just because I know most of them since I play in the fire department's baseball league, and a bunch of us body build and run extreme marathons together."

"You really like the extreme sports, don't you?" he said, casting a quick glance her way. He assumed that the love of adrenalin pumping activities was related to her belief that her life was inconsequential. While he understood how her past and what she'd been through could make her feel that way, he wished there was a way to show her that she was wrong. He meant what he had said last night, the world would be a much worse place if she wasn't in it. Whether anything ever happened between them or not, he thought she was a good person, and he wanted to see her happy.

"Yeah, I do," she said suspiciously like she thought he had something to say on the matter, Zeb wondered whether her sisters had lectured her on all the crazy risk-taking stuff that she did. "You going to go all psychobabble on me again?"

"Oh no, I learned my lesson last night. No psychobabble talk." Something had passed between them last night, something that went deeper than just a physical attraction. He didn't know if that meant they had a future or not, but it meant that he cared about her, and if discussing her love of adrenalin pumping sports was off-limits then he would respect that.

"Good." She huffed, but her eyes darted about nervously like she wanted to say something but wasn't sure how.

Since it seemed that she was uncomfortable if they focused too much on the case, and if they focused too much on her, Zeb decided that he should shoot for a neutral topic. She seemed to love her job, so maybe they could talk about that. "What made you decide to become a firefighter?"

"I don't know." Amethyst shrugged. "I guess I just thought I might be good at it. I was always into sports, even as a kid, and I was a good runner, and I liked the idea of running marathons, that got me into bodybuilding, and then from there I had to do something with my life, and I wanted it to be something that would help others, so I thought that firefighting was a good mix of all of my skills."

"You love your job," he said, a statement not a question since he could see that it was written all over her face.

"I do. I love it, I can't imagine ever doing anything different. You became a cop because of your dad?" she asked.

"I did. For as long as I can remember I wanted to be just like him when I grew up. And then after he died, I wanted to live out his legacy, I wanted to be a cop that he could be proud of, and I wanted to try to stop other people from going through what I had, or at least getting them justice. All my dad's friends, they really rallied around me, supported me. I'm still close with most of them, they've been father figures to me most of my life."

"It was so brave of you to testify against your dad's partner," she said, admiration in her tone.

"Just doing what had to be done."

"Sapphire does that, just brush off what she did, but I always thought it was so brave of her to testify against our parents, and she had to do it all on her own because we were all still missing then."

Zeb couldn't imagine what it would have been like for Sapphire to have to testify against her own parents. He wasn't sure he would have been strong enough to do that. "Your sister is a tough one," he agreed, he and Sapphire had been colleagues for many years, but it wasn't until Gideon had come into her life that he had started to consider her a friend. He got it, she was coping with the trauma she had been through as best as she could, he did the same, and he was glad that she had managed to get the happy ending she deserved.

"She is," Amethyst said. "She's so freaked out about being a mom, but I know she's going to be amazing, and it's nice to see her not as angry and closed off as she used to be."

As much as he would love to continue this conversation, dig a little deeper and find out more about Amethyst and who she really was, not just the persona she displayed, they had arrived at their destination. "This is it," he announced, pulling his car to a stop.

"This place looks creepy," Amethyst said with a shudder.

He was surprised by her reaction. It was just an abandoned building, a little remote, but the industrial estate was only a hundred yards or so from the highway. "It's just an old industrial estate," he said as he got out of the car.

"I know," she agreed but rounded the car quickly to stand closely beside him.

"Is something wrong?"

"What?" She glanced up at him then surveyed their surroundings. "No, nothing is wrong. It's just that this reminds me of something. Something I'd rather not talk about," she added.

"All right," he agreed, although he was sure there was more to it than she wanted to admit. But he'd learned his lesson standing watching her drive off last night, she wasn't comfortable talking to him about herself. Maybe she wasn't comfortable talking to anyone about herself, but she'd opened up a little in the car, and maybe by the time this case was closed he would have earned her trust. "The call said that the body was inside."

"You really think it's him?" she asked as they started walking toward the large and partially dilapidated building.

"We'll know soon enough," he replied. A call had come in that a body had been found in an abandoned building out on an abandoned industrial site, and it sounded like it might be Tucker Goud, the evasive glass guy they had been looking for ever since the James fire two days ago. The call had been anonymous, and no one had hung around to speak with them, so his instincts were on high alert for a possible set up. If this was a setup, then maybe Amethyst should wait in the car, he didn't want her getting hurt. "Maybe you should stay here, in the car."

"No way," she said quickly. "I've watched enough horror movies to know you never stay alone. We are definitely safer together if there is anyone here."

"You know how to shoot, right?"

"Of course."

Reaching down, he pulled his backup weapon from his ankle holster. "Take this."

"You really think the killer might be luring us into a trap?" she asked, blue eyes wide, as she took the gun.

No. Not really. If he had thought they were in any real danger, he would have come with Judah and not Amethyst. He would never deliberately put her in danger. But her edginess was making him edgy. "Better safe than sorry," he said as they approached the building's front door. "Stay close and keep your eyes and ears open."

Cautiously, he stepped inside the building, scanning it for any signs of another person, but the place looked empty. There was trash everywhere, cigarette butts, broken beer bottles, and used condoms, indicating that this place was used by the local kids as their hangout zone. The foyer had several corridors heading off from it, as well as a couple of doors and a staircase. There were plenty of places for someone to be hiding out waiting for them to enter.

"There's the body," Amethyst hissed, pointing up ahead near what had at one point probably been the front desk for the building.

He nodded and whispered back, "We cover each other as we head over there."

"Okay," Amethyst agreed. Now that she had something to focus on, the uncertainty that had been in her voice when they'd been outside was gone. That seemed to reassure him, even though he was the one who was supposed to be in control here, and they crossed the large foyer quickly.

When they reached the body, he looked down and immediately that short-lived reprieve from the growing feeling that the two of them weren't alone here was gone. "It's him."

"Why would someone kill him?" Amethyst asked. "There were other witnesses to the killer, and they're all alive. Why kill the glass guy? And why bring his body out here? And why would someone anonymously call 911 to report it?"

Zeb didn't have answers to any of those questions.

And that only ratcheted up his unease several notches.

Someone had lured them out here, that was clear, but for what purpose remained to be seen.

～

2:56 P.M.

. . .

"Zeb?" Amethyst prompted when he didn't provide answers to any of the questions she had just asked. "Why would someone bring us out here to find the body, but not want us to know who they are?"

He turned to look at her, his brown eyes serious. "Exactly for the reason you think."

"Because this is a trap," she said, scanning the area for the hundredth time in the minute or so they had been inside the building. "You think it was the killer who dumped the body out here because it's quiet and secluded, and then used it to get us out here." This was the second time she had been brought out to an isolated area to be killed, last time she had somehow managed to survive, but that didn't mean that this time she would.

"I think there's a chance that it was one of the kids that hangs out here," he said, waving his hand at the broken glass and condoms that were scattered about, "who called it in and just didn't want to be found out. But, I suspect that's not the case."

"What should we do?" Now that she knew they were most likely in danger, she felt so much calmer, in control, she didn't mind being in dangerous situations, she'd certainly had plenty of practice over the years.

"I want you to go back to the car, lock yourself inside, and wait for back up to arrive," he said, sticking his hand in his pocket and pulling out the keys. "You have a gun so you should be safe enough."

"What did I say earlier about being alone?"

"That was different, that was when we weren't even sure who the body belonged to. But now that we know it is Tucker Goud, we know that we've been lured out here."

"What are you going to do?"

"Search the building, see if there's anyone else here or signs that someone was here recently."

"Then I'm coming with you," she said firmly. What she'd said earlier was true, they were safer together than on their own.

"Fine," he agreed, somewhat reluctantly.

"This place is huge, where do you want to start?" she asked. There had to be close to one hundred rooms, it would take hours to search from top to bottom.

"We'll just do a quick sweep of each floor, and by then, back up should be here, and we can do a more thorough search."

Since the sweeps that she and her team did when they were in a fire searching for any people who may be trapped inside, or were overhauling a building once the fire was out to check for any spots that were smoldering and might reignite, were completely different to the kind of sweep cops did, she just kept close and kept her eyes open for anything that moved.

It didn't take as long as she had thought it would, and about fifteen minutes later they were standing on the sixth—and top—floor of the building. "There's no one here," she said, a little disappointed, she had been hoping that it was the killer and that they'd have him in custody by now, she didn't want anyone else to die.

"At least not that we found," Zeb agreed. "Maybe it really was just kids who had come out here to spend the day and found the body, and didn't want their parents to find out what they were up to."

"But even if it was just kids who made the anonymous 911 call, someone still killed Tucker Goud, and since he is one of the few people who saw this killer I think that's pretty suspicious." She might not be a cop, but to her, it sounded like Tucker had seen more than he should and the killer had decided he was a risk and couldn't be left alive. "You think he's been dead all this time we've been looking for him?"

"Possibly. He might never have even left the scene of his own volition. The ME will be able to give us a time of death, and that might help us set up a timeline."

"So, what do we do now?"

"I thought backup would have been here already, I guess we'll go back downstairs and wait for them."

Still clutching the gun, but now holding it pointing at the ground instead of out in front of her ready to shoot at anything that presented itself as a threat, she and Zeb headed back for the stairs. They were about halfway down the main corridor when she froze.

Smoke.

She smelled smoke.

"Zeb, this place is on fire," she said.

"Are you sure?"

She just rolled her eyes and ran toward the stairs. "You think I'm a firefighter who doesn't know what a fire smells like?"

"He must have been hiding outside somewhere, waiting for us to come up here before he set this place alight," Zeb said, sounding angry.

"What's the point in killing us? It's not like it will stop the investigation, in fact if anything, it would make him even more wanted than he already is."

"He probably doesn't care."

"I can't see the flames, they haven't reached the fifth floor yet," she said as they reached the staircase and hurried down.

"I can smell the fire now," Zeb said.

"It's probably going to come for us quickly," she warned. "He likes to use an accelerant, kerosene, so he no doubt doused this place in it before he lit the match."

True to her words as they started down the next flight of stairs, down to the fourth floor, they saw the flames.

Big flames.

The fire was raging and would no doubt have the entire building consumed into one huge burning inferno within minutes.

Probably before help could arrive.

Pulling her cell phone from her pocket, she texted her lieutenant who she knew would make sure that every available fire truck in the city would be heading their way within the next sixty seconds.

When she looked to Zeb, she saw that he had ripped off his shirt and was covering his head with it. "What are you doing?" she asked.

"Covering my head to block out some of the smoke when we go down there."

"We're not going down, we're going up," she said, grabbing his hand and dragging him along with her back up the way they had come.

"Don't we want to get out of here? That fire is going to be up here soon."

"You really want to walk through those flames?" she asked.

"Of course not, but I also don't want to be stuck up on the sixth floor when that fire comes for us."

"We're not staying on the sixth floor," she said, scanning for the stairs she knew would lead to the roof. "We're going up here," she said when she located what she was looking for.

"Aren't the flames going to reach the roof, or make it cave in?"

"Yep, they're going to do that," she agreed, still holding Zeb's hand as she ran toward the stairs that might be their only chance at surviving this fire.

"So, what are we doing up here?" Zeb asked as they burst out into the hot afternoon.

"Not dying."

Amethyst released Zeb's hand and ran over to the edge of the roof, looking for something that would break their fall if they had to jump, or something they could use to climb down. There should be a fire escape somewhere, but sometimes these older, dilapidated buildings didn't have them, or they were broken or partially destroyed.

"What are you looking for?" Zeb asked as he joined her.

"That," she said as she jogged along the edge of the building and found what she had been looking for. "The fire escape." Just as she had feared they couldn't access it from here, part of it had rusted and broken off somewhere along the way, falling to the ground where it now lay in a tangle of twisted metal.

"We can't reach that."

"You want to go back through those flames and try to find the room on the fourth floor where we can go out the window?" she asked. As far as she could see, this was their only option.

"So, what do you suggest we do?"

"Jump," she said simply. "It's only two floors, then once we land on it we can climb down the steps, it looks like it goes all the way down to the second floor, then we jump the last part."

"We'll break a leg at the very least if we try to jump that," he protested.

"You have a better plan?"

"We wait for help to arrive."

"The ladder will reach up here when the truck arrives," she agreed. "If the roof is still in once piece by then." There was no way to know how long it would take help to arrive, and she didn't plan on dying today. "We can't go back through those flames, we'll never make it. And if we wait it could be too late. We can make it," she said confidently.

"Amethyst," Zeb started, but she cut him off by planting her lips on his and kissing him. If she was going to die today, then at least she would do it having done something she had been obsessing over for the last few days.

Then she turned and jumped.

~

3:26 P.M.

She actually did it.

The crazy woman just jumped off the building.

Zeb couldn't quite believe that she had done it. He wanted out of this burning building just as much as Amethyst did, possibly more given that he had already nearly died in a fire as a child and lost his whole family in one, but jumping off the side of a six-story building wasn't the way to do it.

With trepidation, he leaned over the side of the building, half expecting to see her body splattered all over the concrete below.

But she wasn't.

She'd made it to the fire escape, but she had misjudged the distance, and instead of landing on it, she must have landed right at the edge, the momentum pushing her over, because she was now dangling off the edge of it.

He muttered a curse.

Now he had to jump off the roof whether he wanted to or not because there was no way he was going to let her fall. Jumping down two stories was one thing, but if Amethyst fell four stories, there was no way she was walking away from that in one piece.

Dragging in a breath, he jumped up onto the edge of the roof and dangled his legs over the side. Then he carefully turned around so he was on his stomach and lowered himself down, the drop from the roof to the fourth-floor fire escape was probably approximately twenty feet, he was six feet, and if he lowered himself down carefully he could probably hold onto the small ledge below that would probably take off another two feet. Taking eight feet off the drop, making it around twelve feet instead of twenty, was almost halving it.

Without giving himself time to dwell on what he was about to do and all the possible outcomes—none of them pleasant—he let go.

The fall seemed to last forever.

His stomach felt like it was a couple of feet behind him, and he had to bite back bile, he definitely didn't want to throw up while he was plummeting toward the ground.

In comparison to the fall, the landing actually wasn't all that bad.

He landed on his feet, and felt pain jarring up through his ankles and legs.

For a second he was stunned.

Had he really made that fall without injuring himself?

It seemed too good to be true.

Giving a mental assessment of his body from head to toe, when he found that nothing stood out to him as being particularly painful, he realized that he had.

Straightening, he crossed the fire escape landing in three big steps and looked down at Amethyst, who was staring up at him.

"Told you we could make the jump," she said.

"You call this making the jump?" he asked with an eye roll as he bit back a smile, she was really something else. "So, I suppose you got this then?"

"I could use a little help," she said with a bright smile. She really was an adrenalin junkie, and he wasn't quite sure how he felt about that. While Zeb knew that his job was dangerous, he didn't enjoy extreme sports like Amethyst did, and yet to her it was her reason for living. Despite the physical attraction, he wasn't sure that they were particularly well suited. Still, now was hardly the time to be worrying about that.

Kneeling down, he clamped his hands around Amethyst's wrists and dragged her up and set her down beside him.

She was breathing deeply.

He was breathing deeply.

The fact that she had kissed him right before she jumped flashed through his mind.

Their eyes met, sparks flew ... and then literal sparks flew as the window behind them exploded, and shards of grass and embers rained down upon them.

He'd dropped his shirt inside the building when he'd taken it off, intending to use it to cover his face as they made their way through the flames, and pinpricks of pain dotted his back and side when the glass and embers landed.

"We have to get out of here," Amethyst said, lurching to her feet.

"Whoa," he said, grabbing hold of her when he saw that her t-shirt was smoldering. "You're on fire."

"What?" She looked down to where he was looking, and then batted at the tiny flame with her hand. "It's nothing," she assured him.

Unsure whether she was badly burned or not, she was right, they did have to get out of here, once they were back on the ground, then he could worry about the burn.

They scrambled down the ladder, the entire structure was half eroded with rust and wobbling, and he wouldn't have been surprised if it collapsed beneath them. But somehow they made it all the way down to the second floor where the fire escape ended.

"Don't even think about it," Zeb grabbed hold of Amethyst before she could do something stupid like just jump off without even thinking about the consequences.

"We need to get down," she reminded him.

"I know, but instead of jumping like a crazy person, let's lower ourselves down, we cut off several feet of the fall, so the impact isn't going to be as bad."

"Fine, we'll do it your way," she said with a melodramatic sigh.

"Thank you." He let out a relieved breath.

They both got down on their stomachs and wriggled backward until they were hanging off the edge of the fire escape.

Just as he thought that they had this, the fire escape swayed, causing Amethyst to lose her grip.

She dropped.

He heard the sound of her crashing down, bouncing off the dumpster below them before hitting the ground.

"Amethyst?" he called out.

There was no answer.

That worried him, he didn't think that Amethyst was quiet very often.

As carefully as he could, he aimed for the same dumpster Amethyst had hit, and let go.

This fall seemed to go so much quicker, and the landing was much more jarring as he crashed into the dumpster, and then down onto the concrete beside Amethyst.

As soon as he hit the ground, he was shuffling toward Amethyst, who was just lying there, her eyes closed. He saw blood.

With a shaking hand, he touched his fingertips to her neck, praying that he found a pulse.

"Ouch," she moaned the second he made contact with her skin.

"You're alive," he said, sagging in relief.

"So are you."

"Yeah," he agreed, wondering how they had managed to escape the burning building relatively unscathed. Amethyst tried to move, but he held her down. "You were unconscious, I don't think you should be getting up yet."

"We have to get further away from the building."

"Okay," he said, scooping her up into his arms before she had a chance to protest, and carrying her down toward where they had parked the car.

Sirens sounded, and when he turned he saw three fire trucks, two ambulances, and four cop cars come screeching toward them.

The cavalry was coming.

But it was a little too late, they had already saved themselves thanks to Amethyst's crazy plan.

"I guess we could have waited up there for the ladder," Amethyst said, her voice was a little weak, and her head rested on his shoulder, but that she was joking with him let him know she was okay.

"Now you say that, after we already jumped off the building," he teased back, as all the vehicles came to a stop before them.

"Amethyst?" one of the firefighters jogged over to them. "She okay?"

"She's fine, Theo," Amethyst replied for herself.

"You guys don't look like you came through the fire, how did you get out?"

"We jumped," Zeb replied.

"Jumped? Why do I not have to guess whose idea that was?" Theo said.

"We're alive," Amethyst said. "And we wouldn't be if we tried to get out through the flames."

He couldn't argue with that, the building was starting to crumble. They might not have lasted until the fire trucks arrived and they got the ladder up to them.

Paramedics came running over, Theo went to join his team, the fire-fighters started shooting water at the flames, Amethyst was taken from his arms and put on a stretcher, and he was eased down onto one too.

"I'm fine," he said as a medic tried to take his pulse, his eyes were fixed on Amethyst. He knew she had been knocked out because she hadn't answered him when he'd called out to her, and she had taken a much harder fall than he had.

Zeb wanted her to be okay in a way that went much deeper than just not wanting her to be injured. For the last few days they had been fighting against the attraction they both felt, pretending that the chemistry wasn't there, but today, when she had been about to jump off that building the last thing she had done was kiss him. Whether he agreed with her or not, because of her, they were both alive right now.

She was crazy and wild, and yet she had a big heart that he knew hurt when other people were hurting. He had never wanted a woman more in his life than he wanted Amethyst Hatcher in this moment.

7:50 P.M.

"It's not necessary to walk me to the door," Amethyst told Zeb as they got out of his car. "Just like it wasn't necessary for you to drive me home."

"How else were you going to get home?" he asked.

"Any one of the firefighters who were there," she shot back. "Or I could have called one of my sisters. Or Judah could have."

"I guess, but instead you got me," he said with an easy smile.

Amethyst rolled her eyes but bit back a smile, it really wasn't the worst thing in the world to have Zeb drive her home after the fire and being interrogated all afternoon about everything that had happened and what they had seen and heard, but she wasn't going to tell him that. Not yet anyway.

It had been an exhausting day. Not just the fire, but having to repeat over and over again what had happened, the building had been mostly destroyed so they'd had to try to recall as much as they could about the body and what the building had looked like when they'd first arrived. Thankfully, Zeb had snapped a couple of pictures of Tucker Goud's body before they went upstairs, so at least the medical examiner had something to go with, but no body meant no cause of death and no timeline.

But at least they were alive.

The killer hadn't managed to take them out like he intended.

And now they were all that much more determined to find him.

Although both she and Zeb were alive, they hadn't escaped the burning building unscathed. She had burns and cuts from the shattering window, she had bruises over half her body from falling from the fire escape when she lost her grip, and she had a nasty lump on the back of her head that pulsed with a dull pain, but the EMTs had given her some painkillers and all in all, she didn't feel too bad.

That probably wouldn't last, she would probably wake up tomorrow morning stiff and so sore she could barely walk, but that was tomorrow.

Tonight she was just glad that she was alive and in one piece, and she had one thing on her mind.

It was all she had thought about the whole drive to her house.

It probably wasn't what she should be thinking about right now, but she couldn't help it.

When she'd been ready to jump off that building, knowing that there was a chance that things could go wrong—which they nearly had —and she might die, her instincts had been to kiss Zeb.

Now, her instincts were to take things to the next level.

Or to the *top* level.

Sex.

Her libido was running riot right now, maybe just a response to the high stakes events of the day, plus the buildup of the physical attraction that had been simmering between them for the last several days, and all she could think about was the two of them in bed together.

It was a bad idea.

She knew that.

There were so many reasons why she shouldn't even be thinking about this. And yet, he wanted it, she wanted it, and there didn't have to be strings attached. Tonight could just be about tonight.

Amethyst unlocked the front door of her house and then immediately grabbed Zeb and kissed him.

That was all it took.

Like the lid that had been containing their emotions since they had been thrown together to work this case had been blown off, he grabbed her and shoved her inside, pushing her up against the wall as he deepened the kiss.

They didn't talk, they didn't really need to, they were both just acting out what they had wanted to do for days now.

As they kissed, her hands found the hem of the t-shirt someone had given Zeb to wear back at the scene of the fire and shoved it up, breaking the kiss only long enough to yank it over his head and toss it on the floor. Then her fingers traced over his abs, she loved a six-pack in a guy, not just because it looked super sexy, but also because it said they had something in common. There was nothing wrong with a guy who didn't like to work out, but since bodybuilding and running marathons were such a big part of her life, she liked if they had something in common.

But *did* she and Zeb have much in common?

She really wasn't sure, but this wasn't the time to worry about it.

She just wanted one night of explosive passion, nothing more and nothing less.

Zeb made quick work of unbuttoning her blouse, and it joined his t-shirt on the floor. Then reaching behind her, he unclipped her bra like he had done it a million times before and let it drop, leaving them both half naked, but it wasn't enough. She was hungry, she was greedy, she wanted him inside her now.

His hands closed around her breasts, and she sucked in a breath, he was good, *really* good, no one had ever made her feel so good with something so simple before.

But still she wanted more.

She needed this.

It had been a long time since she had last been with a man because she wasn't so good at the whole no-strings thing. She didn't want strings, but she seemed to either pick guys who said they were good with just sex, but turned out to not be, or she started feeling things that led to strings.

That wasn't happening this time though.

Tonight was about both of them getting what they needed, then maybe they could both just let go of that attraction and move on.

With fingers that were trembling with need, she undid Zeb's pants and pushed them, along with his boxers, down his legs. He was big, and the throbbing pulsating inside her had so far outweighed the pounding in her head that the headache was virtually forgotten.

Since Zeb seemed quite content to take things slow and she definitely didn't want to, she did the one thing she knew would speed things up. Wrapping her hand tightly around him she began to stroke him, and when he groaned into her mouth, she knew that she was about to get what she wanted.

His hands spanned her hips, and he lifted her up, Amethyst wrapped her legs around him as he carried her through the house and up the stairs. He'd been to the house before since she used to share it with her sisters before they all moved on with their lives, so he knew where her bedroom was, and he headed for it, now apparently just as eager as she was to get down to what they both wanted.

He was hard against her center, and she suddenly wished that she had stripped out of her pants downstairs.

In her bedroom, he laid her down on the bed, his hands leaving a trail of fire as he pulled her pants down her legs.

"Condom?" he asked, the first word he'd spoken since they entered her house.

"Dresser drawer," she replied.

When he left her to retrieve it, she felt a pang of loss, she was unnerved by how quickly she was getting attached to him. She wasn't looking for a husband or even a boyfriend, but still Zeb had somehow wriggled under her defenses. It was probably just that they had survived the fire together today. He had saved her life, she had mistimed the jump from the roof and only just managed to grab hold of the edge of the fire escape before she plummeted six floors. If he hadn't jumped down and pulled her up, she would have eventually lost her grip and fallen, most likely to her death.

Zeb returned, and her mind came back into the moment.

He entered her in one smooth thrust, and she gasped as he filled her. It took a moment for the pain to morph into pleasure, but once it did, her whole body began to tingle with anticipation of what was coming.

Zeb took her hands, entwining their fingers as he began to move, slowly pulling out then pushing back in. She moved with him, climbing higher and higher with each thrust.

She was getting close, when Zeb flipped them over so she was on top, his hands left hers and wrapped around her hips, his fingers digging into her flesh, holding her in place as he pumped into her.

The combination of him inside her and the friction against her as he moved had that ball of pleasure building, growing and growing, until it consumed her and she came screaming Zeb's name.

He came with a grunt a moment later and set off aftershocks inside her as she came again, until she was a quivering mess, and sunk down against Zeb's chest.

That was amazing.

It was going to be hard not to do that again.

But as amazing as the sex had just been, nothing had changed for her. She still didn't want a future with Zeb. She didn't want a future with anyone. She was perfectly happy on her own.

CHAPTER
Seven

August 25th
6:13 A.M.

She wasn't alone.

That was the first thing she noticed when she woke up.

There was someone in her bed.

A man.

A *naked* man.

Zeb had spent the night.

Amethyst groaned, this did not bode well for her no-strings plan.

She had no idea what her next move should be. She couldn't just outright wake him up, shove his clothes at him, and tell him to leave. That would be rude, and she had to work with Zeb until this case was closed, and besides, she did like him, she just didn't think that they would make a good couple. Maybe she should just get dressed, go downstairs, start making breakfast, go for her run as usual, and act like this had never happened. That plan only worked though if Zeb was willing to go along with it, pretend that last night had never existed, and move forward with things just the way they had been, and Amethyst wasn't so sure he was going to be able to do that.

She groaned again.

For some reason, she felt more nervous this morning than she had last night when she had kissed Zeb, ripped off his clothes, and made love to him over and over again.

What she should have done was tell him to leave last night, letting him spend the night—in her bed no less—was giving him the wrong message. She hadn't meant to do it. She didn't even remember falling asleep, she remembered making love several times and then nothing. She had been exhausted and must have just passed out eventually and fallen into a deep, heavy sleep.

Now she had gotten herself into a predicament that she couldn't see a way out of.

As carefully as she could, Amethyst slid out of bed, grabbed her clothes, and hurried for the bathroom before Zeb could wake up and see her.

She didn't make it.

"Morning," Zeb said, rolling over.

Amethyst froze, then held her clothes up to cover herself as she turned around to face him. "Morning," she said, knowing her voice sounded cold, it wasn't what she meant, she just didn't know how to put this right without hurting Zeb's feelings.

"How are you feeling now that the drugs the medics gave you have worn off?" Zeb asked, apparently not noticing her tone. He sat up, covering himself with the sheet, but she caught a glimpse of him, and despite her decision that this was a one-time thing, her body stirred, and she had second thoughts.

"Oh, I'm fine." She brushed off his concerns, concerns implied intimacy, and there wasn't going to be anything intimate between them. At least not again. She *did* ache all over but no worse than when she fell off her bike while BMXing, or off her horse when she was out riding, she'd be fine, in a couple of days her bruises would heal, and she'd forget all about the fire and jumping off the building.

Probably the only thing she *wouldn't* forget about yesterday was what had happened here in her bedroom.

"What's wrong?" he asked, finally climbing out of bed and walking over to her.

Why did he have to look so sexy?

This would be a whole lot easier if the amazing sex they'd had last night had doused out that passion, that attraction, but it hadn't. It was still there. And now she wasn't sure if it would ever go away.

"Nothing is wrong," she replied, averting her gaze. This would probably go more smoothly if she stopped looking at him and thinking about how good he had been in bed. He'd made her feel things that she had never experienced before.

"You're lying," he said, grabbing her shoulders and turning her back to face him when she tried to leave.

"You back to playing shrink?"

"No," he said slowly, "but it's pretty obvious that you've woken up in a completely different mood than you went to sleep in last night."

That was fair enough.

She should have done this last night.

She felt like she was leading him on even though that was far from her intention.

She may as well just say it and get it over with. "Thank you for last night."

"Thank you?" he arched a brow. "Why are you thanking me?"

"Because it was amazing."

"But? I sense a major but coming."

Amethyst nodded her acknowledgment that he was correct. Now she just had to think of a way to say this, but say it nicely. "It was amazing, but I see it as a one-time thing."

"So, this was a one night stand as far as you're concerned?"

"Hey, you got what you wanted too," she said defensively. She wasn't the bad guy here, they had both wanted what happened last night to happen, and she was pretty sure that neither of them had envisioned it as being a long term thing.

"You think I'm the kind of guy that sleeps with a woman once and moves on?" he demanded, dropping his hands from her shoulders.

"I don't know. I don't think so, but I don't really know you, we don't know each other," she reminded him.

"There's nothing stopping us from *getting* to know each other."

"No, there's not," she agreed. "But I thought that this was just sex. To both of us," she added. "I didn't think it meant anything beyond both of us have wanted this for days now."

"So you used me?" he growled.

"No," she shook her head firmly. "You wanted this every bit as much as I did and don't even think about denying it."

"Doesn't mean I wanted it to be a one night stand," he shot back.

"So, you see us being a couple? Is that what you want? You want to date me? Marriage, kids, family, is that really where you see us down the line?"

"I don't know," he said, finally dropping the angry frown. "I guess not."

"Then I don't know why you're so upset," she said, fighting the pang of sadness that his words stirred up. That was what she was expecting him to say, she knew that he didn't really want a future with her, he was just caught up in everything that had happened the last few days. She didn't want a future with him, this was what she wanted.

So why did it feel wrong?

Why did it feel like she was making one of the biggest mistakes of her life?

"I guess I'll get dressed and go then," Zeb said, and turning around he began to collect his clothes, she didn't even remember how they got up here since they had undressed downstairs last night.

"What does this mean for the case? Am I still working it with you and Judah or am I going back to the firehouse?"

"Your boss and mine want you on this case," he replied as he shoved his legs into his boxers and then his pants.

Okay, so that was going to be awkward, which was exactly why she had known that this was a bad idea from the beginning. And then once Judah found out—which she was sure he would—it would no doubt make things awkward between them as well. And Judah would probably tell his wife, and Ruby would tell their other sisters, and things would be awkward between her and her siblings too.

This really had been a bad idea.

But she wasn't sure she would take it back even if she could.

"Maybe I should work with Judah from now on," she suggested.

"Fine with me." Zeb yanked his t-shirt over his head and strode to the door. He stopped abruptly. "I called Judah last night and asked him to get your car and bring it over here."

That was sweet. She hadn't even thought about how she was going to get to the station, but her car had still been right where she'd parked it yesterday before she and Zeb had gone in his car to the abandoned industrial estate. "Thank you," she said softly, and she meant it.

She didn't want things to end like this between them.

She wanted to go back to yesterday when there was just sexual tension bubbling between them.

She wanted them to find a way to put last night aside and be friends.

She wanted ...

She wanted ...

Amethyst didn't even know what she wanted, but as she watched Zeb walk out the door, and to all intents and purposes out of her life, she knew that it wasn't this. She was so mixed up, her emotions were all over the place, she wanted things that she didn't think she was capable of having, she had trained herself so successfully—*too* successfully—to think of herself and her life as inconsequential. Now she didn't know how to live any differently. That wasn't the kind of person who got too deeply involved with another person.

Zeb was ...

Well, he was something special, and she had no intention of ruining that.

She was making the right decision, she was sure of it.

It just sucked.

8:48 A.M.

To say he was in a bad mood was an understatement.

Quite possibly the worst mood of his life.

It was Amethyst's fault.

Zeb wasn't sure what he had expected when they woke up this morning, but it hadn't been for Amethyst to tell him that as far as she was concerned last night was just sex, it hadn't meant anything to her, and she didn't want it to happen again.

That wasn't what he wanted.

It wasn't until Amethyst had fallen asleep last night in his arms as they finally wore themselves out after three rounds of sex that he realized that things had changed for him.

Was he ready to commit to a future with her?

He wasn't sure.

And that was the problem.

He knew that he felt something for her. He knew that what had happened last night wasn't a one-off as far as he was concerned, but he didn't know what the future held. He didn't know if he wanted to get married one day, have kids, he liked his space, and he was used to being on his own, but he wasn't against the idea of having a family of his own.

Being unsure of what he wanted himself really didn't leave him in good stead to convince Amethyst that they might have something special going on here. And what good would trying to convince her do anyway? She had made her position very clear. Last night was a one night stand in her mind, she wasn't looking for more, and she didn't want more.

He should leave well enough alone.

Move on and forget that last night had happened.

Write it off as the overflowing of emotions from the attraction that had bubbled between them for the last week, and then the fire, and fighting for their lives together, it had all come to a head, and falling into bed had been the natural progression.

"Morning, sunshine," Judah said, appearing in the conference room door.

"Morning," he muttered. He didn't want to be at work today. He wanted to lick his wounds, slink away and hide out in the peace and quiet of his house. But he had a job to do so he was here. He wanted this pyromaniac killer off the streets before another person died a horrific death, so he wasn't going anywhere as much as he would like to.

"Don't you sound all rainbows and roses this morning," Judah said as he dropped into a chair at the table and handed over a cup of coffee.

Zeb took the cup, drank half of it in one go. Maybe he could drink enough coffee to buzz his brain with caffeine, and he'd stop thinking about Amethyst.

Yeah right.

Like that would ever happen.

Any minute now she was going to come walking through the door, and he would have to spend the day with her, and tomorrow, and the next day, and however long it took to get this guy off the streets. He had no idea how that was going to go, but he would soon be finding out.

"How was last night?" Judah asked.

Why did his partner have to be so nosy this morning? Had they talked about things like this before? Sure they had. Had they discussed Judah's love life when he and Ruby had gotten together? Yep. But that didn't mean he wanted to discuss the colossal mistake last night had been.

"Nothing to say about it? You spent the night, right? So I have to assume that you two did some lovemaking," Judah teased.

"It was just a one-time thing," he mumbled. "Amethyst isn't looking for anything else."

"And you are?"

"I don't know, I guess I just wasn't ready for Amethyst to be so adamant about it the morning after."

"Give her time, she'll come round, she just has this whole risk taking, live life on the edge attitude because acting like she didn't care if she lost her life was how she survived what happened to her as a teenager."

"I know, I get it, I really do, I just don't think she has any plans on changing."

"I don't know about that. I think seeing her sisters all find a way to put the past in the past and heal some of the open wounds they still had from that time in their lives has her thinking. Seriously, give her some time, she might change her mind. You just have to figure out what *you* want. You seem wishy-washy, you don't even know what you want, stop worrying about what Amethyst is thinking, and start worrying about what you're thinking. Amethyst doesn't need me to stand up for her, and she'd probably be mad to know that I'm even saying anything, but she's Ruby's twin sister, and I feel protective of her, so don't mess things up."

Before he had a chance to say anything, the door opened and Amethyst stepped nervously through it. She was deliberately looking anywhere but at him and for a moment he regretted last night.

This was exactly what he had been worried about. This was why he had known that the two of them getting together was a bad idea. Maybe Amethyst had the right idea, move on, it was a one-off, it didn't mean anything beyond one night of passion, best to move forward with their lives.

"Gang's all here," Judah said, trying to lighten the mood. "Morning, Amethyst."

"Morning," she said, sitting down at the table.

"So we have the preliminary report on the fire from yesterday," Judah told them.

At the mention of the fire, Zeb couldn't help but glance at Amethyst and found her watching him. Her gaze darted away when she caught him looking at her. That sexual tension was still there whether either of them wanted it to be or not, but physical attraction wasn't enough to build a foundation for a relationship on, and he really didn't know what the future held for them. All he knew was that he didn't want last night to have been a one-time thing.

"Even though the building was destroyed by the fire, the medical examiner was able to get cause of death," Judah continued.

"Oh?" That caught his attention, and he refocused on his partner. "I thought the fire would have destroyed everything."

"It did a pretty good job, he must have waited until you two headed upstairs then doused the whole place in kerosene before setting it alight. The fire spread quickly, you two were lucky to get out alive."

The only reason they had gotten out alive was because Amethyst had known what to do. If it was up to him, he would have headed down the stairs, tried to find his way out through the flames.

"He was obviously prepared," Judah said.

"We checked the whole of the downstairs before we went up," he said. "He must have had the kerosene cans hidden outside around the back or something, he was obviously sitting there watching us, waiting for us to start checking the building, then he got to work."

"He wanted you guys dead," Judah agreed.

"But he didn't get what he wanted," Amethyst reminded them.

"Because of you," Zeb said, meeting her eyes, and feeling that exact same spark ignite between them that he'd felt all week, and last night when they had made love.

"CSU is going to go through every inch of that building today now that it's been deemed safe, but for now at least, we know that Tucker Goud was murdered. Someone smashed his skull in," Judah informed them.

"He must have seen something the killer knew would be incriminating," Zeb said.

"I think I might know what," Judah told them.

"What did you find?" he asked his partner.

"Tucker Goud's cousin is Curtis Cane."

"Curtis?" Amethyst exclaimed. "He was on our list of suspects."

She was right, Curtis Cane had been one of their suspects, and now they had something that bumped him to the top of their list. Just because Curtis was cousins with their dead witness didn't mean that he was the killer, there were any number of reasons why whoever set the fire might have killed Tucker, but they couldn't deny that this definitely gave them something to think about.

"So what's the plan for today?" Amethyst asked, he heard the hint of nervousness in her tone. She was afraid to be alone with him because she didn't know how to deal with what had happened, and what was brewing between them.

As much as he felt for her because he understood where she was coming from, the ball was in her court. She had made her position crystal clear this morning, and if she had changed her mind, then she needed to come to him and tell him that.

"We'll interview Curtis," Judah answered Amethyst's question. "And continue to work through the list of other suspects while we wait to hear if CSU got anything from the fire yesterday."

"And wait for the call that there's been another fire," he added because they all knew that call was coming.

This guy wasn't finished yet. He had gotten a taste for it now, fire fueled him, it was what he lived for, and there was no way he was going to quit until they stopped him.

∾

11:37 A.M.

There seemed to be a lot more cops on the streets today.

Every time he turned a corner, drove down a street, it seemed that he was passing another police cruiser.

Was it too egotistical to believe that this was all because of him?

He didn't think it was. They knew that he had been setting fires every day, sometimes more than one a day, since he started this, so they knew that he had to be out and about somewhere, just looking for the perfect swimming pool to choose for his next fire.

They weren't wrong.

He *was* out and about looking for the perfect swimming pool to use as the setting of his next fire.

This was exactly what he intended to keep doing until the cops finally realized it was him that they were looking for, and managed to track him down and come after him. When that day finally came, he had no intention of going down quietly. He wasn't going to go to prison, spend the rest of his life behind bars. The ending he had in mind was very different.

His ending was quite obviously flames.

When the cops did come for him, he was going to go down in a blaze of fiery glory. He was going to make the saying going down in flames a reality. That was how he wanted to die, and he was going to take as many cops as possible down with him when he went.

It was nothing personal of course. *None* of this was personal to anyone that he had gone after so far, it was merely relishing the thing that he loved the most. So taking out the cops that would come for him that day was only his way of having one last bit of fun before his life ended.

He was a little disappointed that his attempt to kill the cops at the old industrial estate yesterday hadn't worked out. He'd planned it out so perfectly, keeping the body a few days to make sure the cops would be wondering where the man was, then calling in anonymously to report the body, making sure to describe the man well so the cops would assume that it was who they had been looking for. He had been there the whole time, watching the car pull up and the cops walk inside, he'd watched them through a grimy window as they checked out the body then disappeared off into the building. As soon as they had headed up the stairs, he had sprung into action, unsure just how long he would have before they returned.

As soon as he had doused the place in kerosene and struck the match, throwing it into the building, he had hightailed it out of there. Circling back around to the highway, he had pulled his car over to the side of the road and pretended to be changing a flat tire so he could watch.

The flames had roared to life, consuming the building even more quickly than he had anticipated, and he had been sure enough that the two cops would perish that he had been about to get into his car and drive off when he had seen them on the roof. They had done the opposite of what he had intended and gone up instead of down through the flames, and it had worked in their favor. He had watched as they jumped off the roof, and while he'd wanted to watch to see what happened next, he knew the fire would have been called in, and he had to get out of there.

So that plan hadn't worked, it was disappointing, but he was intrigued by the idea that they had survived. Maybe they were phoenixes rising from the ashes just like he was.

While it was an interesting notion, he didn't really have time to ponder it. He had to get to work, and now that the cops were out looking for him, he had to be even more careful, especially since he didn't want to have to kill another witness. That had been unfortunate but unavoidable, the man had seen him, tried to stop him from leaving, and he'd had no choice but to bash his head in then throw him in the trunk of his car. It wasn't what he'd intended, and although it had been a great tool to lure in the cops, he really didn't want to have to do it again. He wasn't out to kill per se, and having to do so only increased the risks.

He could always go back to more remote houses again, that had its benefits like not having to worry about anyone stumbling on him so he could watch the whole thing, but it also took away some of the fun. What was the point of getting an adrenalin rush when the rush was subpar? So for now, he had to manage the risks as best as he could and go for that rush. Go big or go home, he'd heard that saying before and always thought it was kind of stupid, but it was certainly apt for his current situation.

Pulling his car to the side of the road, he watched as another cruiser rolled past, pretending to talk on his phone, just in case they should happen to look his way, he watched as it passed him. It was annoying that he now had to deal with the increased police presence, but at the same time, it was kind of exciting that he was obviously one of the top cases in the city.

That made him feel special.

He liked being the center of attention.

Growing up the way he had, with a father that had left, two older siblings who were old enough that they no longer wished to spend time with their little brother, he had been left on his own a lot of the time. His mother was an obsessive control freak who wanted to micromanage his every move, in his world it had been his mother who was the center of everything, she had craved attention even more than she craved her next breath of air, and all of their worlds had revolved around her.

But not anymore.

Now *he* was the one who was the center of the universe. The cops were fixated on finding him, and the residents of the city were no doubt terrified that their pool might be the next one he chose. What fun. He'd never had so many people thinking about him, usually he kind of blended into the background, that was how he had survived his youth, but he was done with that. He was never going to blend in again.

Well, he supposed that wasn't quite true.

If he was going to keep setting fires, then he was going to have to blend in enough that no one noticed him slipping into backyards to set fire to their pools.

To that end, he slipped out of his car, and with a glance around, started walking down the block. It was quiet out, it was a hot morning, already the temperature was climbing, and he was sure this was going to be the hottest day of the summer so far, despite the heat, he noticed a frazzled looking mom trying to wrangle three little kids on tricycles down the street.

He pulled out his phone again, pretended he was busy typing out a message, and then waited until the woman and the kids had passed on by. Then he kept walking.

He paused outside a house when he heard the sounds that made his body buzz.

Wondering how many kids he would find when he entered the backyard, he turned and walked down the front path. He was kind of hoping that he might find quite a few kids, it was getting harder and harder to get that same rush that he had the first time he'd done this. It was still exciting, it was still fun, but it wasn't quite the same. He needed more.

Was this how it was going to be from here on out?

Would he keep having to find something more to add to this so that he continued to get that buzz of adrenalin he'd become addicted to?

Maybe he could look into hitting up public swimming pools, that would certainly make things a whole lot harder, but it would also make things a lot more exciting.

What would he do after that wore off though?

Worrying about where this was going to end, he walked through to the backyard, for now at least, he was just going to enjoy the moment.

12:02 P.M.

This was getting ridiculous.

They were driving to fire number six, and although they had two suspects now, they didn't have anything concrete on either of them.

To say he was frustrated was an understatement.

Zeb wanted this case closed for so many reasons. Topping the list was getting this guy off the streets so no one else died, but not having to spend all day every day with Amethyst was definitely on there too.

She was sitting in the back seat of the car right now as he drove the two of them and Judah to the scene of the next fire. She hadn't said much this morning, but the tension between them had only grown. The more time he spent around her, the more he wanted her, and the more he wondered if she was right and things just weren't meant to be between them.

It was getting to the point that it was distracting. He could no longer focus on his work, and he was worried that the lack of attention was going to end up causing him to make a mistake. A mistake that would allow this guy to remain free. Free to keep killing because Zeb knew that this man was never going to stop. If anything, he was going to start looking to make things bigger, more deaths, higher risk situations. If this guy was doing it for the excitement, the adrenalin rush, then sooner or later he wouldn't be able to get that rush unless he upped the ante.

"There's the house, just up there," Judah said as he turned the corner and they saw the fire trucks, police cruisers, and bystanders milling around in the street.

"Do we have any information yet on the fire, how many people were involved, if there were any witnesses?" Zeb asked as he parked the car

"911 caller said there were five kids in the pool," Judah replied.

"Who was the 911 caller?"

"There was a sixth kid there. Apparently, she had gone inside to use the bathroom, she heard the screams, saw the fire and called it in."

"Did she get a look at whoever set the fire?"

"Nothing more than what we already know, a man dressed all in black."

Zeb let out a frustrated breath. It was so annoying that they'd had several people who had seen the killer, and yet no one was able to give them even the most basic of descriptions.

The three of them opened their doors and got out of the car, they walk toward the house in question, just as they reached the edge of the house's front yard a man came rushing toward them.

Heading straight for Amethyst.

Without even thinking, Zeb snapped an arm around Amethyst's waist and yanked her up against his body, turning so he was between her and the man charging them.

"Hey," Judah yelled, managing to grab hold of the man before he slammed into them. "What do you think you're doing?"

"Teaching *her* a lesson," the man growled.

"Teaching who? Amethyst?" Judah asked.

"Do you know who this is?" Zeb asked Amethyst, who was holding herself stiffly in his arms. He didn't know if it was because he was touching her, or because she was upset about the man who was clearly furious with her.

"It's Kel Ingham," she replied. "He worked at the same station as me for a while."

"Until you got me fired," the man fumed, struggling to get free from Judah's grip.

"You didn't get fired, you got put on leave," Amethyst corrected, clearly unconcerned with the angry man who looked like he wanted to beat her to a bloody pulp.

"Calm down or I'm going to put you in handcuffs," Judah told Kel Ingham.

"Fine," the man huffed, holding up his hands in defeat. His partner slowly released his grip on Kel, but stood close to him in case he changed his mind and went after Amethyst again.

"Do you want to explain what happened between you two?" Zeb asked Amethyst, letting go of her.

"He made sexual advances toward me even after I told him no. He wouldn't stop, he kept trying to approach me whenever I was alone. I told him if he didn't stop I was going to go to the lieutenant about it. He got angry, grabbed me, shoved me up against a wall and started touching my breasts, I punched him in the face, broke his nose, then went straight to the lieutenant, and Kel got put on leave until this got sorted out since he denied that it happened the way I said." Amethyst's blue eyes sparkled with fire, if looks could kill, then Kel Ingham would be a dead man.

"You really broke his nose?" Zeb asked Amethyst, pride flushing through him. There was nothing sexier than a woman who could defend herself against a creep.

"Yep, and I'd do it again, enough times until he learns that no means no," Amethyst said.

"What are you doing here, Kel?" Judah asked before Kel could say anything else. "If you're on leave then you aren't here to put the fire out."

"I live right across the street. When I heard the screams I came running over and saw the fire, I did what I could to put it out, there were five kids in there," Kel said, the anger finally leaving his face.

That was a reasonable explanation. *Or* it was Kel Ingham's way of trying to insert himself into their investigation while also trying to look like the hero. The profile of firefighters who started fires said that they often tried to be the hero who showed up on the scene and put the fire out or saved someone. While he hadn't saved the kids from the fire, he might have thought it would both make him look good to his bosses, and he got to watch the aftermath of his fire.

Zeb had his mind fixed on the second.

The man clearly was unable to follow even the most simple of directives like the word no, and being put on leave from his job when he believed that he was the one in the right could have been the trigger that started all of this.

With Kel, they now had three suspects. Joaquin Burton who had been the firefighter who was first on the scene of one of the previous fires, Curtis Cane who was cousins with their dead glass guy and witness to one of the fires, and now Kel Ingham who had also been first on scene at one of the fires. While Zeb's instincts said that the man they were looking for was Kel, he suspected that had more to do with the fact that the man had assaulted Amethyst than anything else.

While he wanted to slap the man in handcuffs and haul him down to the station, technically, he hadn't done anything. They couldn't say for sure that he would have attacked Amethyst if given the chance. Maybe they could hold him for a little while at least, his lawyer would no doubt have him out in a couple of hours tops, but it was better than nothing, and they might be able to use it to try to find something on him that would prove he was the killer.

Zeb was about to pull out his handcuffs when tires screeching behind them drew his attention. He looked over at Judah and saw the same thing written on his partner's face that he was thinking.

That could be the killer.

"Amethyst, go in the backyard with everyone else," he said when she started to follow him and Judah to the car. There was no way he was bringing her with them. If this *was* the killer, then he didn't want her getting hurt, after yesterday he was benching her on anything that might wind up being dangerous. "And stay away from *him*," he added, nodding his head in Kel's direction.

Trusting that she would do as he'd asked, Zeb jumped into the driver's seat of the car and took off, his own tires screeching down the street in the same direction that the car had gone. There was no guarantee that it was the killer, but it definitely bore looking into.

"Did he turn left or right?" he asked Judah.

"Right," his partner replied confidently.

Turning right, just as he was straightening the car, something came crashing straight into them, and immediately the vehicle was engulfed in flames.

For the second time in as many days, he was confronted with fire.

Only this time he didn't have Amethyst by his side.

That seemed to make a difference to his brain.

He froze.

Memories of being trapped in his home as a child flashed through his mind. Being dragged out of his bed in the middle of the night, being tied up and carried down to the living room. Watching his father's partner—a man he had known all his life—beat his father until he could barely recognize his face. The kerosene being thrown about, and the flash of bright orangey-red as the fire sprung to life.

Zeb thought he was going to die that day and for a long time after he wished that he had.

That day, he had been frozen just like he was today.

It was his father who had grabbed him, somehow managed to untie his wrists, and shoved him toward the laundry telling him to climb up onto the washing machine and then out the window.

His father had told him he could do it, that he could get out, and that he would be okay. The last words he had heard before he left his parents and baby sister behind, were his parents telling him they loved him.

Fire should have taken his life that day.

Fire should have taken his life yesterday.

Maybe today it would finally get what it wanted.

∿

12:14 P.M.

As soon as Zeb and Judah got into their car to follow after the one that had just rocketed off down the street, Kel turned and ran off.

Should she go after him?

Amethyst thought that probably wasn't the best idea given how angry he was with her.

Kel was a disgusting, filthy slimeball who thought that his big baby blue eyes, thick dark hair, dimples, and sculpted physique made him God's gift to women, but did that make him a killer?

She wasn't sure. She was trying to be objective since she was playing at being a cop these days she was doing her best to work this as hard as Judah and Zeb were, she didn't want to be the weak link that kept this guy on the streets where he was free to kill at will.

Now that Kel was gone and no longer a threat to her—even though she could totally take him on her own anyway—she decided to go to the backyard and find out whatever she could about the scene. She wouldn't interview the girl who had watched her friend's horrific deaths, she wasn't that good at being a cop yet, but she could talk to her colleagues, see if they had anything helpful to tell her.

It felt weird being at the scene of a fire as a cop and not as a fire-fighter, and although she felt a little more at ease in her new role, she still couldn't wait to get back into her comfort zone. As much as she was a risk taker and loved crazy adrenalin pumping activities that most people balked at, she still liked her routines and being in her safe place. While home had been her twin sister's safe zone, her safe zone was her job, she always felt at ease there, just one of the guys, she laughed and talked with her friends, and they were such a well-oiled machine that as soon as it was time to go to a fire they just clicked and got things done.

Before she could go back to doing what she loved, she needed to help Zeb and Judah find this guy, but unfortunately, instead of narrowing down their suspect list and focusing in on one person, they were adding in more suspects. Now it wasn't just Joaquin and Curtis who were top of their list, Kel was there as well.

The pressure was really getting to her, people's lives depended on her, and that was a scary thing. Walking through flames to rescue someone was easy, but unraveling clues to find a killer was the hardest thing she had had to do in a long time.

Amethyst didn't know how Zeb and Judah did this every day.

Sapphire had always made being a cop look so easy, she saw things other people didn't, and she obsessed over every little detail until she found its significance, and she trusted her instincts. That was something she was still learning about, she didn't have to trust her gut the same way as a firefighter, but doing this was making her really learn how to listen to herself.

When it came to this case anyway.

Listening to herself when it came to her personal life, now that was a whole other thing.

She still didn't know what she was going to do about ...

Her train of thought trailed off when she heard the unmistakable sound of a fire igniting.

Amethyst didn't even think about it, she just started running. This time she didn't need to worry about listening to her instincts, they were screaming at her that Zeb was in trouble.

Since running was her thing, it didn't take her long to reach the end of the block, and immediately she saw it.

Zeb's car was on fire.

One door of the car was open.

The passenger side door.

But Zeb had been in the driver's seat.

And Judah was rounding the car, heading for Zeb.

Had this been a job and she was here with her team on the scene of a random car accident, she would have approached slower, more cautiously, but since this wasn't just some scene her team had been called to, she threw caution to the wind and bolted toward the car.

Just as she was about to reach it, the driver's door finally opened, and Zeb staggered out.

Relief almost knocked her to her knees.

She could hear footsteps behind her, and voices yelling, but she kept running toward her goal.

Zeb.

She saw blood on him, and he was staggering like he was dazed, was it just because of shock and the smoke he had no doubt inhaled, or had he been seriously injured?

Amethyst didn't have time to think about it, the front of the car was burning, and she knew it could explode at any second.

Reaching Zeb, she grabbed his hand and began to run with him away from the car. The two of them and Judah made it a few yards away before a loud roaring bang ripped through the air.

The force of the explosion threw all three of them to the ground.

Metal rained down around them, and for the second time in two days she felt something burning against her flesh, on her back this time.

She was a firefighter, and she knew what to do, she rolled over onto her back, smothering the flames before they could consume her.

Someone snatched her up, and she was carried further away from the burning debris. Amethyst scanned the area looking for Zeb. Was he okay?

"Amethyst, you with me?"

She blinked as a face came into focus before her.

It was Theo.

As much as she loved her friend that wasn't who she wanted to see at the moment.

"I'm fine," she assured him. "I just got a little burn on my back."

As soon as she said that, Theo set her down and turned her around and lifted the back of her t-shirt so he could see the burn. "First degree," he told her.

"Good," she murmured, only half paying attention. She could see Zeb, he was standing ten feet away talking to Judah, Greg, and Oz, paramedics were heading toward him and she was sure that soon one would come over to her. Her back stung but she didn't care, Zeb was okay, and that was all that mattered.

"Do you know what happened?" Theo asked her.

"No, by the time I got here the car was on fire, I was worried it was going to explode, and Zeb was still inside. He got out, and I just remember grabbing his arm and running then flying through the air and hitting the ground." She had to stop to take a steadying breath. If Zeb hadn't already been out of the car when she got to him, then they would both probably be dead right now. There was no way she could have gotten him out of the car and both of them away from the vehicle before it blew up.

Thankfully, everything had worked out. This fall on top of the fire yesterday and jumping off the roof was going to leave them even stiffer and sorer in the morning, but at least they were alive.

It was kind of an unusual thought for her. Usually, she didn't worry about whether or not she was still alive, she went into things having calculated the risks and decided that it was something she wanted to do anyway. Her job, her extreme marathons, all the adrenalin pumping pursuits, with all of them she knew that her life was on the line, and while she was as careful as it was possible to be, that had always been an acceptable risk.

Only now she was rethinking things.

Her life had always seemed disposable because she didn't really have anything that was so important that she felt that passion to be alive. It wasn't that she wanted to be dead, because she didn't, it was more that she was neutral, it didn't matter to her one way or the other, she just wanted to have fun, get that buzz, and whatever happened, happened.

But Zeb made her reconsider that.

He made her wonder if she had been looking at things wrong all these years.

Maybe she should go over there, talk to him, tell him that she was confused, that she didn't know what she wanted, but she knew she didn't just want to let him walk away.

She should go over there.

She should.

And yet her feet didn't move.

Something was holding her back.

Fear, maybe.

Maybe she wasn't as tough and always in control as much as she would like to think that she was. Maybe she wasn't quite as confident as she liked everyone else to think she was. Maybe she had more insecurities than she would like to admit.

Whatever the reasons, she stayed right where she was.

This whole thing with Zeb left her feeling so out of her element that she wanted to just run away and hide like a little girl in her bed under her blankets.

But she wasn't a little girl.

She was a big girl.

A woman.

A woman who it turned out was a coward.

❧

7:37 P.M.

Zeb flipped over the next page in a photo album and smiled when he saw a picture of himself holding his new baby sister. He'd been six when Lucy was born, and he couldn't have been more excited about becoming a big brother. When his mom had gone into labor, he'd been taken to his grandparent's house for them to look after him, they had intended to take him out to the circus for the day, to keep him busy and occupied, but he had begged and pleaded to be allowed to wait in the hospital until the baby arrived.

As soon as she had entered the world, he had been in that hospital room with his parents, holding the red, squishy little baby in his arms. From that moment on he had been smitten.

For the next two years he had doted on Lucy, cuddling her when she cried, playing with her, teaching her new things, she was his baby sister, and he'd been protective of her. If she hadn't died, he would have given any boy who wanted to date her a hard time, they would have had to prove that they were good enough for her, and he wasn't sure any of them would have measured up.

He was sure Lucy would have hated that.

His baby sister had been such a little tornado of sass, and spunk, and energy. She could go from zero to one hundred in a second, she made him laugh, she was always so excited when he came home from school at the end of the day and would greet him with the biggest, squeeziest hug.

Losing her had been hard.

She was such a tiny little thing, small but with a personality big enough to fill a room. His life had seemed so empty after that, if he wasn't a big brother, and he wasn't a son, then who was he?

For a long time he had felt out of place in the world.

He didn't have a family.

Well, he did of course, he'd had grandparents on both sides who had doted on him and showered him with love. He'd had aunts and uncles and cousins who had made sure to include him in everything that they had going on. And he'd had his father's family of blue, they had all rallied around him and made sure he knew that he had a family there as well as his biological one.

But none of it was the same.

He didn't have parents, he didn't have siblings, it was just him.

Bit by bit he had managed to rebuild himself, he had found his place in the world, he'd taken up football, been part of a team and made a new family there, then he'd joined the police force, solidifying that family as it became his own and not just an extension of his father's life. While he might have become a different person had he not lost his family at such a young age, and in such a horrific way, he had family, friends, and colleagues who he cared about, loved and trusted.

And yet still that feeling of loneliness lingered.

His family, who had never once let him down, were his family, and yet they weren't *his* family. They were extended family, they didn't give him that same feeling that his parents and sister had. His friends were an important part of his life, but they all had families of their own, and while he didn't resent it and knew it was the way it should be, he was secondary in their lives, behind their partners and children. He would lay down his life for his partner, or any one of the cops in the department, but again, they were just colleagues, friends, people he liked and cared about but not people that he *loved*.

There was no one in the world who he felt was his. No one for whom he was the number one person in their life. No one that should he die tomorrow would grieve him with a hole in their heart that would never heal like the one he had from losing his mom, dad, and Lucy.

He wanted someone that could be the center of his universe. He wanted someone that would roll over in bed in the middle of the night and be concerned if he wasn't there. He wanted someone that even after years and years, was still excited to be with him. He wanted someone that he could build a family with, a family that wouldn't replace what he had lost, and yet in some ways it would.

It had taken nearly dying twice in two days, in the exact same way that his parents and sister had died, to make him realize this. He had thought he was doing okay, he had thought he was happy with his life, he hadn't thought he was missing out on anything, but now it felt like he was only living half a life, and that the things he should have been focusing on he had ignored.

That had to change.

Of course, the first thing that came to his mind when he thought of changing, of falling in love, getting married, having a family again, was Amethyst.

He couldn't stop thinking about her.

She had saved his life twice now.

Yesterday at the fire, then this afternoon when someone—presumably the killer—had thrown a rock soaked in a burning rag at the car, causing the engine to explode. He'd been dazed by the flames and the memories that they brought up, it had taken him several moments before snapping to attention enough to open the door, undo his seatbelt and get out of the burning car.

As soon as he was out of the car the first thing he had seen was Amethyst running toward him, no fear of the flames and the explosion she had known was coming. All she had been thinking about was him. How could you not love a woman who would gladly throw herself to the flames to try to save him?

But that was also part of the problem.

Amethyst had grabbed his hand and dragged them both far enough away from the car before it blew up that they had only received minor injuries, and he knew that she would do it again if she had to, but he had already lost a family once before, and he wasn't sure he could take it again. Amethyst liked to take risks, she didn't mind putting her life on the line to do things that she thought were fun that most people balked at. Skydiving, bungee jumping, drag racing, BMX biking, extreme marathons, to her that was a fun way to spend her time, but to him, it was a disaster waiting to happen.

Did he want her to change who she was because of him?

Of course he didn't.

Did he want her to give up all the things she enjoyed just because he didn't think the risks were worth it?

No. He didn't want Amethyst to be anything other than the person that she was, and she loved all of those things.

The problem was he didn't think he could deal with all of those things that she loved. That left them at an impasse. Even if she decided that she was willing to give them a chance, he didn't think they would work out.

She was right.

This morning Amethyst had asked him if he saw a future for them, it was clear that she didn't, she thought they were too different, and as much as he hated to admit it he thought that she was probably right.

He should just let go of this whole thing.

If he wanted to fall in love there were a million women out there, he could find someone who he was more compatible with.

So why couldn't he stop thinking about Amethyst?

They'd slept together now, if all there was between them was physical attraction, then he should be able to move on.

But he couldn't.

And it wasn't just because he wanted to sleep with her again.

It was more than that, he cared about her, if she'd been killed today trying to get him away from the car then he would have been left with another hole in his heart that would never completely heal.

Zeb set the photo album down and picked up his phone. He should call her, ask her to come over so they could at least talk things through properly before either of them made any final decisions.

He opened his contacts and scrolled down to her name. Touching her name, his finger hovered above her phone number. It was so easy, call her, talk to her, sort this out.

But he didn't do it.

Part of him was afraid that when he called her, and they talked that she would agree that maybe they'd been wrong and maybe they could make a great couple.

And part of him was afraid that she wouldn't.

Risking your heart again after such a big loss at such a young age wasn't easy. And risking it for someone who could very well get herself killed because she believed her life wasn't anything important was even harder.

With a sigh, he set his phone back down.

~

8:14 P.M.

"Thanks for dinner," Amethyst said, pushing back from the table. She was having dinner with her sisters and their husbands and kids, and although she always loved spending time with her family, tonight she just kind of felt like being alone. She had debated turning down the invitation, but knew her family was worried about her, given that she had almost died twice in two days, so she'd come but now she was ready to say her goodbyes, go home, take a long, hot shower—or given the seemingly never ending heat, maybe a cool one—then curl up in bed and mope.

Usually, she wasn't much of a moper, she just got on with it. Took an extra long workout, hung out with friends, researched a new activity that met her requirements for being as adrenalin pumping as it got, but today none of that sounded appealing.

She felt like she was making a big mistake letting Zeb walk away, and yet she still believed that they weren't compatible.

Opposites attract.

She had heard that so many times before, and she had to admit that while Ruby and Judah, and Diamond and Elijah were similar, Sapphire and Gideon were opposites, and yet here they were, happily married and now with a new baby to raise. They seemed happy, even when they bickered, they never seemed to take anything to heart.

Maybe it wasn't so big a deal that she and Zeb didn't share many things in common.

"You leaving already?" Sapphire asked, looking disappointed.

"It's been a long day, I was just going to head home, make it an early night," she replied, although she'd probably be in bed within the hour she doubted she was going to get much sleep.

"We haven't even had dessert yet," Diamond added.

"And it's not even eight-thirty," Ruby chimed in. "I know you've had a rough couple of days, but we'd love it if you stayed a little longer."

They were triple teaming her.

Amethyst was sure that they suspected that she wasn't worried about yesterday's fire or today's explosion, and that there was really much more going on inside her head right now. The last eighteen months or so had been a time of change for all of them. Sapphire meeting Gideon, then Ruby and Judah getting together, followed by Diamond and Elijah, she was sure that they were just waiting for her to follow suit.

"I'm going to go check on Leo," Gideon announced.

"I'll check on Archie," Elijah said, standing up, and nudging his teenage foster daughter's shoulder. "Brooke, why don't you come with me?"

"Upstairs? Archie's sleeping, what do we need to check on him for?" Brooke asked.

"Smooth one, Brooke," Elijah said.

"Oh." The girl's eyes widened. "You want me out of the room, gotcha. Sure, I'll go check on Archie with you."

Amethyst couldn't help but laugh.

She knew why her sisters wanted to get some alone time with her and what they wanted to talk to her about, and while it wasn't necessary —she didn't need a pep talk—it was nice to know how much they cared.

"Come on, you." Elijah took Brooke's hand and tugged the teenager to her feet.

"Well since Brooke already obliterated the subtle and tactful approach, I guess I don't need to make an excuse to leave you four alone, I'll just go upstairs and check on the kiddies with the others," Judah said with a grin.

Once they were alone, she said to her sisters, "I know what you guys are going to say and it's really not necessary, I'm fine, I don't need a pep talk, and I don't need convincing to go for anything or do anything different with my life. I really am fine."

"You gave each of us a pep talk," Diamond reminded her.

"Right," she agreed. "So I know exactly what you're all going to say. What happened to us when we were teenagers doesn't have to define us. That a decade has passed, that even though we're always going to have scars, it's okay to leave the past in the past and move on. That I deserve a future, and that just because I had to find a way to become hard to survive Nikos, now I have to find a way to become soft again so that I can have the future that I want. Did I cover everything?"

"Pretty much," Sapphire said.

"You got everything that I was going to say," Diamond said.

"Me too," Ruby agreed.

"So, I guess this little secretly coordinated chitchat doesn't really need to go ahead. Can I head home now? Call a rain check on dessert?" It wasn't that she meant to sound sharp, although it kind of was her way most of the time, it was just that she really wanted to be on her own tonight. The last few days had been such a rollercoaster ride of emotions, and it had worn her out, she needed some time to just try to process it all, and allow herself to really feel it instead of just trying to brush it all away.

"I don't think so," Ruby said.

"But I thought we just covered everything that you wanted to say," she said.

"You covered the pep talk part of the evening," Diamond told her.

"We also have a we're concerned about you part to the night," Sapphire added.

"Concerned about me?" she echoed, confused. She didn't know that her sisters were worried about her. That made her uncomfortable. She was fine, she had always been fine, she had dealt the best of all of them with what had happened, and the idea that anyone—even her sisters—should worry about her left her feeling really unsettled.

"Yes, concerned about you," Sapphire said. "You think that what happened didn't affect you all that much, that it just made you into this risk taker who doesn't care about what happens to her, but that's not true. In a lot of ways, I think it affected you the most because you're the one in denial. Diamond, Ruby, and I, we all knew how it affected us, we might not have broadcasted it to everyone around us, but we weren't living in denial. I think it's time that you finally open your eyes because if you don't, you're going to miss out on so much."

"And we don't just mean falling in love," Ruby said. "Sure, that would be nice if it's what you want, but it's not what this is about. This is about you. We want you to be happy, and right now you're not, you're just moving from one adrenalin overload to another so you don't have to feel anything else. You can't live in denial forever."

"You keep saying I'm in denial, but I'm not," she protested. She didn't get where all of this denial talk was coming from, she knew her strengths and weaknesses, and she didn't lie to herself.

"The thing with denial is you're not doing it on purpose," Ruby said as though reading her mind. "You believe that you like the adrenalin because it's the only time that you feel alive, and you think that you take all those risks because you don't care if you live or die. But that's not true. If it was, then you wouldn't have survived Nikos. You did what you had to do to survive because you *wanted* your life. Now you have it, so you need to stop acting like you don't care if you lose it tomorrow because I know that you do."

Her initial response was to disagree.

Of course, her twin sister was wrong.

She knew why she chose the hobbies that she had, and she knew her own thoughts and feelings. She didn't lie to herself, she didn't pretend, she was who she was, and whether her life would include Zeb, or someone else, or no one but herself, she was going to make the most of it.

"Don't say anything," Diamond said. "Don't disagree with us, don't argue your side of things, don't try to convince us that we're wrong. Just go away and think about what we said. Consider it. Really consider it, let it sink in, over the next few days and weeks every time you go and do one of your crazy activities, think about why you're there. There's nothing wrong with any of those things, and none of us think you should stop, but really think about why you're there. At some point, if you want to truly move on, then you have to feel all those emotions that you've bottled up for a decade. You stopped feeling so you could survive Nikos, but you *did* survive, and now if you want to have the life you fought for, you're going to have to fight against yourself, and feel every single one of those emotions so you can finally let them go."

"It's not easy," Sapphire said. "I know because I bottled things up too. I want more for you than this, I want you to be happy. I want you to be free."

Amethyst still disagreed with her sisters, but a tiny little voice in the very back of her head told her that maybe it was her who was wrong and not them.

Had she bottled up her feelings, convinced herself that they didn't exist?

She didn't think so, but what if she was wrong?

Had she really fought so hard, endured so much pain, to survive Nikos only to not live her life to the fullest?

If she had that seemed like a waste.

A waste that she should rectify.

CHAPTER

Eight

August 26th
9:18 A.M.

He was running late this morning. He'd slept in which was something he hardly ever did, but given the fire, and then the explosion yesterday, and everything with Amethyst. Plus the fact he'd been up half the night going through the old photos that family and friends had put together in an album for him after he lost his family and everything else that was in the house, Zeb had finally crashed.

He'd slept straight through the night not waking until after eight-thirty, around the time he was usually leaving the house. After taking a quick shower, he'd thrown on some clothes, fed his pet rabbit, Pebbles, and jumped in the car. He'd skipped his morning run and not bothered to stop to grab a coffee on the way to work, and had managed to arrive only twenty minutes late.

As he walked up to his desk, he scanned the room looking for Amethyst, but he didn't see her. Maybe she had crashed and slept late this morning too, they'd both had a rough last couple of days.

"How're you feeling?" Judah asked as he approached their desks.

"Fine," he replied, still trying to look about to see if Amethyst was here without making it overly obvious what he was doing. "You?"

"Fine, but I wasn't the one who was in two fires back to back," Judah replied. "And I'm not the one who has a bad history with them."

His partner knew about his past, it wasn't something that he had ever tried to hide, they never really talked about it, but that was because there really wasn't a lot to say. Yeah, it sucked that his father's partner had been a crook and tried to set his dad up by killing them all, but talking about it didn't change anything. When he'd gone to live with his aunt and uncle after losing his family, they had sent him to see a therapist who specialized in childhood trauma, and that had helped with the nightmares and the flashbacks, but it had also made him realize that no amount of discussion could change facts.

"I'm fine," he said firmly, wanting to assuage his partner's fears, he didn't want Judah's focus anywhere but on this case, and besides, he really was okay, it wasn't the fires it was Amethyst that had his head all messed up. "I just want this guy off the streets so we don't have any more deaths."

"Me too," Judah agreed. "Hopefully, we have our guy here at the station right now. If we can get him to trip up, say something incriminating, then we might get what we need to keep him here."

They were starting off the day by interviewing Kel Ingham, the firefighter who had been put on leave because he'd sexually assaulted Amethyst. The man had run off yesterday as soon as he and Judah had gotten into the car to take off after the car they'd thought might be the killer. They didn't get the license plate of the car, and it had been long gone by the time the hoopla of the explosion died down. There was no evidence that it had been the killer driving that vehicle, and if Kel had taken a short cut, he could have been the one that threw the rock covered in the burning rag at their car.

"Where's Amethyst?" he finally asked, he still couldn't see her anywhere, and he wanted to know if she was alright. He was sure that if it turned out her injuries were more serious than they appeared yesterday and she'd been taken to the hospital, that Judah would know since he was her brother-in-law, and Zeb was sure that Judah would have mentioned it, but he had to know for sure.

"She went back to work," Judah replied. "She spoke with her boss, said that she had done all she could for us, she'd given us background on every firefighter in the city and helped us narrow things down to three main suspects."

"Oh," he said, feeling empty. It was ridiculous of course, these last few days aside, they had never worked together, and while their jobs occasionally overlapped, it was unlikely that them working together would have continued past the closing of this case. And yet knowing that he wasn't going to see her today left him feeling disappointed. Things might be messed up between them, but at least this case was one connection they shared. Now that was gone.

"Things any better between you two?" Judah asked.

"Things aren't anything between us," he shrugged. "Let's go interview Kel." With that, he walked off toward the interview room, obsessing over his relationship—or lack thereof—with his partner was the last thing he wanted to do right now.

As he opened the door to the room where Kel Ingham was waiting for them, the first thing he noticed was the burn on the man's arm. He didn't remember noticing that yesterday, although at the time he had been preoccupied with making sure that the man didn't get his hands on Amethyst.

"How'd you get the burn?" he asked as he took a seat at the table.

"The burn?" the man echoed, following his line of sight. "Oh, this one," he said, touching his fingers to the freshly scarred skin. "It was a family barbecue, one of my nephews was setting off fireworks, managed to set himself alight, I was putting the fire out."

Not that it mattered how the man got the burn, but they would speak with family to see if they could confirm it, prove Kel had lied to them once, and it threw into question everything else he told them.

"So am I here because I was first on the scene yesterday, or because of a certain blonde someone who thinks she's better than everyone else?" Kel asked.

Zeb bristled.

His partner must have noticed because he felt Judah's eyes on him telling him to hold it together.

This wasn't about Amethyst, they already knew about the animosity there and that Kel blamed her for being benched from his job. They needed to find out if Kel was their killer, and getting distracted— as no doubt had been the man's intention—by the case with Amethyst was going to hamper their ability to do that.

"This is about yesterday's fire," Judah told Kel.

Kel ignored him. "You like her," the man said, zeroing in on Zeb. "I recognize that look. She's like that, she draws you in with that aloof stare, she's hot, and she knows it, she advertises herself but the second you take her up on that offer she rescinds it."

"That's what all sexual predators say," Zeb replied haughtily, refusing to be baited. How many times had he heard rapists blame their victims? This man was filth, and he was sure that whether he was the killer they were looking for or not, he would eventually find himself behind bars.

"You think I approached her just because she's hot? I know all about her and Theo, the two of them have been at it more than once, and there are plenty of rumors that she's slept with other men at the firehouse, I just thought I'd make myself available to be next."

Kel was taunting him.

Zeb knew that and despite his best efforts not to get sucked in, he couldn't help it. Amethyst had slept with Theo Black, a fellow fire-fighter on her team? That was none of his business, nothing to do with Amethyst's sex life was, but it did make him wonder, was he just a spur of the moment thing? They'd both felt that sexual tension between them, they'd both wanted more, neither of them had discussed the future before falling into bed, and she had been the one to say that as far as she was concerned it was just a one-time thing. Maybe this was what she did, maybe she just slept around with men she was attracted to and truly didn't want a future with any of them.

Or maybe that was just what Kel wanted him to think.

He had seen the vulnerability in Amethyst's eyes on more than one occasion, he didn't think that she would just use him like that.

"We're not here to discuss Amethyst," he informed Kel. "This is about the fires. Six of them so far, we have evidence to say that we're looking for a firefighter, and since one of the fires just happened to occur right across the street from your house, we think it might be you."

"You were suspended from duty," Judah continued. "What do you do with your days now? Specifically, what have you been up to this last week?"

"I'm no killer," Kel scowled, no longer smooth and in control now that he realized he wasn't going to be able to sidetrack them.

"So, what do you do with your days?" Zeb pushed. "You want to prove you're not a killer then tell us what you do each day, give us someone to talk to, someone who can give you an alibi for the times of the other fires."

"I don't do anything really." The man pouted. "And since you don't have any proof that I've done anything wrong, I'm out of here." With that, Kel Ingham stood and stormed out of the interview room.

They let him go because he was right; right now, they didn't have anything on him.

But that would change.

They were going to go digging into every aspect of the man's life until they found what they needed to nail him to the wall.

~

2:50 P.M.

She watched as the foam poured out of the hose.

It puddled on the water, and slowly, the flames began to dampen.

Beneath the fire and the foam, Amethyst could see the bodies floating.

The lifeless shells of what had just an hour ago been four teenage kids.

This time the victims were a little younger than the others, according to the frantic mother who had met them at the driveway, they ranged in age from thirteen to fifteen.

They were just babies.

They were supposed to be enjoying their summer, the break from school and essays and homework, a time to chill out and relax and have fun, a time where they shouldn't have a care in the world besides the nearing end of freedom with the beginning of the new school year looming over them just a couple of weeks away.

Now they would never have to worry about that again.

They'd never get a chance to start a new school year, or graduate and go on to college, they'd never have a first real job, or buy their first car, or their first house. They'd never fall in love, get married, have kids, and watch them grow until they were old enough to have kids of their own.

They'd never get to do anything.

Their young lives had been cut down far too soon, and it was so unfair.

That thought kept floating through her mind.

Unfair.

Why did life have to be so unfair?

Why did life dangle something wonderful in front of you but not let you reach out and grab hold of it?

Why did people kill others?

Why did these kids have to die?

Why them, why not someone else?

"Fire's out," Theo said softly from behind her, and she nodded. He was right, the fire was out, but once again, they were too late.

This morning when she had gotten up early and spoken with her lieutenant about returning to her team she had felt so positive. Zeb and Judah had three suspects, surely they would be able to find out which of them was the killer and arrest them. Surely there wouldn't be any more fires.

In case there was, she and her team had been driving about, keeping an eye out for anything suspicious, as she knew every cop in the city was also doing, and wanting to be ready to go should another fire occur so that hopefully this time there might be a different outcome.

But there wasn't.

It was the same outcome as all the other fires.

Dead kids.

That made sixteen now.

Sixteen people who had lost their lives.

How many more would there be?

How long would this killer roam free?

She was starting to feel like they would never catch him. What if they were wrong, and it wasn't Joaquin, Curtis, or Kel? Then this guy could go on and on killing all summer and then again when the weather thawed out and people started using their pools again next year—and the year after, and the year after that.

"You okay?" Theo asked his hand on her shoulder.

"Fine," she said, probably a little harsher than she should have since she knew that they were all getting hit hard by this case, but she was the only one who had worked it from both sides, and she was quickly reaching the end of her rope. "Really, I'm fine," she said, shrugging off his grip. "I'm going to go take a walk around the yard, make sure there aren't any sparks or anything that might start another fire."

Leaving the rest of her team to pack away their things ready to head back to the firehouse to no doubt await the news of another fire, Amethyst went to check out the yard. She knew that this guy wasn't stupid enough to have left a burning match anywhere, or anything else stupid like that, he was too controlled, he knew what he was doing, and that made him all the more terrifying.

Tears welled up in her eyes, and she didn't bother trying to stop them from chasing each other down her cheeks. Her heart was breaking for all of these victims, she couldn't shake that sense of responsibility for their deaths. She had failed as a firefighter and as a cop on this case and their deaths weighed heavily on her.

It was like they had formed a noose around her neck and they were pulling her deeper and deeper down, down into a place that she hadn't visited in a long time.

A place that was too full of emotion.

Life had been so much easier when she spent it jumping from one adrenalin rush to the next, never giving herself time to dwell on anything else.

Maybe her sisters were right, maybe the whole adrenalin junkie thing did have something to do with avoidance. It really was easier to just focus on that rush that she got jumping out of a plane, or flying down a hill on skis, or going sixty miles an hour on her BMX bike.

"Hey."

She startled at the sound and spun around to find Zeb standing watching her.

For a long moment, they just stood there and stared at one another. She thought about lifting a hand and brushing away the tears that still tumbled down her cheeks like a little wet avalanche, but she didn't.

She didn't feel the need to.

Then Zeb stepped forward and enclosed his arms around her, drawing her close.

He didn't say anything, he just held her.

Amethyst curled her arms around his waist and pressed her face against his neck and let the last of her tears drain out of her.

"I'm sorry," she whispered at last.

"For crying? You don't need to apologize for that, I know how hard this case has been on you."

"Not for crying, for the other morning, for telling you that what happened between us meant nothing, because it wasn't just mean it wasn't true," she explained. He tried to pull her back, but she resisted, this was easier to say if she didn't have to look at him while she said it. "I can't tell you that I know what I want because I don't. I'm confused, and I don't know if I'll ever want to get married and have kids and do the whole family thing. I like you, and I know there's something between us, but I don't know what my future looks like, I can't expect you to want to be with me knowing that."

"Don't you think that's up to me?"

It was probably egotistical of her, but no, she hadn't thought of that.

She was too busy being wrapped up in herself, and her insecurities, and what she wanted, and what she thought Zeb wanted, to actually ask him.

"I guess you get a say in the matter," she joked.

"Good, I'm glad we agree on something." She still wasn't looking at him, but she could hear the smile in his voice, and she'd felt his body relax. "Look at me," he said, gently grasping her arms and easing her back, then he hooked a finger under her chin and tilted her face up so she was looking at him. "None of us know what the future looks like, but I like you too, and whether you're ready to commit to something right now or not, I'd like to get to know you better. Even if nothing ever develops between us at least we'd each get a new friend. This is a risk I'm willing to take because *you* are worth it, *you* are a risk worth taking."

That was quite possibly the nicest thing anyone had ever said to her.

Her eyes misted over again.

"Thank you," she said, it didn't sound like enough because those words had given her a confidence she hadn't even known that she was lacking.

"Can I take you out to dinner tonight? Just a date, no pressure for anything more," he added.

"I can do dinner tonight, I'm doing ten-hour shifts this week, so I'll be off at six," she said with a smile. A date sounded nice, and she liked the idea of no pressure and just taking things slow. Just because Ruby and Judah, and Diamond and Elijah, had had rocket speed relationships, didn't mean that she had to do the same thing. She had never been in a serious relationship before and the idea of dating, having fun together, was a nice one.

"I'll pick you up at your house at seven?"

"Seven would be fine."

"Until tonight," Zeb said, but didn't move. His eyes met hers, and he sought permission to kiss her. When she nodded, he dipped his head and touched his lips to hers. The kiss was sweet, not hot and heavy like their kisses had been at her place the other night, and somehow this kiss was better. Maybe because it was more intimate, it was more than just a burning desire for sex.

"Until tonight," she echoed as he released her and with a last look walked away. There may still be a killer out there, and there might even be more deaths before her shift ended, but her day had just gotten a whole lot better.

~

7:24 P.M.

. . .

"So, where are we going?" Amethyst asked for probably the tenth time since he'd picked her up thirty minutes ago. He'd been a little early because he just couldn't wait any longer, but she must have been every bit as anxious as he was because she answered the door about half a second after he knocked, dressed and ready to go.

"Didn't I answer that already?" he asked lightheartedly.

"You *did* answer," Amethyst agreed, "but you didn't really tell me anything."

"I did, I told you that you'd know where we were going when we got there," he reminded her with a grin.

"Do you enjoy torturing me?" She sighed melodramatically.

Zeb couldn't help but laugh. "Is it really torture to not know where we're going until we get there?"

"Yes," she said with a small pout, but he heard the mirth in her voice and knew that she was excited. This might be the first time he'd actually seen her excited about something, it was a nice change of pace.

"Do your sisters know we're going out tonight?" he asked. He knew that Sapphire had been tough on Judah when he first started dating Ruby, and while Sapphire had definitely mellowed a lot over the last year, he knew that she was protective of her sisters and he wanted her family to be supportive of this. Yes, they had decided to take things slow, but Zeb couldn't deny that he was hoping things worked out.

"Those busybodies know everything that goes on in my life," she said with an eye roll, but then she laughed, "but I guess I know everything that goes on in their lives too."

He liked that she was so close with her sisters, it was the relationship he hoped he would have had with Lucy had she lived past the age of two. While there was no way to know if they would have remained close the older they got, he hoped that they would have become friends as well as siblings as adults.

"You had a sister, right?" Amethyst asked.

"Her name was Lucy, she was such a sassy, bubbly little girl, I miss her and our parents every day." Zeb didn't think that a single day had passed in the last twenty years that he hadn't thought about them at least a few times a day. "It's tough losing people that you love, but you know about that. Do you know anything about Emerald and what happened to her?" He was sure that it was a touchy subject for her, but if they were going to be a couple, even for a short time, then he wanted them to be able to talk about anything.

"They found a trail early on, but it went cold, I know that Sapphire looks into her case all the time, but so far we don't know anything, not even if she's still alive."

"The not knowing must be the hardest." He couldn't imagine not even knowing what had become of someone you loved. Knowing that his family was dead and were never coming back was hard, but at least it was closure, he didn't have to live on that precarious sword of hope.

"It is," she agreed.

Zeb reached over and took her hand, Amethyst curled her fingers around his and smiled at him.

"You don't need to ask me where we're going again," he told her.

"Why?"

"Because we're here." He turned the car down onto the road that would lead them to their destination.

"Are we going to the beach?" Amethyst asked, her blue eyes growing wide and a huge smile breaking out on her face.

"The beach, and then the carnival," he said as they drove past it. "This was where we used to come during the summer when I was a kid, we'd swim at the beach and make sandcastles, then as it started to get dark, we'd leave and go on all the rides, try to win stuffed animals and toys playing carnival games. We would eat so much cotton candy, and pretzels, and snow cones, and kettle corn, that it felt like we were going to burst, and then we'd fall asleep on the drive home, and our parents would carry us into bed. Those were good days," he said with a wistful smile. It was hard to know that he could never get those days back, sometimes you really didn't know what you had until it was gone.

"We can make new memories here," Amethyst told him, squeezing his hand.

He didn't miss the way that she had phrased it. "We?"

"I might not know exactly where this thing between us is going, but that doesn't mean that I'm not all in. I only do things one way, and that's with everything I got. So I think of us as a we," she said with a smile.

"Good to know," he said as he parked the car. He'd told Amethyst to dress casually, and she'd put on a simple pair of jeans shorts and a pink tank top, the outfit showed off her long, toned legs, and those lean, but muscled arms, and while she looked amazing, he hoped she wasn't going to get cold once the sun went down and the temperature finally started to drop. "You want to take my jacket with us, in case you get cold later?"

"Thank you, it's been hot, but it's meant to rain tomorrow, so it's probably going to start cooling down, I should have remembered to bring a jacket."

"It's no problem, I have a blanket in the trunk too so we can grab that if we need it."

"Zeb?" she asked as they got out of the car.

"Yeah?"

"Do you think if it does rain tomorrow that our killer will take a break?"

There was no way to know that. Just because it made sense that if no one was out using their pool that the killer wouldn't attempt to set any more fires, there were no guarantees. He might decide to find a way to branch out since he couldn't do what he usually did, and it could actually end up hurting them in the long run. At least for now he was predictable, but if he decided to mix things up then getting ahead of him would be even harder.

"It's okay, your silence gives me my answer."

"Hey," he said, grabbing her shoulders and turning her to face him. "Tonight is not about work, tonight is just about having fun, it's just about the two of us, okay?"

"Okay," she agreed.

Hand in hand they left the parking lot and walked down onto the soft white sand. Since it was still hot, the beach was packed, there were families and kids running about everywhere, couples were lounging on beach towels. There were people tossing around Frisbees, and balls, people were laughing and chasing each other, he could see water skis out in the deeper water, and a couple of boats. Although being here at the beach brought back a lot of memories, seeing everyone enjoying themselves made being here easier, it made it a good thing instead of a bad thing.

Since he'd just told Amethyst that tonight was about letting go and having fun, he snatched her up, threw her over his shoulder, and ran across the sand down to where the waves were lapping, then he threw her into the water. She landed with a splash, a moment later her head broke the surface and water streamed down her as she fixed her eyes on him.

For a moment he thought he was about to get a tongue lashing, but then Amethyst burst out laughing.

"You are going to regret that, mister," she told him, then dived down under the water.

Zeb wasn't surprised that Amethyst was a good swimmer, she seemed to be good at everything that she put her hand to. As he waited to see where she was going to pop back up, he walked out into the ocean. The cold water was so refreshing, and it was so nice to take a little time out and just enjoy himself for a change.

All of a sudden something latched onto his back, causing him to lose his balance and he went crashing forward into the waves getting a mouth full of salty seawater.

"Told you, you were going to regret throwing me into the water," were the first words he heard when he stood up. Amethyst stood there, grinning at him.

She looked happy, relaxed, not like the Amethyst he was used to. He liked seeing this side of her, he liked seeing her let go, be in a place where she didn't have to be her usual tough girl self. He liked that she could be tough, he loved that she was passionate and threw herself one hundred percent into everything that she did, but he also wanted to see her enjoy herself without it needing to be something that got her adrenalin pumping.

"You just instigated a battle," Zeb told Amethyst, lunging at her.

She shrieked and darted away, dodging in between people as she raced away from him. With a laugh and a lightheartedness that he hadn't felt in a long time, nearly a lifetime, he dashed off in pursuit of her.

~

11:17 P.M.

"How are you still eating?" Zeb asked.

"Still hungry," Amethyst replied with a shrug.

"I don't know how you manage to stay in such great shape when you eat as much as you do."

"You'd know how if you see how many hours I'm going to have to put into my workout tomorrow," she told him as she took another bite of cotton candy. "You sure you don't want any more?"

"I couldn't eat another bite if my life depended on it," he said with a groan, taking a hand off the steering wheel to press it to his stomach. "Maybe if you hadn't made us ride that rollercoaster over and over and over again I wouldn't feel so bad."

"You're surprised about that?" she asked with a grin, she thought Zeb would have guessed that she would zero in on the craziest ride at the carnival.

"Nope, not surprised in the least, ten years ago I could have ridden that ride and not batted an eye, but today," Zeb groaned again, "I'm getting old."

"So I guess you're dropping me off and going straight home to bed then?" she asked in a teasing voice, trying to hide her apprehension. She was new to the whole dating scene, she never usually cared about where things went with a guy because she never saw it going anywhere serious, but this time was different. This time, she *did* want things to go somewhere, she was just nervous about it because she really liked Zeb and she would be upset if it didn't work out. But she'd been the one to make a big deal out of wanting to take things slow, and as much as she wanted to rip off his clothes and make out as soon as they got to her place, she didn't know if it was what he wanted.

"If that's what you want," he said, leaving the ball firmly in her court.

Since he wasn't going to let her wriggle out of being the one to make the decision, she said, "If you want to you can hang around for a while."

Zeb laughed. "Such enthusiasm, good thing my ego doesn't need stroking."

Amethyst giggled too, she liked that Zeb was easygoing because she knew that she wasn't. She was too intense, too serious, especially when it came to things like this, hanging out with friends was one thing, but dating was something else. "Tonight was so much fun, playing in the water, it felt like being a kid again, and going on all those rides, it was the perfect first date."

"Don't forget the stuffed tiger I won you," Zeb added.

She picked up the stuffed animal that was sitting on her lap and held it up. "I will treasure it as my most prized possession for as long as I live."

"You better," he shot back.

She giggled again. "I'll put him on my bed, and that way he'll be the first thing I see each morning and the last thing I'll see each night."

"Perfect," he said as he pulled into her driveway.

Nervous butterflies started up in her stomach.

They were home.

That meant that it was time to go inside.

And that meant that they would make out.

As much as this was what she wanted, she couldn't deny that Zeb turned her on like no one else she had ever met, this was different than last time. Last time had been the culmination of days of sexual tension and the explosive release of pent up emotions caused by the fire.

But this time would be different.

This time meant something on an emotional level.

Parking the car, Zeb got out, walked around and opened her door for her. "You're quite the gentleman aren't you?" she said, a little breathily, as she climbed out of the car.

"I try," he said, his eyes meeting hers. "You look gorgeous with your hair down," he said, running his fingers through it, his hand settling on the small of her back.

"I usually leave it up so it's out of the way," she said, brushing off the compliment because they always made her feel uncomfortable. "I only took it out to let it dry after you threw me into the water," she said, giving him a playful punch on the shoulder to try to lighten the mood because things were starting to get heavy.

"You should let your hair down more often," he said, drawing her closer, and she got the feeling he didn't just mean letting her hair hang down around her shoulders.

"Maybe there are a lot of things I should do more often," she admitted, maybe her sisters weren't completely wrong when they'd told her last night about her using all of her extreme sports as a barrier to feeling anything else. Amethyst had a feeling that Zeb was going to change that. She had a feeling he was going to end up changing a lot of things in her life. Okay, maybe she was a little more invested in this blossoming relationship than she wanted to admit.

"Maybe there are a lot of things we should *both* do more often," Zeb corrected, as he whispered his lips across hers.

Despite the storms that were meant to be coming early tomorrow morning the sky was still clear, and with the moonlight and the billions of twinkling stars shining down upon them, Amethyst couldn't think of a more romantic setting for what felt like their first real kiss.

Taking her hand, Zeb led her down the path to the front door and waited while she unlocked it, as soon as they stepped inside, Amethyst expected the same explosion of passion that they'd shared last time. Her hands went immediately to the buttons of his short-sleeved shirt, intending to rip off their clothes as quickly as possible because that burning inside her had already started. It seemed like however much she got of Zeb it was never enough.

"Uh, uh, uh," Zeb said, his hands closing around hers, stilling them from their near frantic attempts to get the shirt unbuttoned in record time. "This time we do things slowly."

Scooping her into his arms, he closed and locked the door behind them, set her purse on the table by the door, then proceeded to carry her up the stairs.

"Where did all the candles and rose petals come from?" she asked as he stepped into her bedroom.

"Your sisters."

"You called them?"

"Yep."

"I thought you weren't sure whether or not you were coming in?"

"I hoped you wouldn't want the night to end that soon."

"What would you have done if I'd kissed you goodnight on the doorstep?"

"I would have had to tell you that you were going to get a surprise when you walked into your bedroom."

"Pretty cocky of you," she said with a teasing smile.

"I was pretty confident that things were going to turn out the way I wanted," he grinned back.

"You got lucky," she said.

"I'm about to," he winked.

Amethyst rolled her eyes at him, but that burning inside her intensified. Zeb carried her over to the bed and laid her down, trailing his fingers down her arms as he straightened, leaving a trail of fire everywhere he touched.

While last time everything had happened in a rush, an explosion of uncontrollable passion, tonight Zeb took his time as he removed her tank top and bra, then slid her shorts and panties down her legs. He touched and kissed each inch of her as he went, and every time his fingers or his lips made contact with her skin it was like another little spark ignited inside her.

"I was wrong earlier when I said I couldn't eat another bite," he told her, his eyes dark with desire as he looked up at her.

Her mind had already started to zone out, focused on every sensation that Zeb drew out of her and she didn't realize what he meant until his head dipped between her legs and his tongue touched her.

She flipped out.

A barrage of memories assaulted her.

Time and place melted away, all she knew was that she wanted it to stop.

She wanted those memories, those feelings out of her head, out of her body, out of her soul.

"Shh," a voice murmured in her ear. "It's okay, you're okay. Shh."

Arms were wrapped around her, rocking her, and slowly she felt herself begin to return to normal.

It had been a really long time since she had freaked out like that, not since those first few days that she had been back home, and even then, it had only been a couple of times. The first time she saw herself after seven months of living in hell, the first time she left the hospital and realized that she had to go back to living a normal life even though she was no longer a normal teenager, when the cops came to tell her that they had Nikos in custody and that all the girls who had still been alive were now free.

Those times had only been witnessed by doctors, cops, her sister, and family, never by another person who her relationship with was still a little up in the air. This was why she needed to control her emotions so tightly, so this never happened again.

Embarrassed, Amethyst tried to move away, but Zeb tightened his grip on her. He was sitting behind her on the bed, she was pressed against his chest, and he'd pinned her arms down as he'd circled his own around her.

She should feel trapped.

Pinned down.

It wouldn't be the first time she had been pinned down by a man, but this was different, Zeb was about as opposite of Nikos as it was possible to be, and instead of his hold being stifling, it made her feel safe.

Probably because she knew that she *was* safe with Zeb.

Not knowing what the future held didn't mean not knowing that she would be lucky to end up with a guy like Zeb. He'd suffered his own trauma, which made him sensitive to that same pain in others. And she liked that he was physically strong and muscled, she could look after herself, and she had never needed a man to save her, but it still made her feel secure to know that she was with someone bigger and stronger than she was.

"You okay," he asked, his voice soft and soothing but not patronizing.

"Yeah, sorry about that." She closed her eyes, mortified, she might feel safe with Zeb, but she was never going to be able to have sex with him again without thinking of this moment.

"No need to be sorry," he assured her, but he was just being nice. There was no way he could have expected her to react like that because they'd already slept together.

But that night had been different.

That had been just sex.

This was making love.

To most people, it sounded like semantics, but to her they were two very different things. She had sex; she did *not* make love.

"You don't have to explain if you don't want to, but if you do want to talk I'm right here. It's up to you."

That he didn't push her to talk actually made her want to open up. "I don't know how much you know about my past. I mean, you're friends with Sapphire, so you obviously know that the five of us were sold, I mean specifics about what happened to me."

"I don't know anything, beyond that your parents sold you and your sisters. I would never breach your privacy by looking into that."

"I was bought by a man named Nikos, he was a collector, paintings, sculptures, antiques, jewelry, and people. Girls. He had this huge room full of seventeen cages, and each one had a blonde-haired, blue-eyed girl in it, the youngest was just one year old, and he bought me to replace the oldest who had died. Each one was a different age, one all the way up to seventeen. You know that I have scars." Zeb had loosened his grip on her, and she lifted a hand to run a finger along the mark on her neck from the knife that had very nearly ended her life.

"You never hide them," he noted, touching a scar on her shoulder.

Amethyst shrugged. "No need to. They exist, and they're constant reminders that I survived. A lot of people who end up victims of human traffickers don't survive, I know how lucky I was, and I don't ever want to forget. The scars, they weren't because Nikos liked to hurt us, in reality he didn't, he fed us, he gave toys to the little girls, books to the older ones, he only used to hurt me because I wouldn't give in to him, I was defiant, I knew that it would make him angry, but I never backed down. When he was angry, he would lash out. But I think in his mind we were precious to him, just as valuable as his artworks and other things. When he used to rape me, it was always so gently, like he thought he was my lover, and tonight, we weren't just having sex, we were making love, you were being so gentle, and I don't know, it must have just brought on a flashback. I really don't usually have them," she assured him, positive he must be just about ready to run for the hills.

"I told you that you don't have to worry about it," he said, but his voice had gone strange. He was just trying to be nice to her, but how could he ever see her in the same way again? He'd seen her at her most vulnerable, and now he no doubt thought that she was some broken doll who needed someone to put her back together.

But that wasn't who she was.

It had never been who she was.

She had stood up to Nikos, she had never once cracked in her composure, and she had held it together no matter what he had done to her. And this last decade, she had survived that too, she'd graduated high school, then college, gotten a job she loved, had hobbies she loved, and cherished the family she adored. She had issues, you couldn't go through what she had and not have a few lingering ill effects, but she wasn't broken, all her pieces were together and intact, maybe just a little chipped and cracked in spots.

"You see me differently now," she said, turning her voice hard. Nikos hadn't broken her, and Zeb wouldn't either.

"No," he said firmly.

"You sound different, and your body, it's all stiff," she contradicted.

"Because what you just told me makes me want to do very bad things to Nikos, things that would make me just like the people I arrest," he said, and she could tell he was making an effort to relax. "But I don't see you any differently, if anything, I think you're even more amazing than I already did."

"Really?" she asked, wiggling around so she could see him, then her mouth dropped open, and she touched her fingers to a bloody split in his lip. "Did I do that?"

"You did," he smiled. "You have a mean left hook on you."

She offered a watery smile. "Sapphire said since most people are right-handed, an attacker would be expecting you to hit with your right hand, so your left should be equally as strong, that way you can surprise him, hopefully get the upper hand."

"Why am I not surprised that Sapphire had something to do with that? Remind me to remember that next time."

"Next time?" she arched a brow. She wasn't sure there would be a next time after this mess.

"I don't care that you have baggage, I knew you would, I do too. I don't care about that. When I saw you at the first swimming pool fire, I just felt something, then when you started working with us, I couldn't think of anything else but you. At first I thought that it was just about physical attraction, but even after we slept together, that feeling didn't go away. It's only growing. I know that you need time, I know you're not ready for a commitment, and I'm fine with that, but just know that *I'm* serious."

Maybe she was a little more ready for a commitment than she thought she was.

Kneeling between Zeb's legs, Amethyst took his face between her hands and kissed him.

"Thank you. I know you don't want me to thank you," she added, "but I don't think there are a lot of guys who would just accept that like it's no big deal."

"It's not hard to do when the woman is as amazing as you." He gave her an appreciative once over, and she realized she was still naked. She was confident in her body, and it did stroke her ego a little when she saw the fire in his eyes. "And have I mentioned that you're also gorgeous?"

"A couple of times maybe." She laughed. "You know you're not bad to look at yourself."

"Why, thank you." He grinned. "So would you like me to leave?"

"No," she said immediately.

"You want to go to sleep then?"

"Nope. I think we should finish what we started before we even think about calling it a night."

"I'm not going to argue with that."

Moving them both so they were lying on the bed, he kissed her, then trailed a line of kisses down her neck, between her breasts, and along her stomach, making her shiver in delightful anticipation. He paused when he got between her legs, waiting for her permission to go further.

When she nodded, his mouth claimed hers. Amethyst closed her eyes and didn't let her past pull her out of the moment and just focused on the amazing things his tongue was doing.

She came in a rush, gasping as he tossed her off the edge of a cliff and into ecstasy.

When she was able to think again and managed to pry her eyes open, she found Zeb looking smugly down at her.

"You're pretty proud of yourself aren't you?" she asked with a lazy smile.

"Oh, yeah," he nodded.

"You know I can make you come like that too," she told him.

"I look forward to that, but not tonight. Tonight I think we're both worn out."

Amethyst was going to argue, but a yawn nearly split her head in too, and she nodded, maybe he was right, maybe it was time to go to sleep. "Tomorrow night," she told him.

"Can't wait. Am I going home or spending the night?"

"Do you really have to ask?" She wriggled sideways to make room for him. Zeb stretched out beside her, and she curled into his side, she didn't usually spend the night in bed with a man. After sex, she usually left or sent them home, but tonight this was exactly what she wanted.

Cuddling.

She'd never really seen the appeal in it before now.

But cuddled up against Zeb, with her head on his chest, listening to his heartbeat and the rise and fall of his chest as he breathed in and out, his arm around her shoulders, this was perfect.

11:40 P.M.

He really shouldn't be doing this.

What was he going to gain by stalking Zeb Tuck and Amethyst Hatcher?

Nothing.

It was as simple as that.

He wasn't going to gain anything by following them around, by sitting outside Amethyst's house, and yet he didn't leave.

For some reason, he wanted to know what the two of them were doing together. As far as he was aware, they barely knew each other, one was a firefighter, and one was a cop, and yet the two of them had been spending most of their days together. Had they been told to work together to find him?

If they had that was quite the compliment. The cops couldn't find him on their own, so they'd had to team up with the fire department, and that the two of them together hadn't been able to do that basically showed how inept both departments were.

It was definitely quite the ego boost to know that he was still walking around a free man when half the city seemed to be looking for him. He wasn't delusional though, he knew that his luck wasn't going to last forever, sooner or later they would find something on him and arrest him, hauling him off to prison and throwing away the key. Well, they would come after him and *try* to arrest him, but he was definitely not going down that route. Any cops that came after him were going to find themselves blown to smithereens.

Just like the cops almost had been yesterday.

Concerned that they were starting to get too close, he had decided to try to take them out. It was a little disappointing that it hadn't worked out the way he wanted because that was twice now, but that didn't mean he was giving up. If an opportunity presented itself, he was definitely going to grab hold of it and use it to his advantage.

Maybe things would have worked out yesterday if he'd used more accelerant on the rag. It had been an on the fly thing, he hadn't had time to prepare, and that wasn't like him, usually he prepared things down to the tiniest detail because he hated when things didn't work out and go to plan. He'd just grabbed a rock that was lying around, ripped off a piece of his t-shirt, and tipped some of the accelerant in his container onto the material then tied it around the rock, set it alight, and thrown it at the car.

He had hit his target at least. That was one positive, and he did like to focus on the positives.

Right now though, he wanted to figure out what was going on between these two. Amethyst had been at the fire today in her firefighter gear, so she was obviously no longer working with the cops, so there was no reason for Zeb's car to be parked in her driveway.

The two of them had driven out to the beach, spent hours playing in the water then ridden the rollercoaster at the carnival over and over again. He knew this, of course, because he had followed them out there and watched them the entire time.

They looked like they were on a date.

That was an interesting development.

This had nothing to do with them, but since they were hunting him, he wanted to know as much about them as he could.

Know your enemy.

That was the way he had survived his childhood. When you lived with a narcissistic control freak like his mother had been, then you learned to do whatever it took to try to stay out of their crosshairs. That was what he'd had to do on a daily basis, from the time he got up in the morning until he went to bed in the evenings. It had been exhausting, but it was better than finding himself as the target of her wrath, so he had done it, and as it turned out it was a useful skill for life as well.

Now, he had to implement that skill for a whole different purpose.

This wasn't about protecting himself and keeping himself out of the line of fire. This was about finding out as much as he could about these people in case he found something that he could use against them if the need arose. He supposed in a way that was still about protecting himself, but he was no longer that scared kid who was always worrying about putting a foot out of line. Now he was a man, a man who knew how to get what he wanted, a man who wasn't afraid to go after what he wanted rather than hanging back because he didn't want to hurt anyone.

Life was about pain. There was no avoiding it, there was no running from it, there was no hiding from it, it was there, and the quicker you accepted it and stopped being afraid of it, the happier you were. It had taken him decades to learn that fact, but now that he had, he found life to be so much more pleasurable.

It was freeing to let go of that fear.

It was like being born again, starting a new life, one that didn't have the constraints of societal obligations and expectations. When you weren't afraid of pain, and instead you just prepared yourself to deal with it when it came, then a whole new world of possibilities opened up to you.

He was taking full advantage of that.

And while he had accepted the "pain" of this situation, which was his inevitable downfall, he was still going to fight to keep doing this for as long as he could, and to that end, he wanted to know as much as he could about his opponents.

Climbing out of his car, he walked across the street to the Hatcher house. It was silent, but he could see a light glowing from one of the upstairs rooms at the front of the house, which he assumed was a bedroom.

Interesting.

Were Zeb and Amethyst a couple?

That certainly seemed like something he could use to his advantage at some point. If one of them came after him, maybe he could threaten the other to get them to let him go. It was a possibility and one that he would store away to use if the opportunity presented itself.

For now though, he wanted proof that they were together, maybe he could snap a couple of pictures, that way he could use them as proof that they were together if he had to make an escape at some point. If he had photos, there would be no denying it, no pretending that it was a pointless bargaining chip.

There was a gate at the end of the driveway, but they hadn't closed it when they returned here thirty minutes or so ago, so he was able to get easy access to the property. There was a large tree in the front yard, and he was pretty sure that if he climbed it he would be able to see into the bedroom.

Climbing trees was simple for someone who had to be able to climb ladders, and rescue people as a firefighter, so he shimmied up it in no time at all. Now he just had to get out on a branch close enough to the window that he could see inside and snap a few pictures, but also make sure that no one would notice him. It was late, and there wasn't really anyone about, but he was pretty sure that Zeb and Amethyst were awake in there so either one of them could see him at the window.

Picking a branch that looked like it was strong enough to support his weight, and also leafy enough to keep him covered enough that no one could see him, he crept along it, cautious now. One wrong move and he would be going down in flames.

Literally.

He carried accelerant and matches with him everywhere he went, so if they noticed him and managed to get outside before he got down from the tree and into his car, then none of them would be making it to tomorrow.

Reaching the window, he looked inside. "Bingo," he murmured with a smile. He had been correct, the couple were in bed, and Zeb had his head buried between Amethyst's legs. Quickly pulling his phone from his pocket, he snapped some photos, he couldn't have asked for a better scene to get some pictures of, neither of them could deny that they were a couple when he shoved these photos in their faces.

While he hadn't known what was going to come from following the two tonight, he was certainly walking away with more than he could have hoped for. Climbing down from the tree, he walked back to his car, he should head home, get some sleep, because he was sure that tomorrow was going to be another big day.

CHAPTER
Nine

August 27th
8:48 A.M.

"You're chipper this morning."

"Yep," Zeb agreed cheerfully, he felt like he was flying today. Waking up in Amethyst's bed this morning was completely different than last time. This morning, she had woken up bouncy and full of energy, she'd been in a great mood, greeted him with a kiss. She'd taken a shower, then he'd taken one, although he had tried to convince her that they should take one together, then they'd driven to his house so he could put on clean clothes, and grabbed a quick breakfast at her favorite café before he dropped her off at work and came here.

It was a simple morning, and yet it was amazing.

It was amazing because it was so simple. It was like they were just a couple going about their morning routine, and the more time he spent with Amethyst, the more he realized that that normalcy of sharing your life with someone had been missing from his life. He hadn't even realized that he was missing out, but now it seemed so obvious. He was so glad that this case had brought him and Amethyst together, but he still wanted this guy off the streets.

Today hopefully.

"Is Curtis Cane here waiting for us?" he asked Judah.

"He should be here in about ten minutes."

"I'm hoping we can either pin him down as our killer or eliminate him, which means that all our focus will be on Joaquin."

Yesterday afternoon they had been able to eliminate Kel Ingham as a suspect in the swimming pool murders, but that didn't mean he would be staying out of a jail cell. The man had been keeping busy while he was on suspension by sexually assaulting his neighbors. He hadn't just heard the screams from his house two days ago like he had implied, he had been leaving the house next door to the one where the fire had been set, having broken in there to rape the seventeen-year-old girl who was home alone at the time.

When they had been interviewing the residents of the houses around the fire, the girl had sent up immediate red flags when she'd opened their door terrified, and with red-rimmed eyes that had suggested she'd been recently crying. It hadn't taken much to get the girl to admit what had happened, and as soon as they had taken her statement, called her parents, waited with her until they arrived, given her a card for a trauma counselor they had gone straight to Kel's house and picked him up.

The man had been irate, screaming and threatening them, blaming Amethyst and claiming that he would find a way to punish her. Zeb was sure it was all idle threats, but he would make sure that Amethyst knew to keep an eye out just in case the guy got out on bail and made good on those threats. Now that they had Kel for rape, they would start interviewing more residents who lived around him, and Zeb was sure that more victims would turn up.

But today they were focusing on the swimming pool case because unless they found this guy, there would be more victims dead by the end of the day. The rain and storms that had been forecast for today didn't look like they were going to turn up, and that meant the killer would be out searching for a pool to set his next fire in.

"Amethyst's instincts were right about him," Judah said. "It was lucky that she was with us that day, otherwise we might have liked him as a suspect in the fires, but we wouldn't have been looking at him as a sexual predator."

"Amethyst has been a big help to this case," he said. He wasn't sure they would have been able to narrow down a suspect list without her. Between going to the scenes of the fires he and Judah had been working through the list that he and Amethyst had come up with that first day, and had managed to cross most of them off with alibis, leaving another three that were still suspects. If both Curtis and Joaquin turned out to not be who they were looking for, they would move on to those three.

"She has, and I take it by your upbeat attitude today that things are going better between the two of you."

"They are. We're taking things slow, but I'm fine with that, we have our whole lives ahead of us, we don't have to jump into anything too serious too quickly. We don't all do things as quickly as you do, Mr. married three months after you started dating," he teased his partner.

"Hey, when its love its love and there's no point in waiting," Judah said with that same dopey smile he had on his face whenever he talked about his wife. If things did work out with Amethyst, then he and Judah would end up being brothers-in-law and not just partners.

"Detectives?" A blonde man with hazel eyes approached them, Zeb knew from his driver's license photo that it was Curtis Cane.

"Mr. Cane, thanks for coming down to speak with us. I'm Detective Tuck, and this is my partner, Detective Willow," he said, making the introductions.

"Nice to meet you," the man said gravely. His face was serious, as were his eyes, and he didn't give off any vibe that Zeb could zero in on.

"Why don't we go and talk in here where it's quieter," he suggested, steering them toward the nearest interview room. They had brought Curtis down here under the guise of discussing his cousin's murder, no need to tip the guy off that they were on to him if he was the killer.

"Sure," Curtis agreed. He didn't appear to be a man of many words, which would make it harder to trip him up and get him to confess to something that he hadn't intended to confess to. The more someone talked, the more likely they were to incriminate themselves.

Inside the interview room they all took seats at the table, then Zeb shot the man a grave look of his own. "I'm very sorry for the loss of your cousin, Tucker Goud," he said.

"Thank you." Curtis gave a courteous nod.

"We believe he may have been murdered because he saw the face of the killer who has been setting fire to backyard swimming pools," he told Curtis, gauging the man's reaction.

Curtis gave another nod. "I'm sad to hear that. I know my cousin doesn't have the cleanest record around, but he's a good man, and I'm sure he would have tried to do the right thing."

The man didn't give much away, he didn't seem particularly upset about his cousin's death, or the connection to the fire, or seem to be worried about them thinking that he might be the killer.

"You've heard about the fires I'm sure," Judah said.

"Yes."

"Seven of them so far," Zeb added, trying to draw some sort of reaction out of the man, he was like a clam and if they couldn't get enough to gauge whether he was the killer or not, then their chances of getting this guy today dropped.

"It's awful," Curtis said, but his face didn't match his words, this guy was a stone, he didn't seem to feel anything about anything.

"It is," he agreed. "We believe that we might be looking for a fire-fighter," he finally just came right out and said it, see if that finally shocked the guy into giving something away. Curtis was the only other firefighter, besides Kel—who they had already eliminated—and Joaquin, on their suspect list who was currently on leave of some kind, meaning that they had the ability to set the fires without needing to wait until they were off duty.

"And you think that I'm a suspect? Because my cousin was killed?" Curtis asked them. Both his face and his tone remained emotionless, not giving anything away, but that in and of itself told them something. Most people who were unjustly accused of a crime were outraged by the accusation and vehemently denied it. Curtis hadn't done that at all.

"We think it's a possibility," Judah told him.

"I didn't set any fires, and I didn't kill my cousin," the man said evenly.

That was probably the worst denial he had ever heard in all his years as a cop. "Mr. Cane, you're currently on leave, may I ask why?" Zeb asked, he knew why but he wanted to see what the man had to say about it.

"I took family leave to care for a dying relative," Curtis replied.

"You're her full-time carer? Do you have a nurse aid who comes and helps during the day? Or at night? A sibling who helps share the responsibilities?" They needed to know if Curtis was truly at home all day caring for his dying mother, or whether he had time to be out starting fires while someone else took care of his mother.

"We have a nurse," the man confirmed. "She's there most days."

That was exactly what he had expected to hear. "Mr. Cane, we're going to need alibis for the times of each of the fires."

"I don't know that I can do that. During the day, while the nurse is there, I'm often out and about running errands."

No alibi, a reason to have killed Tucker Goud when none of the other witnesses who had seen the man in black had been killed, and Curtis Cane was a firefighter, it looked like the strange man was three for three and sitting at the top of their suspect list.

1:03 P.M.

Amethyst lay on a bed at the firehouse trying to read a book but failing miserably.

Usually, she wasn't a big reader, not like her twin sister anyway, Ruby read like a book a day, sometimes more, while she was lucky if she read a book a month. Still, it was usually a good escape from reality, and she always kept a couple here at work in case she needed something to do to pass the time.

Today it wasn't her work that had her all anxious and twitchy, it was the *lack* of work.

She was only working a ten-hour shift today, usually those flew by, but today there hadn't been any call outs, not even one for a backyard swimming pool fire.

It was only one in the afternoon, and she knew that there was still plenty of time for the killer to strike, some days he didn't start a fire until two or even three o'clock, but the fact that he hadn't done anything yet today had her on edge. Did his lack of activity mean that he was planning something bigger, more extravagant, with more victims?

She hoped it didn't, but she didn't really know a lot about criminal psychology. She put out fires, she didn't catch the people that set them. While it definitely wasn't her area of expertise, she did have a sister and two brothers-in-law who were cops, as well as a brother-in-law who was a criminal psychiatrist, and her boyfriend—if that was what she and Zeb were calling each other now—was a cop, so she had definitely spent a lot of time around people who worked cases like this every day of their lives. If she had to guess as to whether or not the killer would soon start to expand upon his small swimming pool fires because they no longer gave him the rush he desired, then she would have to say yes he would.

In a way she understood that.

In a way *she* was like that.

After she had come back home after Nikos tried to kill her, she hadn't started out jumping out of airplanes, she'd started skateboarding, from there she had moved onto BMXing, then progressed through a series of extreme sports before moving onto things like skydiving. Some of those activities she still did, but a lot she had given up because they no longer gave her the adrenalin rush that she loved. She had had to keep finding new and bigger and better things to do if she wanted to get that rush, and it became addictive. She was sure the killer felt the same way.

"Hey."

She jumped at the voice, dropping her book and sending it skidding across the floor. "You have got to stop walking up on me like that, what do you wear, like silent boots or something?" she asked as she turned to find Zeb watching her with a bemused smile.

"Sorry, I thought you heard me come in."

"You don't sound sorry," she grumbled as she got down on her hands and knees to fish the book out from under the bed beside hers where it had landed.

Zeb just laughed and came and wrapped an arm around her waist when she stood back up, drawing her in for a kiss. While she would have liked to deepen the kiss, fool around a little, she was at work, and this wasn't the place for that.

So after one chaste—*way* too chaste—kiss she took his hand, and they both sat down on her bunk. "What are you doing here? Not that I'm not thrilled to see you, but I thought you were at work."

"Judah and I are taking a quick lunch break, and I decided to stop by here and say hi."

"Oh, well, hi, I'm glad you stopped by. Did you speak with Curtis?"

"We did, he doesn't have an alibi."

"He's a weird guy, right? Don't you think so?"

"I do," Zeb agreed.

"Do you think he's the killer?"

"Judah and I like him as the killer, but we don't know anything for sure yet."

Amethyst let out a frustrated sigh, why did everything have to take so long? She wasn't used to this. In her line of work, you went to a fire, and you stayed there until you put it out. She could probably count on one hand the number of times she had ever left a fire before it was out, and that was because it was so fierce that it had taken them days to finally extinguish it. This case had been going for a week now, and really, they still didn't have anything concrete pointing to anyone.

"What's wrong?" Zeb asked, obviously sensing her distress.

"There haven't been any fires yet today."

"Isn't that a good thing?"

"You tell me, you're the cop, to me it feels like a bad thing, I know he's out there somewhere, waiting, preparing, and I hate it." She stood and began to pace around the room. "I want him behind bars, I want him where he can't hurt another innocent person. I know he's up to something. I'm sure he's planning something bigger. I don't want anyone else to die."

"Hey." Zeb stilled her, his hands on her shoulders, gently kneading. "I know this case is stressful, and you might be right, he might be planning something bigger, but for now, let's just be grateful that no one else has died at his hands so far today."

"Yeah, okay." She drew in a shaky breath and tried to calm herself down, but she felt on edge, she had that feeling that said something bad was going to happen soon, and there was no way to stop it.

"Trust us, trust *me*, I know how to do my job," Zeb assured her, cupping her cheek in his hand and brushing his thumb across her cheekbone.

"I do trust you," she told him, and she did. It wasn't trust that was the problem here, it was just that bad feeling that she couldn't shake.

"Dinner tonight?" he asked. "Because I believe someone owes me some fun in the bedroom," he winked.

His teasing had the desired effect, and she couldn't help but smile, a little of her apprehension faded away. "I would love to have dinner, but it would have to be a late one because I'm going BASE jumping with some of my friends, up at the cliffs just north of the city."

"BASE jumping?" he echoed. "Isn't that like ridiculously dangerous?"

"It can be dangerous," she admitted. "But I wouldn't call it *ridiculously* dangerous."

"You jump off things and plummet toward the earth," he said skeptically.

"We jump off things wearing a parachute or a wingsuit, having practiced what we're doing and made sure we take all the necessary precautions," she added, starting to get frustrated. Zeb knew that she liked extreme sports so why was he making such a big deal out of this? "Are you going to act like this every time I want to go and do something fun?"

"Act like what?"

"Like this," she waved her hand at his face, which was wearing a lecturing mask like he was about to tell her how reckless she was being.

"I really don't know what I'm doing that has you all upset."

"Pretending you don't know what I'm talking about is even more infuriating. Just because we went on one date doesn't mean that I'm going to give up everything that I love."

"I never thought that it did. I never asked you to give up anything, nor did I ever expect that you should. If you like risking your life with extreme sports then that's up to you."

"See the way you just phrased that by saying that I like to risk my life just proves my point. You want me to stop BASE jumping and every-thing else that I like just because you disapprove."

"I really don't," Zeb insisted. "And I don't know why you're getting so upset."

"I'm getting upset because you want me to change. You said last night that you knew I had baggage when you asked me out, so you can accept that, but you can't accept this side of me. Maybe I was right all along, maybe we're just not compatible."

"If that's how you feel, then I'll go," Zeb said quietly, turning and walking away.

Stop him, she screamed at herself internally.

Amethyst knew she was freaking out, she was being unreasonable, starting an argument over nothing and she didn't even know why.

What was wrong with her?

Instead of stopping Zeb, apologizing, telling him that she just had this bad feeling she couldn't shake and it was making her act crazy, she watched him go with a sinking feeling in her stomach that said she was sabotaging herself.

This was what her sisters were talking about.

Instead of feeling anything, she always tried to brush it aside and instead shove herself into the most adrenalin pumping situations that she could, and right now that was an argument over something stupid with a guy she really liked because her messed up brain thought that was better than feeling anything else.

She really was messed up.

She liked to think that she was too strong, too determined, too tough to let anything get to her, but apparently she didn't know herself as well as she thought she did.

She was ruining her own life.

Dropping down onto the bed, Amethyst buried her head in her arms and continued to berate herself.

～

6:44 P.M.

. . .

"You got this," Amethyst told herself as she parked her car.

All day she had obsessed over this, she hadn't been able to concentrate on anything else, and it turned out to be a good thing that they hadn't been called out to any fires. She had messed up earlier this afternoon, and she was always one who owned her mistakes, Amethyst just hoped that Zeb wasn't too angry with her and was willing to accept her apology.

Climbing out of the car, she walked up to Zeb's front door and knocked. Sucking in a breath, she held it as she waited for him to answer. Just how angry was he going to be? That he was going to be angry was a given, and she deserved it, but she didn't know just how upset with her he was going to be.

Had she already ruined this?

She truly hoped that she hadn't because she really liked Zeb, and she wanted to see what could grow between them.

After what felt like an eternity, the door was opened, and Zeb stood there in a pair of shorts and nothing else.

Don't get distracted, she warned herself. She wasn't here to make out, she was here to apologize and try to explain.

"Hey," she said with a sheepish smile. "Is it possible I could come in and talk to you for a bit?"

"Sure," he said, holding the door further open to let her in.

She had never been here before so she followed him through a small living room and into a kitchen dining room, there was a weight set in the corner, and she could see he had been working out before she arrived.

"You want something to drink?" he asked, opening the fridge and pulling out a bottle of sparkling water.

"Yes, thanks."

Zeb brought two bottles, and a carrot over to the table and set the water down, then he took the carrot over to a hutch in the corner, and she saw an adorable little brown rabbit with ears sticking straight up. It scurried over when it saw Zeb, and eagerly began to nibble at the carrot when Zeb put it inside the hatch.

"You have a bunny," she exclaimed. She'd had a pet rabbit called

Thumper when she was in elementary school and had been devastated when he passed away.

"Pebbles," he said as he took a seat at the table.

"She's cute," Amethyst said, joining him at the table, her hands shaking and she quickly picked up the bottle and unscrewed the lid in an attempt to hide how nervous she was. If she had blown this then she was never going to forgive herself. It was time to stop running, stop hiding, stop pretending that she didn't feel anything and that she needed an adrenalin rush to feel alive.

It was time to be honest with herself.

And that started by being honest with Zeb.

But first, the apology.

"I'm really sorry, Zeb," she said quickly, wanting to get the words out before she lost her nerve. "I don't know what came over me today. I don't know why I started an argument over something so stupid. I know that you wouldn't want me to change who I am just because we're dating, well, assuming we still are."

"It's okay, you can relax." He reached over and gently pried her fingers off the bottle of water. "I'm not angry with you, just a little perplexed, I don't get where the argument came from, I wasn't expecting that."

"I wasn't either," she admitted, curling her fingers around his and clinging to his hand as though he might change his mind and decide she was too high maintenance for him to bother with.

"Then talk to me, let's figure this out together."

"Together? You haven't had enough of my freakouts already?" Three times now she had shoved him away, Zeb was a good guy but if she kept pushing him away, then sooner or later he would assume that it was what she really wanted, and he'd just walk away on his own.

"You have baggage, I'm not expecting you to get rid of it in just a couple of days, I just don't want you to keep pushing me away, if something is bothering you then just tell me what it is."

That was fair enough, if they were going to be a couple, then she had to learn to trust him. Completely trust him. With everything. Maybe even with things that she didn't admit to herself. "That night that my parents sold me and my sisters, we were taken to this house, it was where they kept the girls until they were sold. But Nikos had already asked for a blonde, blue-eyed, seventeen-year-old, so I was already marked as his. They took me to a bathroom where I was stripped and washed like I was a new car or something. Then I was taken into a bedroom, and there was a woman there, she was supposed to do my hair and makeup and help me get dressed. Before I got into that room I was crying, hysterical, panicked, I was a mess."

"You say that with a tone of voice that says you think that was a fault on your part," Zeb told her.

"I guess I did, for a long time anyway, but lately I've been rethinking things. The woman that I met that day, she told me to give in, to give up, to let whoever bought me do whatever they wanted to me, she wanted me to agree with them that I was nothing, just an object to be used and abused. As soon as she said that to me it was like a switch had been flipped. I knew that there was no way I could do that. It wasn't who I was. So instead, I did the opposite. I fought. I knew that it was going to provoke Nikos, I knew it was going to make him hurt me, I knew that I was going to die there and I wanted to die knowing that he had never truly owned me. I learned how to shut down my emotions, and at the time, I didn't think that it mattered because I never expected to survive."

"But you did."

"By some fluke. I should be dead right now, if those people hadn't found me, then I would be dead. When I first came home I was so angry, and then I found extreme sports. That made me feel alive, it was the only time I felt something other than anger, at least that's what I thought, but then I was talking to my sisters the other day, and they had a different opinion."

"Whatever they said made you rethink things."

"Yeah it did," she said, this was hard to talk about, she was used to keeping everything bottled up inside, but she was trying to show Zeb that he was important enough to her that she could tell him what was going on inside her head. "My sisters told me that maybe it wasn't that getting my adrenalin pumping was the only time that I felt something, maybe it was just a way to hide what I was really feeling. Adrenalin is such a strong thing that it's easy to use it to mask other things."

"Now, you think that's what you've been doing?"

"I don't know, I really don't, I think that they might be right, but it's scary to let go and find out. If I stop with all the extreme sports then I take away my crutch, and when I take away my crutch, what am I going to find?" She let the vulnerability that she was feeling show because this was Zeb, and he had already proved that he was a dependable guy. He hadn't held anything that she had done so far against her, he'd forgiven a lot from her in just a few days, and if that didn't show her what kind of man he was then nothing would. This was the kind of man you could build a life with because you knew that he was going to be there for you no matter what.

"What have you got to lose if you take away that crutch?" Zeb asked, moving his chair closer so he was sitting beside her and not across the table from her.

"I don't know, my sanity?"

He gave a small smile. "I don't think you have to worry about losing that. You still have lingering feelings from being abducted and sold, tortured and raped, I think that's normal, I don't think it's anything that you have to fight against. What are three things that you think you're going to find that your adrenalin junkie ways are hiding?"

"Anger," she said immediately, that one was easy. "Anger at my parents and anger at Nikos. Violated I guess, I was able to block out the rape for the most part because I was too busy not letting Nikos beat me, but I know I have unresolved issues about it. And I suppose ... fear."

"That bothers you the most," Zeb said, reaching out and catching a lone tear that rolled down her cheek.

"It does," she admitted. "If I'm afraid, then it feels like Nikos won. It feels like all the times I stood up to him knowing that he was going to hurt me, all the cuts, and burns, and broken bones, it was all for nothing, in the end, Nikos won anyway. And if Nikos won anyway, then it feels like the last decade of my life had been a waste, I'm just some poor pathetic girl who was sold and abused, I'm not strong, I'm not tough, I'm nothing."

Tears began to flow down her cheeks in a torrent, and Zeb folded her into his arms, holding her, letting her cry, just being there for her, and in that moment, that was exactly what she needed.

~

6:59 P.M.

Amethyst wept in his arms, and he just held her. Zeb felt like she didn't need words right now, she didn't need assurances, she just needed someone to be here, and that was something he could give her. It was something he could *always* give her.

He hadn't been lying earlier when he told her that he wasn't angry with her, he truly did understand that she had issues associated with the ordeal she had suffered, and he was prepared to be there for her and help her however he could. But she had to be prepared to open up to him. He had already lost one family, and if he was going to build another, then he had no intention of losing it as well.

When Amethyst's tears dried up, he began to stroke her hair, letting her hide her face for a little longer. "You are, without a doubt, the toughest, strongest person I have ever met. I don't want you to ever doubt that. Ever. Being afraid doesn't negate the way you rebuilt your life, it just makes you a human being. Human beings feel things, they doubt themselves sometimes, and sometimes they get afraid. But Nikos didn't win, because he ended up in a prison cell, and you are a smart, beautiful, compassionate woman who spends her life helping people, literally walking through flames to save strangers, does that sound like someone who is nothing to you?"

"I guess not when you say it like that," she admitted, straightening her back and wiping at her wet cheeks.

"I say it like that because it's true. Would I lie to you?"

"Maybe," she said with a half-smile. "Because I think you like me a little."

"More than a little," he corrected, leaning forward to kiss the tip of her nose. "But I still wouldn't lie to you. Some things in life are just too big, they leave too big an impact on you that you just can't ever get rid of. Like these scars," he said, touching a fingertip to the red line that marred her neck. "This scar is never going to completely fade, and I like how you told me that when you look at your scars, you're reminded of your fights, your strength. Your internal scars are the same, they're always going to be there, they're always going to affect you, but they should remind you of your victories. Not a lot of people could have survived what you did and still managed to not just survive but to thrive."

"You make it all sound so simple, so wonderful, you make me sound like some sort of hero in a book or a movie or something."

"It's not simple, and it's not easy, but you are a hero. I have scars too, I have struggles too, losing your whole family when you're eight-years-old, blaming yourself for it because you couldn't get them out, that's rough, but I rebuilt my life, just like you rebuilt yours, and now, who knows, maybe we're going to get our happy ever after."

"I hope so," she said. "A week ago I didn't even know that I wanted one. I thought I was happy being on my own, even with my sisters getting married and moving on with their lives I didn't feel like I was missing out on anything, and then you came into my life."

"It only takes one second to change your life."

"Isn't that the truth," Amethyst agreed.

They both had learned that lesson the hard way, but Zeb hoped that those hard times were behind them, he hoped their future was bright, and he had no reason to believe that it wouldn't be.

"Is it too late to go to your BASE jumping thing?" he asked. While he couldn't imagine jumping off a cliff, if it was important to Amethyst, then he'd go and watch her do it, cheer her on, try to learn about it so that it was something they could share even if he was never going to do it.

"I'm not really in the mood now."

"It's only seven, we could go out for dinner, see a movie or something?"

"You know what I really want to do?"

"What?"

"Just hang out here, have a quiet evening. I believe I owe you something in the bedroom, then maybe we could do a workout together, go for a run or something, I'm exhausted, and an early night sounds like heaven."

"I like the sound of that," he agreed. Just like this morning had felt like the two of them were a real couple, this did too, making out, working out, falling asleep in each other's arms, that was the kind of simple evenings that he had missed. "But I have to warn you, I'm not so good at sitting on the sidelines in the bedroom."

"Oh yeah." She arched a brow, the desolation that had been in her eyes when she wondered it her whole life wasn't what she thought it was had faded, and while he knew she would battle that insecurity for a long time at least now she was facing it rather than hiding from it.

"Yep." Before she could protest, he snatched her up, finding her lips, and she wrapped her legs around his waist and kissed him back with the same passion he felt. Despite their differences, they shared something that was more important than those externals. They both knew pain and suffering, and they both knew what it was like to have to fight for your life, in both the physical sense and the psychological sense.

Carrying her through to his bedroom, he laid her down on the bed, but before he could remove her clothes, she had her hands on his shorts, shoving them down his legs, taking his boxers with them. Her hands claimed him, teasing him, moving slowly and lightly, then increasing the pressure only to drop it right back down as soon as he started to peak. As much as he wanted to shove that pretty blue sundress up over her hips, rip off her panties, and enter her body so both of them came in unison, he gave her her moment, her moment to be in control.

Zeb held off for as long as he could, and because he knew that she was egging him on, waiting to see how long he could hold off, when he couldn't take it anymore he did exactly what he knew they both wanted. Pushing her down so she lay on the bed, he shoved that dress up, yanked those panties down, and entered her in one swift thrust.

Together they moved in harmony, building each other up, driving each other wild, until that climax came in a rush of power and emotion, that left them both breathless.

Pulling out of her, he lay down at her side, spooning her against him, his hands settled on her hip and one of her breasts, claiming her in his own way. From the way she nuzzled backward pressing closely against him, she let him know that she was claiming him too.

"I don't think I can even get out of bed for a workout." Amethyst sighed contentedly.

"How are you going to work off all of that cotton candy?" he teased.

"Hey" She swatted a hand over her shoulder at him. "We do that a couple more times and I'll have worked off everything I ate at the carnival."

"I think I can probably help you out on that one, take one for the team and make out with you a few more times." Zeb let his fingers slide from her breast down her bare stomach and nudged their way between her legs.

Amethyst arched back against him, moaning her pleasure, and that was all he needed to hear. He could do this forever, just lying in bed, this amazing woman in his arms, reminding her just how beautiful, and how sexy she was. He didn't want a lot in life, just someone who made him feel wanted, needed, to share a life with him. Someone who would be excited to spend each day with him, to work through problems with him because there wasn't any problem too big to drive a wedge between them. Someone who even when they were old and gray still wanted to make out with him because that passion and desire never died.

Zeb truly believed that Amethyst could be that woman. She confused him sometimes, but he respected her, and he enjoyed spending time with her, and he couldn't deny that the attraction he felt for her only grew each time their bodies joined together.

In the end, what he wanted most of all was to not feel alone anymore, he wanted to find his place in the world, he wanted to feel connected, and when he was with Amethyst, he felt all of those things.

You could never guarantee the future, but he thought they stood a pretty good chance of finding happiness together.

CHAPTER
Ten

August 28th
10:16 A.M.

She was sick of being so hot.

All summer the temperatures had soared all day, and there had been little relief even once the sun set.

Today the weather was supposed to finally cool down, there was supposed to be rain, and thunder and lightning, storms that would bring some relief from the heat. Storms that would keep people indoors and out of their swimming pools. Storms that would eliminate the killer's victim pool.

But it didn't look like that was going to happen.

The sky was blue, Amethyst couldn't see a single cloud, and the sun was shining so brightly that there was no relief from it no matter where you went.

Today she and her team—and every other team in the city—were circling their local neighborhoods, going from block to block and sending anyone who they found in a backyard pool back inside. She couldn't believe that after seven fires in a week, there were still people who thought that it wouldn't happen to them, that they were so special that they could cheat death, and were still lounging around their pools, and splashing about in the water like they didn't have a care in the world.

Already today, she had personally sent a dozen teenagers back to their homes.

A dozen.

Twelve kids who thought they were invincible.

She remembered those days when she too had thought she was untouchable. But the thing about believing that you were invincible was that eventually, you came crashing back down to earth. Reality could be a harsh blow. Coming face to face with your mortality was a difficult thing at any age, but particularly when you were young, when your body and your spirit were strong, when you felt like you had an eternity to live before you too would get old.

When the sounds of cheerful voices echoed from the house she was walking past, Amethyst veered off the sidewalk and through the yard, heading around back where she found a group of four teenagers laughing and chatting like there wasn't a possibility that a psychopath with an obsession with fire might turn up in their yard. Hadn't they heard the news? Didn't they realize that kids just like them had lost their lives while they were just having fun and enjoying their summer vacation?

These kids could be next.

But not if she had anything to do with it.

"Hey, guys," she said, turning off the music playing on an iPad, "what are you doing out here? Didn't your parents tell you not to go swimming today?" she demanded as she stalked over to the pool to find that the kids were younger than she expected.

"We weren't going to stay long," a boy whined at her.

Now was not the time to be easy on these kids. The world was a tough place, and they needed to be prepared for it. "There is a killer out there who is pouring kerosene on the water in swimming pools and setting them alight, while there are people in there. Did you know about the murders?"

"Yes," they said, looking sheepishly from one to the other.

"Did your parents tell you that you should stay indoors today?"

"Yeah," one admitted, staring firmly at his feet.

"I know when you're a kid you think you know everything and that parents only exist to stifle your fun, but you know what? Sometimes they know better, they're older, they have more life experience, and they want what's best for you. And you," she turned her gaze onto Brooke Frasier, her fourteen-year-old foster niece, "does my sister know that you're here?"

"No," Brooke said in a small voice, refusing to make eye contact.

"Where did you tell Diamond that you were spending the day?"

"At a friend's house."

"This house?"

"Yes."

"Does Diamond know that there's a pool here?"

"No."

"So you lied to her?" Amethyst didn't want to make the teenager feel bad, she knew that the girl had had a rough start in life, but Brooke was a part of their family now, and she didn't want to see anything bad happen to her. If the only way to accomplish that was with a little tough love, then that was what the girl would get.

"I didn't lie exactly," Brooke stammered, looking to her friends for help, but her friends smartly kept their mouths shut.

"You three, inside," she ordered the other girl and the two boys. "Now, and when I'm done here, I'm calling your mothers to tell them what you've been up to." The teens scampered off, their worried faces indicating they were going to try to come up with what excuses they wanted to give their parents for lying to them and disobeying orders. "Why did you lie to Diamond and Elijah?" she asked Brooke once they were alone. "They really care about you, and they only want the best for you, they want to be parents to you so don't you think you should show them the respect of listening to them?"

Brooke just shrugged and picked up a towel, wrapping it around herself and then dropping down onto one of the lounges.

Amethyst joined her. "What's going on, Brooke? You're a smart kid, you work hard in school, you're great with Archie, you're polite and well mannered, why did you lie today?"

"Just wanted to hang out with my friends," the girl replied.

"Not buying it. Diamond would have let you spend the day with friends at your place or at their place, so why lie? I mean, you're wearing a swimsuit, so you obviously planned to go swimming today which means you deliberately tried to hide that from Diamond and Elijah."

"I don't need to tell them." Brooke huffed. "I make my own decisions."

"Not while you live with my sister you don't. They're your parents, that means they have a say in what you do."

"They're not my parents," Brooke countered, but her tone wasn't bratty or defiant, instead it was almost wistful.

"No, not biologically," she agreed. "But I'm sure you know that Archie isn't biologically related to either Diamond or Elijah, that doesn't stop them loving him."

"I guess," the girl said slowly.

"You used to being on your own?" She didn't really know much about what Brooke's life had been like before she entered the system, but the girl was part of their family now, and she wanted to help her in whatever way she could.

Brooke nodded. "I never knew my dad, he split before I was a year old, and I don't have any siblings, at least none that I know of, so it was always just me and my mom, only ..."

"Only what, honey?" she asked when the girl trailed off.

"Only she wasn't around all the time. Sometimes she would disappear for days at a time, and sometimes even longer."

"She'd leave you all alone?" Her parents hadn't been the best of parents even before they'd sold her and her sisters. Her dad had a gambling problem, and her mom was addicted to shopping, they were distant and not very warm and loving, but they had always made sure there was food on the table, clean clothes, and that they went to school every day.

"Yep."

"How old were you?"

"The first time I remember her being gone, I was seven. By then, I already knew how to cook, and do laundry, and clean the house. I knew the way to school, so I still went every day, and I never told anyone that my mom was gone. I was scared that if anyone found out that she would get into trouble, and then the cops would take her away, and I really would be all on my own because she wouldn't be coming back. And that's what happened in the end."

"That was brave of you to try to protect her, but you're not on your own any more, and you don't need to hold things in. My family is a little crazy, but we love each other, and you're one of us now. I know that you must be scared, not knowing what your future holds, your mom could try to get you back when she gets out of prison, or the system might decide to send you to another family, but even if that happens, you always have a home with us, okay?"

"Okay." Brooke smiled at her.

"Now, I'm going to call your friends' parents and tattle on them, then I'm taking you home."

"Diamond is going to be mad."

"She sure is."

"She's probably going to ground me," Brooke added, although she didn't sound like she was particularly upset about the prospect, in fact she looked almost pleased. Maybe having parents who cared enough to discipline her was what she had been craving all her life.

"Oh yeah, you're going to be grounded for a while, and I suspect you might find yourself head babysitter of your little brother these next few weeks."

"I hope she doesn't take my phone," the teen said, finally looking like that would be a punishment too big to bear.

With a laugh, Amethyst put her arm around the girl's shoulders and led her over to the house. It had been a pretty productive morning, sixteen kids moved out of harm's way, and she thought she had gotten through to her new niece, shown the girl that she finally had a family.

Now she hoped the rest of the day was as productive.

∽

11:39 A.M.

. . .

"This doesn't feel like a very scientific way to work this case," Zeb said dubiously as they parked their car and got out.

"Nothing else we've tried has worked, maybe this will," Judah said.

He couldn't argue with that. So far they had barely made any progress, besides the footprint that told them they were looking for a firefighter, they hadn't found any other physical evidence. They had whittled down a suspect list to include three people, one of whom was now in prison on other charges, but so far, they didn't have anything concrete on either of their remaining suspects. Neither Joaquin nor Curtis had alibis for the fires, and since they didn't have enough to even get a warrant to look into their homes, cars, or bank accounts, both men were still wandering the streets.

Which meant that another fire was coming.

It wasn't a matter of if, it was simply a matter of when.

Since forensics and interviewing suspects wasn't getting them anywhere, they were trying something different.

Something that still felt odd to him, maybe because it was so simple and not what they usually spent their days doing when they were working a case.

"I would have thought you'd be all in with this plan since it seems to have been mostly instigated by Amethyst," Judah said with a sly grin.

Zeb rolled his eyes at his partner, but he couldn't deny that he was proud of Amethyst rallying the entire fire department in addition to pretty much every cop in the city into patrolling the streets themselves. Maybe if they couldn't find this guy any other way, then just walking the streets in the hope of stumbling upon him might work.

Might.

But he wasn't convinced.

It seems like they should be doing more ... he just didn't know what that something more was.

"I see our girl in question up ahead." Judah pointed further down the street, and following his partner's finger, he saw Amethyst walking down the sidewalk. "I'll go this way, you can go that way, give you two a chance to spend a little time together," Judah said with a wink, then disappeared off in the opposite direction.

Zeb sighed, but wasn't going to pass up an opportunity to spend time with Amethyst, even if they were working. It just didn't seem like they *should* be having fun working. They were hunting a sociopathic killer who found it enjoyable to sit and watch as someone perished either by flames or drowning, that should surely wipe a smile off anyone's face, and yet as he jogged down the street, he knew there was a smile firmly planted on his.

Amethyst caught sight of him when he was about halfway to her, and raised a hand to wave at him.

"Hey," he said when he reached her, giving her a quick kiss.

"Hey, yourself," she returned.

It had only been a couple of hours since he'd seen her, she'd spent the night at his place, and this morning he'd been able to talk her into a little shower sex before they went to her house for her to grab some clean clothes, but he'd missed her in those hours.

"You've really rallied everyone in this march the streets approach," he said, taking her hand.

"I thought you thought this wasn't the way to go about this," she said, but she didn't sound angry, and she threaded their fingers together.

"I said I thought that we should be doing more than just walking the streets because there are too many streets, too many houses, and there's no guarantee that we're going to find him," he corrected. On the drive to her house this morning they had discussed the case, and she had told him of her plan to speak with her lieutenant and get every team in the city out looking for this guy.

"Well, you were a little more negative about the idea than that," Amethyst said. "What you actually said was that it was a waste of time."

"Did I say that?" he asked sheepishly. He hadn't meant to be so negative about Amethyst's idea, he knew how rough this case had been on her and how badly she wanted this guy caught, and he didn't want anyone else to die either.

"Yep, you did."

"Sorry." He reached for her other hand, entwined their fingers, then tugged her closer. "I didn't mean to make you feel like I don't respect you or your ideas. I'm just frustrated. Judah and I are cops, we should be able to do something to get this guy, and yet it seems we're down to this, just walking around and hoping that we bump into him."

"You've worked this case as hard as you could," she reminded him. "I know because I spent a few days with you and Judah. You're both great cops, and you both did everything you could to find this guy. Taking a chance doesn't mean that you're not working hard, and even if all we do is get kids out of swimming pools, then we've done something."

"I guess you're right," he relented. Did it really matter how they found this guy so long as they got him off the streets? If it turned out that they were able to find him just by walking the streets and stumbling upon him he'd still be caught.

"I'm always right." Amethyst grinned up at him, her blue eyes twinkling and an easy look on her face he hadn't seen before.

She was happy.

Because of him.

He was happy too.

Because of her.

While he would take this relationship as slow as she wanted, as far as he was concerned, they were a couple now, and he saw them having a future. A great future, where maybe both of them could finally find some peace. He knew that they both needed it, he needed to feel like he belonged somewhere, and she needed to finally start being honest with herself. She was getting there, she'd opened up to him last night and started looking at herself more objectively than just believing the same thing she'd been telling herself for a decade. He didn't think she'd quite gotten to the bottom of her need to put herself in dangerous situations yet, but he knew she'd get there, and he had a feeling he knew where there would be, but it was something she needed to figure out for herself.

"Always right, huh?" he hooked an arm around her waist to draw her up against his body. If they were alone right now and not both at work, and in the middle of a neighborhood street where kids, and parents, and the elderly were enjoying another hot summer's day, then he'd be ripping her clothes off. But they *were* at work, and they *weren't* alone, so he settled for planting another kiss on her mouth.

"Always."

"Want a chance to prove it?"

"Of course. What do you have in mind?"

"Well, I'm pretty sure I remember a certain someone bragging last night that she could beat me at poker in her sleep."

"You really want to end up giving me all your money?" she asked smugly.

"Oh, I'm not going to lose to you, princess," he shot back, just as smugly, his dad had taught him to play poker when he was four, and by the time he was six, he could beat his father more often than not.

"You are going down," she bragged confidently.

"We'll see," he said, just as confidently, maybe after they'd played for money they'd play a round of strip poker. "What about I take you out for dinner then we can go to your place or mine, and play poker until I own every dollar you have in your purse."

"Pretty cocky for a guy who's going to be broke by the end of the day." She grinned up at him.

"I don't think so, princess," he kissed her again, then reluctantly released his hold on her.

"You have to go back to work?" she asked.

"No, at least not right away, we have people staking out both Curtis Cane and Joaquin Burton's houses, but neither of them is there, which means ..." he didn't even want to say the words.

"That one of them is out here now, just looking for his next victims," Amethyst finished for him.

Both of them sobered as they remembered why they were out here and not at the firehouse or the police station.

"I can't believe people are still using their pools, do you know how many kids I've already sent back indoors today? Around twenty. Do they have a death wish or something?" Amethyst said as they started walking down the street.

That she could see a death wish in others but not in herself didn't go unnoticed, but now wasn't the time to bring it up, he was sure sooner or later she would figure it out on her own anyway, no doubt sooner rather than later. "You were right when you said that even if we don't find him today, at least we're eliminating his victim pool."

"Which is better than nothing. You'll never guess who I found at a pool earlier. It was Brooke, she'd lied to Diamond and Elijah, neglected to tell them she planned to go swimming, but it turned out we had a great talk and—"

Amethyst broke off when a shrill screech filled the air.

They exchanged glances, both in agreement.

It was the killer.

Without a word, they took off in the direction of the scream.

12:06 P.M.

He was buzzed this morning.

How exciting was this?

Not only were most of the cops in the city out looking for him, but it looked like the entire fire department was too.

That was quite an accolade. At least that was how he was choosing to look at it. He'd known that they were both looking for him, but today he saw that they were going all out.

They were everywhere.

And he did mean everywhere.

They were patrolling the streets, walking up and down, going in and out of houses, presumably getting people out of swimming pools as if that was all that it took to stop him. They were also stopping people on the streets, he had noticed from driving around that they were focusing on single white males, no doubt because they believed that was who they were looking for. They weren't wrong, but he was hardly going to be walking about looking like himself, he wasn't stupid after all. There might be nothing he could do about the white male part, but he had put in colored contacts, put a color rinse through his hair, and he'd stolen a stroller from one of his neighbor's front porches. He was hoping that was enough.

Hoping, but he couldn't deny that he had a feeling.

A feeling that said today was the day.

The day.

The day where all of this finally came to an end.

He wasn't sad about it, or even angry, but he had hoped that he would have more time. The more he did this, the more he enjoyed it, and he wasn't ready for it to end. If there was anything he could do that would help him get away alive today, then he was going to do it, but if not, then he was prepared to accept the consequences of his actions.

Since he really did hope to eke out a few more days—or if he was really lucky weeks—out of this, he was trying to be as smart as he could. He'd waited until a bunch of firefighters finished up on a street before parking his car and getting out. He set the stroller up and then started walking, he tried to look like any dad out for a stroll, but he was pretty sure he didn't. He felt awkward with the stroller, and he had to keep looking about to see if there were any more cops or firefighters coming his way.

Thankfully it didn't take him long to find a house where he heard voices.

It was beyond baffling that people were continuing to be so stupid and still using their swimming pools, even though he had been killing people every single day, sometimes more than once a day. But he was glad that they were stupid, or they thought they were indestructible, or whatever other reason they continued to go swimming when there were a million other things they could be doing with their time, including swimming at any of the local pools in the city or driving out to the beach, but whatever, he was certainly happy that there were still plenty of people willing to play Russian roulette with their lives.

Turning into the house, he dumped the stroller behind a bush and then crept closer. The voices he heard were bubbly, chirpy, and full of youth, exactly his favorite type. While he didn't discriminate, he certainly liked it when it was teenagers that he found, maybe it was because of their youth and their propensity to believe that they were immortal that drew him to them. He remembered being that age and in no way, shape, or form, had he considered himself to be invincible. These kids should learn that same lesson.

"You think those firefighters will come back?" he heard a girl ask.

"I hope not," a boy replied.

"My parents are going to flip out if they find out I went back in the pool," another girl said with a nervous giggle.

"Mine won't," a boy bragged. "My dad said that if anyone came into the yard while I was swimming, that I should just get out of the pool, run inside, and get the gun out of the safe. He said he didn't pay all this money for a pool to let some loser with a small penis that got his jollies off by setting fires keep us out of it."

Loser?

Small penis?

He wasn't a loser, nor did he have a small penis, and he didn't get his jollies off setting fires, he got them off the same way as any attractive man in his thirties did, by sleeping with a woman. He didn't struggle in that department, not at all, he was good looking, and he knew it, and women knew it, he had never in his life had to do more than ask to get a girl to have sex with him.

This was about finally climbing out of the box his mother had worked so hard to lock him up in, and doing something that he wanted to do. He loved fires, and he loved the buzz he got whenever he set one, but just starting fires was no longer enough to get him buzzed. So he had started using fire to kill, and thankfully, that buzz had returned, now he was starting to lose some of that buzz again, and already planning what he could try next.

But for today, he was going to exact great pleasure from killing these kids.

Today he wasn't wearing his usual black sweats because he knew that would be a dead giveaway to the cops and firefighters patrolling the streets that he was the man they were looking for, which meant that the kids and anyone who came running at the sounds of their screams would see his face, but he didn't care. If he had to, he would just kill them as well, the more the merrier.

The sounds of splashing told him that the kids had jumped back into the expensive pool that was apparently worth more to the couple who owned it than their kid's life.

Striding through the backyard, he didn't even pause, just went right up to the pool and began to throw kerosene into it.

"Tyler," shrieked one of the girls, clinging to one of the boys.

"Hey, get out of here, we're not afraid of you," one of the boys, the one who had just repeated his father's insult, yelled.

"Uh, uh, uh," he cautioned when the kid made a move to get out of the pool. He pulled out his matches and struck one, holding it up so the kids could see the tiny flame.

The kids stopped moving, one of the girls began to scream, and he was just about to throw the match into the pool and watch the fire ignite when footsteps pounded across the yard, and two people appeared on the other side of the pool.

"Amethyst, Detective Tuck," he said, surprised by their presence.

"Curtis?" Amethyst stared back at him in shock. He didn't know why she was so surprised, the cops had already had him at the top of their suspect list.

"You've arrived just in time to have a front row seat for today's fiery action," he smiled.

"Put the match down, get down on your knees, and put your hands behind your head," Detective Tuck ordered, gun pointed squarely at his head.

"You shoot me, Detective, and the match goes into the pool, then these poor kids go up in flames," he warned. He knew cops, and he knew there was no way the Detective would risk him setting the pool with the teenagers in it, on fire. But he also knew that within minutes this place would be swarming with police officers and firefighters, and there was no way he would walk out of here alive.

Which meant he had to make a choice.

He could try to find a way to get them to let him go, or he could accept that this was the end, and take Amethyst and the Detective down with him.

Before he even had a chance to decide which way he was going to go, Amethyst stepped closer. "Put the match down, Curtis, leave these kids alone, and I'll go with you."

"Amethyst, no," Detective Tuck said, grabbing for her when she started to walk around the pool.

This was an interesting proposition and one that he hadn't been expecting. Would he accept her as a trade? The idea could be intriguing, he wasn't quite sure what he would do with her, but he *had* been looking for a way to get more fun out of this, maybe he could use Amethyst for that.

"If I go with you will you let the kids live?" she asked.

"I might," he agreed. What did he have to lose? If Amethyst was willing to go with him then he could walk out of here alive.

"Are you crazy?" Detective Tuck fumed.

"You let me walk out of here with Amethyst, and the kids live," he said, agreeing to her terms.

"Cops will be here within minutes," Detective Tuck told Amethyst. "You don't have to sacrifice yourself."

"Not in time to save the kids though," she said, stepping close enough for him to grab.

Yanking her up against his body so he could use her as a human shield, he dropped the match to the ground and stomped on it, putting out the tiny flame. "You try anything stupid, and I'll set your girlfriend on fire. I know you don't want that, then you won't get another chance to put your head between those sexy legs of hers and make her scream your name when she comes."

The Detective's face drained of color. "You were watching us."

"You put on quite the show." He grinned. "Let's go," he told Amethyst as he began to walk her toward the front of the yard, they had to get out of here before anyone else showed up. Amethyst was a good bargaining tool, but he wasn't sure she was enough to get him out of here when more objective cops arrived.

As they walked out of the yard, Detective Tuck stood looking helplessly after him. The gun was still aimed at them, but Amethyst was between the two of them, and he knew the cop wouldn't risk putting a bullet in his girlfriend.

Nor would he risk her being set alight.

So he had no choice but to let them go.

This certainly wasn't how he had expected the day to turn out, he hadn't killed anyone, nor had he had to kill himself, but Curtis couldn't wipe the smile off his face as he ran towards his car with a hostage in tow.

~

12:11 P.M.

This couldn't be happening.

Zeb's mind was spinning, trying to figure out a way to change what was happening but coming up empty.

What had Amethyst been thinking?

If she had just waited a couple of minutes, then backup would have arrived and they'd have Curtis Cane in custody right now.

But if they'd waited, those kids would most likely have died.

That was something that Amethyst couldn't stomach happening, so she had traded herself.

Her for them.

Now she was gone.

Instead of having Curtis in handcuff sitting in the back of a cruiser ready to be taken down to the station, booked, and put where he belonged, the man had grabbed Amethyst and dragged her away with him.

And he hadn't stopped it.

Because his hands were tied.

If he had fired off a shot at Curtis the man would have dropped the lit match into the pool, setting those kids on fire. Once Curtis had gotten his hands on Amethyst he'd used her as a human shield, and even if he'd been able to get a clear shot, which he hadn't, he'd been afraid that the man would follow through on his threat to set her on fire. He had no idea if Curtis had rigged something that could explode if he was hit, and since it was Amethyst's life they were talking about, he couldn't risk it.

Which was what Curtis had been banking on.

Zeb had no idea how long the man had been following them, but he'd obviously watched them the other night while he and Amethyst had been making out. Amethyst's bedroom was on the second floor, which meant that the man must have climbed the tree in the front yard to look through the window.

"What happened?" Judah asked, running up to him, other cops, and a couple of firefighters were also starting to swarm the block, but it was too late.

Curtis was gone, and he had Amethyst.

That the man wasn't going to hurt her wasn't even a consideration. He would hurt her, if he had to guess, then Curtis would probably burn her, and the thought of that made him feel physically sick. He had already lost his parents and baby sister to a fire, and he didn't want to lose the woman he was falling in love with to one as well.

"Zeb, what happened?" Judah repeated.

Forcing himself to focus before he went completely off the deep end, he met his partner's eye and tried to work this like he would any other case. Of course, that was easier said than done because this couldn't be less like any other case. Someone he cared deeply about was in danger. Since the only way to bring Amethyst home was to cling to sanity, he made himself do it. "We heard screams, went into the yard, found four kids in the pool and Curtis Cane standing there with a lit match in his hand. I had my gun on him, but he threatened to throw the match in the pool if I fired, his hand was above the water, even if I shot to kill the match would have landed in the pool. Then Amethyst said she'd trade her life for the kids and go with him."

"She did what?" Judah exclaimed.

"Traded herself," he repeated even though he knew his partner had heard what he'd said.

"I'm not looking forward to telling Ruby. Strike that," Judah said, rubbing his temples, "I don't want to be the one to tell Sapphire. She's going to go ballistic."

He couldn't imagine how Sapphire, Ruby, and Diamond were going to feel when they found out that their sister was now in the hands of a dangerous fire-starting psychopath.

Actually, he could.

And that was worse.

"How did he get out of here?" Judah asked.

"He used her as a human shield so I couldn't get a clean shot, and he threatened that he would set her on fire if I tried to stop him from leaving. There wasn't anything I could do," he finished helplessly. Although, logically, he knew that there hadn't been anything he could do to stop Curtis taking Amethyst hostage it didn't mean he wasn't crushed by guilt.

He'd been the only other one there, and he was a cop, it was his job to get people out of dangerous situations, not into them.

And yet he hadn't been able to save Amethyst.

Even if he got her back alive, he doubted he would ever erase either the guilt or the image of Amethyst with Curtis's arm around her neck, from his mind.

It could be the last time he ever saw her alive.

The panic was back.

It was suffocating him, it was like being back in his house that night as an eight-year-old little boy, the smoke was thick, choking him, the flames were bright, blinding him, the heat seemed to get inside you, making you sluggish and uncoordinated. Today he might not be trapped in a burning house, but his fear and panic were affecting him just the same way that the smoke and flames had.

"Try to hold it together," Judah said, laying a steadying hand on his shoulder.

"I *am* trying," he said.

"Amethyst is a strong woman, she can hold it together, and if anyone can find a way to bring this guy down then it's her. And, at least we know who we're looking for now, that has to help, we'll keep people on Curtis' house in case he goes back there."

"He's not that stupid," Zeb snapped, not because he was angry with his partner, but because he was angry with himself. How had *they* been so stupid, he was a cop, he should have noticed someone following them, he should have noticed someone watching them through the window.

This was on him.

"We'll start looking into him, see if he has another property, check out his family, speak with everyone who knows him and see if there's anywhere he might go when he knows that the walls are closing in on him. Because the walls *are* closing in on him," Judah said firmly.

"He was stalking us," he told his partner. He wasn't sure what it meant, or how long Curtis had been doing it, or whether or not it was going to be pertinent in finding him, but he may as well give everything he had because it could be the smallest thing that ended up leading them to Curtis.

"Stalking you? You and Amethyst? How do you know?"

"Because he told us. He was watching Amethyst and me the other night, he saw us making out, he knew that I was going to let them walk away rather than risk Amethyst getting hurt." He hated that Curtis had been able to use his feelings for Amethyst against him.

"You did what you had to do to make sure everyone stayed alive. From what you said you didn't have any other options. You couldn't shoot while he had the match held over the water without sacrificing those kids, and you couldn't shoot while he had Amethyst between you."

He knew his partner was trying to make him feel better, but the words just sounded hollow.

He *should* have been able to do something.

Something.

Just thirty minutes ago, he and Amethyst were planning their second date, teasing each other about who was going to win at poker, and now he didn't even know if she would still be alive tonight.

More cops were coming, having responded to the call he'd made to his partner as he and Amethyst headed towards the screams, they would start interviewing residents and the teenagers to see if anyone had seen anything that might be useful. The crime scene unit would be here soon, searching for evidence that might help, but he couldn't think of anything they could find that would give him what he needed.

What he needed was the address of wherever Curtis had taken Amethyst, but he wasn't sure anyone could give him that. He wanted to do something, but he didn't know what his next move should be, he didn't know where to look for her, he didn't know how to find where to look for her. While he would gladly knock on every door of every house in the city to find Amethyst, he knew they didn't have that kind of time.

She could be dead already.

That thought kept echoing in his head.

Why did Amethyst always have to run toward trouble instead of away from it like a normal person?

Why did she have to sacrifice herself for other people?

Why did she have to have that burning need to push herself as close to death as she could get?

And why did he only respect and admire her more because of it?

Amethyst was one of a kind, smart, sassy, strong, and sexy, she was everything that he could want in a woman to share his life with, and he'd had her. For all her talk of wanting to take things slow, he knew that she was as hooked on this relationship as he was.

There was no way he was going to sit back and let someone take her away from him.

A fierceness rushed through him, it felt like a piece of Amethyst was coming to him right when he needed it the most.

He wasn't giving up.

She would never do that, and neither would he.

I'm coming for you, he told her, hoping that she knew he would never give up on her.

~

12:13 P.M.

Amethyst had faith that Zeb would find her.

If she didn't, then there was no way she would agree to trade her life for those four kids.

Or maybe that wasn't entirely true.

She probably would have traded her life for those kids even if she thought that she was going to die at Curtis' hand.

Those kids were young, they had their whole lives ahead of them, lives that they hopefully wouldn't mess up the same way she had messed up her own. Now that she was facing death, maybe more closely than she had since Nikos had slit her throat in that abandoned lot, everything was so clear to her.

Crystal clear.

Like finally after over a decade, she had agreed to put on the glasses of self-enlightenment, and now she could see exactly what had been hidden at the back of her mind.

She wanted to die.

Maybe not outright wanted, she wasn't suicidal, and she hadn't even realized that it was what she wanted, but now she realized that that was what she had been trying to do these last several years. She didn't do extreme sports because they gave her an adrenalin buzz and made her feel alive, she did them because she wanted one of them to end up claiming her life.

Only now that she had finally figured that out and stopped lying to herself, she realized that it wasn't true anymore.

She *didn't* want to die.

She was done with kidding herself that she was happy on her own and that she didn't want what her sisters had found, she wanted it, and she had it.

If she could survive Curtis to return home to Zeb.

Amethyst weighed her options, she had no doubt that if she tried to do anything other than walk along where Curtis was dragging her, that he wouldn't hesitate to set her on fire. She also didn't have any doubts that she would be dead before anyone could get to her. It would be a horrific and excruciating death and one that she wouldn't wish on Zeb. He had already lost his family to fire, and to lose her the same way would be a devastating blow.

So for now, it seemed that the only thing she could do was play this out, trust in the man she was falling for, and be the perfect hostage.

Curtis stopped beside a car. "You try to make a run for it, you do anything to attract attention to us, and I will kill your family. One of your sisters has a newborn right, you want to see that tiny little baby go up in flames?"

"You're a monster," she hissed.

"Not a monster. I don't *want* to kill the baby, I just don't mind doing it if it gets me what I want, and this was *your* plan after all. I was happy with dropping the match into that pool, then blowing you, Detective Tuck, and myself to smithereens. But you changed that, you decided that this wasn't over yet, all because you couldn't bear to let those kids—those strangers—die." He said that like it was an insult, like there was something wrong with her because she didn't want another human being to suffer a horrendous death.

"You could have turned yourself in," she reminded him.

"Yeah, right," he scoffed. "That isn't happening. This is only ending in one way, me and whichever cops are unlucky enough to be the ones trying to arrest me going down in flames. And now you're going to be joining us. Still think trading yourself was a smart idea?"

Smart?

Nope.

The only thing she could have done under the circumstances?

Absolutely.

There wasn't a single other thing she could have or would have done, and given the same situation, she would have made the same choice a million times over.

Zeb wouldn't shoot Curtis so long as he was holding the match over the water and those kids were in the pool. Waiting for the cops would still have meant that those teenagers would have died, as Curtis would have thrown the match into the pool and tried to use the ensuing chaos to escape. There hadn't been any other way to ensure that those kids lived, besides this.

"I still would have done this," she said quietly.

"Then you're an idiot," the man shot back. "Since I wasn't planning on walking away with a hostage today, I don't have ropes or anything to tie you up with. Usually, I would never do this, I am a gentleman after all, but I don't see another way to keep you quiet in there."

With that, he turned her around then slammed her head into the back of the car.

Once, and she saw stars.

Twice, and the world began to spin around her.

Three times and she was knocked out ...

She was moving.

It wasn't the moving in and of itself that yanked her out of unconsciousness, it was the vicious pounding in her head, and the sickening swirling feeling in her stomach that said she was about to throw up.

Turning her head to the side, she vomited.

"Yuck," a voice said, and Amethyst realized that she wasn't moving, someone else was moving her.

It seemed important that she remember who, and why, but she was tired, and it seemed so much easier to just slide back down into the quiet, inky darkness.

She very well might have, but she was moved again, and once again she threw up.

"Maybe knocking you out wasn't such a great idea after all," the same voice said, tone distasteful.

She groaned, and prayed that he would stop moving her, maybe if she could just be still she could figure out what was going on.

That she had a concussion was evident. You didn't do all the crazy extreme sports that she did and not get a couple of concussions. How she got this particular concussion, that she still wasn't sure of.

Finally, she was set down on something hard.

The floor maybe.

Something cool was snapped around her wrist, and she heard a click like handcuffs being closed.

Handcuffs?

If she'd just been handcuffed to something then that was not good news.

Think, she commanded herself.

Thinking was a near impossibility with a concussion, but it wasn't like she had a choice.

The last thing she could recall was telling Zeb that she was going to leave him broke at their poker game tonight. They'd been on the sidewalk when they'd had that conversation because she had rallied every firefighter in the city to be out looking for the killer.

Screams had led her and Zeb to a swimming pool.

And the killer.

He'd been holding a lit match above a swimming pool with four kids in it, and she had traded herself to keep them alive.

"Curtis," she groaned.

"At your service," he mocked.

"Where are we?" she asked, trying to open her eyes, but the light—dim though it was—seemed to slice right through her.

"Nowhere you need to worry yourself about."

"What are you doing?" Amethyst managed to crack her eyelids up enough to see that they were in a house, in a sitting room, she was on the floor handcuffed to the thick oak leg of a table, and Curtis was standing over by one of two windows. He'd drawn all the drapes, and although it was light enough to see, it had dimmed the room enough that she could open her eyes without screaming in pain.

"Keeping watch for our visitors," he replied.

"What visitors?"

"I doubt your cop boyfriend is going to just sit by and let me keep you," Curtis answered, turning around to look at her. "He'll find where we are, and he'll come running to your rescue like the knight in shining armor he thinks himself to be. When he comes, I'm going to set this place on fire, and he can watch you burn to death, knowing you're alive and feeling every second of it. Or ..."

"He can come in here, try to save me, and die too," she finished for him. If she knew Zeb, there was no way he would stand by and watch her burn alive, he would rather come in here, attempt to save her, and perish right along with her. Maybe this whole giving herself up as a hostage idea wasn't one of her best. At the time it had seemed like the only option, but now she wasn't so sure. Everything had happened so quickly, there hadn't been time to run through every scenario looking at the pros and cons.

But things were what they were, she *had* traded herself, and now she had to make the best of things. With her head feeling like her brain was trying to rip its way through her skull, she couldn't concentrate enough to figure out a way to escape, which left her with one option.

Get him talking.

Maybe if she got him talking about why he was doing this, and what he hoped to achieve, then she could find something that she could use against him.

It might not work, but her options were limited, and it was better than sitting here and doing nothing, just waiting to die.

"Curtis—"

"Don't do it," he warned. "Don't be so cliché as to ask me why I'm doing this."

"Isn't that why you agreed to take me as a hostage? So you could tell someone why you'd done all of this before you, to quote you "go down in flames"?"

~

12:39 P.M.

Well, she had him there.

Curtis hadn't really given it a whole lot of thought. Amethyst had presented herself as the sacrificial lamb, and he had jumped at the opportunity to use her to get away because he was having too much fun to end things today.

But maybe there had been a little more to it.

Maybe part of him had liked the idea of being able to tell someone about his childhood, and about why he was doing this.

Amethyst would certainly give him an outlet, a person to hear his pain and suffering, maybe validate it a little.

It wasn't like he had anything to lose. She wasn't walking out of this house alive, and he had never intended to walk away from this alive, simply to play the game for as long as it lasted, ride it out, have fun, and then when it was all over allow the flames to return him to what he had been in the beginning. Ashes to ashes, and dust to dust, and all that jazz, he was simply returning to his original state in the way nature intended it.

Letting the drapes fall closed, he took a few steps away from the window and dropped down into one of the armchairs. Amethyst was squinting at him, and he could tell she was in pain and struggling to focus, but he appreciated her attempts. It was nice to have a captive audience to finally unleash the anger he had been holding onto since he was a small boy.

"My dad ran off when I was four, well almost four, just a couple of weeks before my birthday. We never heard from him again, but I heard later on that he remarried and had more kids. Kids he hung around to raise," he added bitterly. How did the man think it would make him feel when he had disappeared out of his life but stayed around to raise the kids of his second wife? With a male role model like that was it any wonder that he had grown up to be obsessed with fires?

"I'm sorry," Amethyst said, resting her head back against the wall.

"Thank you," he acknowledged, because he felt that she was being sincere and not mocking him, or just telling him what he wanted to hear because he was the one with all the power here.

"Did you have any siblings?"

"I had two, an older brother and an older sister, but they were a lot older than me. My sister was eight when I was born, my brother ten, they were never interested in hanging around with me. They didn't really care that our father left, they were twelve and fourteen by then, it didn't hurt them as much as it hurt me, they'd already had him around for most of their childhoods."

"Maybe they just wanted to pretend it didn't bother them so they could be strong for you and your mom," Amethyst suggested.

Brushing off her suggestion, he shook his head. "No, they didn't care. My sister was more interested in boys, she wound up pregnant at thirteen, a mother at fourteen. And my brother was always carrying on about how glad he was that dad was gone, and how much he hated the man. He liked playing at being the man of the house, he would boss me and our sister around, telling us what to do, pretending that he had the right to try to control our lives. He was just like our mother."

"Your mom was a control freak?"

"She wasn't just a control freak, she was a narcissistic, cruel, bitter, angry old cow," he spat out.

"Did she abuse you?" Amethyst asked softly, her eyes were open, and although he could see that they were shadowed with pain, there was empathy there too. He knew that her parents had sold her and her siblings to human traffickers when they were teenagers, and while Amethyst never talked about it, she wore her scars like a badge of honor. To her, they were a sign of her survival, and for him, fire was the same thing. Every time he set a fire he proved that he was no longer under the control of a horrible, scheming, nasty old woman who continued to try to control those around her down to the very end.

His mother was old now, seventy-four, and her health was deteriorating quickly. Both his older siblings had refused to have her come and live with them since they were both married with families and claimed they didn't have space for her or the time to care for her. So he had gotten lumped with her. He had tried to put her in a nursing home, but a couple of months ago the old woman had manipulated and schemed her way out of it and into his house. He had been forced to take some time away from the job he adored to care for her full time, and he hated it.

Curtis wanted to finally be free of his mother.

He was tired of her keeping her claws stuck into him.

She could whine and wail all she wanted that he was her precious baby boy, but he knew what she meant. What she really meant was that he was the one who had always taken the brunt of her abusive, neglectful, controlling ways, and she wasn't going to let go of that until her final breath was ripped from her lungs.

"She didn't physically abuse me," he answered Amethyst's question. "But she was emotionally abusive, neglectful, and controlling. She would threaten me into doing what she wanted me to do, or I would be punished. Punishments were things like being chained up outside overnight, being forced to eat dog food for dinner, being kept home from school—a place that I loved and adored—being made to sit in ice baths. She wanted to control every aspect of my life, what I wore, what I ate, who my friends were—if I was even allowed to have a friend—who I dated. I had to do my homework in front of her, even when I was in high school, I had to ask permission to do even the simplest of things like have a snack or go to the bathroom. It was hell. It was like being constantly treated like a toddler even when I was old enough to be able to do things myself and make my own decisions."

"That's awful," Amethyst said, her eyes had fallen closed, but she was obviously still listening because her face was creased with pain. "When did you start liking setting fires?"

"My older brother used to smoke, that's one of my first memories, playing out in the backyard and finding him right down the back, behind the shed, cigarette in hand. I remember the little glowing circle of orangey-red and wondering what it was and what it would be like to touch. Then after my third birthday, I tried lighting a match for the first time, and after that I was hooked. I liked that fire was out of control, my life was so structured, so orderly, everything happened in the same predictable routine. The only thing that was ever up in the air was whether or not my mother was going to wake up in a good mood, meaning we would all have a good day, or in a bad mood, meaning that a punishment was coming it was only what and when. But fire wasn't like that. You can't control it, it does as it pleases, and that was refreshing to me, even as a small child."

"I'm very sorry that you had to live your life like that, I'm sorry that you were hurt and abused, and I understand why you like fire, but what I don't understand is why you started killing people."

"Setting fires was my escape, it was what made me feel alive, it was what gave me that buzz of adrenalin that made me feel happy." Amethyst pried her eyes back open, and this time in them he saw a deep understanding that he hadn't been expecting.

Maybe she actually understood.

Maybe it was fate that had brought her here today.

Maybe it was life's way of giving him what he needed before it all came to a fiery end.

"It wasn't enough anymore," he said softly. "That buzz was fading, and it was the only good thing going on in my life. I needed to find a way to bring it back."

"And killing people did that."

"It did."

"But that buzz won't last, you'd need to keep moving on to bigger and crazier things."

"It's already wearing off," he admitted.

"And you don't know where to go next. That's why you're prepared to end it all. One last big fiery hurrah, taking down as many people as you can with you."

Curtis nodded his assent. "When I was following you and Detective Tuck around, and watching the two of you in bed together, I planned to try to use it against you, and I did. But if I had known that you and I are a lot more alike than you would probably care to admit, I wouldn't have brought you here."

"Does that mean you're going to let me go?" Amethyst asked, her blue eyes lighting with hope.

"No," he said firmly, letting her go was out of the question. Just like those people had had to die to satiate his need for adrenalin, so Amethyst had to die here with him to bring things full circle. To put an end to both of their suffering, to give them that last rush that they both craved, and to send them both off into the next world, where he was sure that they would both rise out of the flames like the phoenix.

Standing, he walked over to her and then knelt at her side, gently touching the sticky, clotting blood that marred her blonde hair.

In many ways this gorgeous woman was his other half. Curtis hadn't realized that there was anyone out there like him, someone who had risen from the harsh hand life had dealt them to come into their own and take control of their lives.

However, here she was.

A woman, that under other circumstances he might have fallen in love with, perhaps finding himself on a different path.

But the path he was on was this one.

There was one last thing he would like to do before the final act of his life was upon them.

Curtis reached for the zipper on her cargo shorts and undid it.

"Don't, please." Amethyst's eyes met his, and her bottom lip trembled.

"Close your eyes and pretend it's your boyfriend," he sneered, angry now. They were alike, more alike than the Detective she was dating, and yet she would let that man taste her but not him?

No way.

He'd never been turned down by a woman before, and he didn't appreciate it starting now. Curtis shoved her shorts down her legs and threw them across the room.

"So, what, you're a rapist now, too?" she asked when his fingers curled around the hem of her panties.

He slapped her. Hard enough that her eyes rolled back in her head and he thought she had passed out.

But she was a tough one, this woman, and that only made him want her more. She stiffened her spine, met his gaze squarely, and said, "We're not alike, you and I. We both got addicted to that adrenalin rush, but I don't need it anymore. I'm tired of living my life trying to see how close I can get to death before it comes for me. If you're going to kill me, fine, but I'm not just going to sit here and let you do it. I'm so sick of men like you, like Nikos, who think they are entitled to just take what they want. There are good men out there, men like Zeb, men who respect women, who care about other people, who are good, and kind, and dedicate their lives to helping others. When I die, there are going to be people who mourn me, who miss me, who will think about me every day, but you're just a murdering rapist, and when you're gone the world will be a better place."

Curtis growled in frustration, hating that she was right.

Who would miss him when he was gone?

Not the father who had walked out on him, not the siblings who weren't interested in him, not the mother who had tried to control him.

There would be no one to give him a funeral, no one to stand crying around his grave, no one to mourn, no one to grieve, not a single person on the face of the earth who would care that he was no longer alive.

This had always been about ending in flames.

And if he was going down, then he was going to get one last bit of pleasure before he did.

If Amethyst didn't want one last bit of pleasure, then she could just miss out. Yanking off his board shorts and boxers, he tossed them across the room and reached for Amethyst's face. Realizing what he was going to do, she clamped her mouth shut, pressing her lips together in a thin line.

"I bet if your boyfriend wanted this you'd be all over him," he sneered. "Think you're too good to suck anyone else?"

Kneeling above her, he put his thumb on one cheek, his fingers on the other, and was about to squeeze until she gave in and opened her mouth so she could take him deep inside when he heard what sounded like cars approaching.

It looked like there wouldn't be time for this after all, but Amethyst's unwillingness to give him what he wanted only meant that he was no longer regretful about killing her. The selfish, conceited witch thought she was superior to everyone else, she was going to get what she deserved, and he was going to enjoy hearing her screams as the flames claimed her.

The final act was upon them.

1:04 P.M.

"How much longer is it going to be?" Zeb asked to no one in particular as he paced up and down Curtis Cane's living room. They were waiting to speak to the man's mother, but the nurse had insisted they wait until she made sure the elderly, sick woman was strong enough to be interrogated.

"The nurse said ten minutes," Judah reminded him.

He didn't want to be reminded.

He wanted to pace frantically.

He wanted to get things moving.

He wanted to find Curtis.

He wanted to get Amethyst back.

Hold it together, he reminded himself.

They would find Curtis and get Amethyst back, but to do that, they needed to speak with Curtis' mother. To get anything useful out of the woman he needed to remain calm enough to interview her.

"The ten minutes was over eleven minutes ago," he said, dragging in a breath in an attempt to calm himself, but it did little to help. How could he remain calm when the woman who already owned a very large piece of his heart was in danger? That he wasn't falling apart, that he wasn't a screaming, ranting mess was a testament to how hard he was working to hold it together.

"It's been eight minutes," Judah corrected.

"Are you trying to annoy me?" he demanded.

"No, I'm trying to help you hold it together the best way I can," his partner said. "I know it's terrifying that Amethyst is with Curtis right now, and that we don't know what—if anything—he's done to her, but we have to work through this the same as we would with any case. Let's interview Mrs. Cane, see what she gives us, then go from there. Try not to think more than the next step ahead, if you're looking too far down the road you're going to get overwhelmed. If you're overwhelmed then you might miss something important. One step at a time. I know it sounds trite, but the only way to get through this is one step at a time."

His partner was right.

As much as he hated it, if he got bogged down obsessing over what was happening to Amethyst this second, and how they were going to get her back, and what would happen if they didn't get her back alive, then he was going to paralyze himself.

One step at a time.

He could do that.

He *had* to do that.

"All right, detectives, Mrs. Cane is ready for you," the nurse announced, entering the living room. "You can follow me down to her room."

Walking a little closer than was necessary behind the woman in an attempt to make her move faster, they followed the middle-aged nurse down the hall and into a bedroom. The room smelled like a hospital and looked like one too. There was an oxygen tank, there were heart and pulse monitors, there was a table filled with medications and instruments, and the elderly woman in the hospital bed in the middle of the room looked as close to death as he had ever seen a living human being be.

Since they didn't have time to waste, he jumped right into things. "Mrs. Cane, we need to ask you some questions about your son."

"Curtis," she said, her voice was raspy and weak, but the eyes that looked back at him were clear.

"Yes," he said, standing close beside the bed. "Did you know that your son loved starting fires?"

"Yes, he's been doing that ever since he was a small boy."

"Did you know that he's been setting fires to kill people?"

"No."

"But you don't look surprised," he noted. "Is there a reason why you're not lying here trying to convince us that we must be wrong, that we have the wrong man, that your precious little baby boy is perfect?"

"Do you know for sure that it's my son?"

"Yes, I found him at a crime scene with a match in his hand, and he took a firefighter hostage to escape." Zeb left out the fact that Amethyst was also his girlfriend because he was trying to set that aside for the moment to do his job.

"Then I believe that my son did what you're saying he did."

"Why aren't you surprised, Mrs. Cane?" Judah repeated.

"Because my son isn't a ..." she paused, seemed to think about her choice of words, then said, "my son has some issues."

"What kind of issues?" Zeb asked.

"Ever since he was a child, he had a very high opinion of himself. He believed that he was the center of the universe, he believed that he should be showered with love and attention every second of the day. My husband left me to raise three children on my own, I had to work three jobs to pay the bills, then my daughter got pregnant and had a baby at fourteen, that was another mouth to feed, another person to care for, I didn't have a lot of time, and Curtis would lash out at me for it."

"Lash out how? Physically? Verbally? Emotionally?" he asked.

"Never physically, but verbally and emotionally. My son was a narcissist. He believed that he was the most important person in our family, he would get angry if he felt like his siblings or niece got any attention. He struggled to make friends because he would get angry at other children for having things that he didn't, better toys, more time with parents, better grades. Everything he did, he thought he was the best at, even if the evidence said otherwise, and if anyone dared to offer him even constructive criticism he would lose it. He doesn't care about other people's feelings, they're irrelevant to him. He liked to punish me, he would spend the night outside in the doghouse because he said I treated him no better than the dog. He would take ice baths because he said I didn't work hard enough and earn enough money for us to use the air conditioning every day in the summer. Life with him was difficult, he felt like whatever he wanted he should get, so if he felt that killing people fulfilled some need for him then he would feel entitled enough to do it."

That this was coming from his mother was telling.

If what she had just told him was even partially true then he knew one thing for certain. Reasoning with Curtis was not an option. There was no way the man was going to be persuaded to surrender or let Amethyst go alive.

"Where would he go, Mrs. Cane?" he asked, trying not to sound as desperate as he felt.

"To the house where we lived when he was a child, before his dad left and we had to move somewhere smaller, more affordable," the woman replied without hesitation.

That was as good a place as any to start. If Curtis wasn't there, they could always come back, speak with her again, see where else she thought her son might go. "Thank you for your time," he said, ready to be out of here.

"I'd ask you not to hurt my son, but I know that's the only way to stop him," Mrs. Cane said quietly, a lone tear trickling down her cheek.

"If we can end this without hurting him we will," Judah assured her.

Knowing they didn't have a single second to spare, he asked the woman for the address then he and Judah left. Neither of them spoke on the drive to the house, there was nothing to say. They both wanted to get Amethyst back alive, and they both knew that with each second that passed, the chances of achieving that dropped. If Curtis was a narcissist, then he was likely to react irrationally to anything he perceived to be a threat to him getting what he wanted with little to no care of the consequences.

The ten minutes it took to drive to the house felt like way too long.

He had never been more aware of seconds ticking by than he was right now.

Losing Amethyst would be a crushing loss for her family, her sisters had already lost so much, and they didn't deserve another blow.

Losing Amethyst would be a crushing loss to him too. It would be losing all of the dreams he was starting to have for the future. He'd begun to think about just how great life for the two of them as a couple could be, and he wanted a chance to make that a reality.

"Next left and we're there," he said as they approached a T-intersection.

"We need to go in carefully," Judah said as he switched on the indicator. "He's most likely going to threaten to set Amethyst alight if we don't leave, we need to keep him talking long enough to get back up here, and the house surrounded. I think it's unlikely that we'll be able to talk him down so I think having a sniper in place might be our best option."

"I think I'll have the best chance at keeping him talking, he knows that Amethyst and I are a couple, and he's not going to be able to resist throwing that in my face."

"Maybe you should go in alone, I'll circle around through the back, maybe if you keep him busy he might not notice me, and I'll be able to get off a—"

His partner never finished his sentence because the house they had just pulled up in front of suddenly burst into flames.

Zeb didn't even hesitate.

He jumped out of the car, and ignoring his partner's screams that a fire truck would be here in less than five minutes, he rushed for the front door.

Amethyst might not have five minutes.

And whether they were her team or not, when the fire truck did arrive, they would have to follow their procedures.

He didn't care about procedures.

All he cared about was getting Amethyst out of this house alive.

The heat as he threw open the front door was almost unbearable, and he stumbled backward.

Recovering quickly, he forged forwards.

The smoke was thick, no doubt Curtis Cane had doused the place in an accelerant so it would burn quickly, and it was hard to see more than a foot or so ahead of him.

"Amethyst?" he yelled, straining to hear over the flames.

He didn't hear her call out to him.

Was she already dead?

Unable to accept that, he walked further into the house, scanning left to right as he went. Not only was Amethyst in here somewhere but Curtis was as well. He had no doubt that the man intended to go down in flames.

"Amethyst?" he called out again, standing still so he could focus on listening.

"Zeb." The voice was faint, but he would recognize it anywhere.

"Amethyst, where are you?" It was hard to place the direction of the voice when smoke billowed around him, and flames were springing up everywhere.

"Straight ahead of you," came the reply.

Moving slowly, cautiously, he made it another seven steps, and then he saw her. She was down on the ground by the wall.

Throwing caution to the wind, he ran the last few yards and dropped down at her side, grabbing her face between his hands and cradling it. "Are you okay?"

"Concussion," she told him.

A concussion combined with the smoke meant that smoke inhalation was going to hit her quickly. He had to get her out of here. Hooking an arm under her legs and his other around her shoulders, he went to lift her, but when he tried to pull her into his arms he couldn't move with her.

"He handcuffed me to the table," Amethyst explained. In the orangey glow of the fire her eyes shone, and he could see blood on her head.

Fumbling to get his handcuff key out so he could unlock her and get her out of here, he put a hand on her shoulder and ran it down her arm until he found the handcuff. His hands were shaking so much that as he tried to line up the key with the lock, which he could barely see thanks to the smoke that was making his eyes sting and water, he dropped it.

Muttering a curse, he asked Amethyst, "Can we just lift the table and slide the cuff off it?"

"Don't you think I would have done that already if I could?" came the wry reply, that managed to tug his lips upward in a smile. To hear her saying things like that reassured him a little, she was on shaky ground, but he still had time to get her out of here alive.

"You always have something sassy to say, princess," he joked, as he felt about on the ground for the key. "Do you know where Curtis is?"

"No," she said. "But I'm sure he's here somewhere."

"Got it," he said triumphantly when he located the key. This time he willed his hand to remain steady as he slid it into the lock and freed Amethyst. "Now, let's get you out of here." That she didn't protest when he gathered her into his arms worried him, but he didn't have time to examine her right now, they needed to get out of the smoke because he could feel it affecting him, and it wouldn't be long until he succumb to it.

"Twenty-five steps straight back the way you came should get us to the door," Amethyst said as her head rested heavily on his shoulder.

Tilting his face sideways he pressed a quick kiss to her forehead. "Hold on, okay?"

"You know me, I'm too tough to let a fire take me out," she said, but her voice was raspy, and she hung limply in his arms.

He started walking.

Counting as he went.

He was at twelve steps when a body suddenly appeared in front of him.

Curtis.

"Oh no, Detective," Curtis sing-songed, "you don't get to leave. You came in here, and now you get to die with us."

Arguing with the man was only going to waste time, time that Amethyst didn't have. Zeb was debating how he was going to juggle holding Amethyst while also pulling out his weapon when he felt a hand at his waist.

Amethyst pulled out his gun, raised it, and fired it.

Curtis dropped.

Just like that, the man was dead.

Clutching Amethyst tightly, Zeb staggered for the door.

As soon as he burst out into the fresh air his lungs seized, and he broke out into a hacking coughing fit.

Hands grabbed hold of him, dragged him away from the inferno, although he tried to hold onto her, Amethyst was pulled from his arms.

He tried to see who had taken her and where, but tears were streaming down his face, and his vision was blurry.

He was pushed down to sit on something, and an oxygen mask was put on his face. Zeb inhaled a few breaths, felt his lungs settle a little, then shoved it away and searched for Amethyst.

He saw her on a stretcher, she was lying still, an oxygen mask covered her face, and there were three EMTs bustling about her.

Unsteady on his feet, Zeb pushed away the well-meaning hands of whoever tried to hold him down. He had to get to Amethyst. He had to know if she was alive.

She'd just saved his life once again. Just when he thought he couldn't be more impressed with her, she managed to shoot a suspect while down with a concussion and smoke inhalation.

"Is she going to be okay?" he asked when he reached her.

The medics just shot him concerned looks and continued working.

Zeb grabbed Amethyst's hand and held it tightly. "You are not going to give up on me. Remember what you told me in the house? That you were too tough to let a fire take you out, you better not have been lying to me," he warned. "Because I don't want to lose you." Ignoring the medics who looked like they wanted to shoo him away so they could do their jobs, he leaned over Amethyst and touched his forehead to hers. "I can't lose you," he whispered, then pressed a kiss to her forehead.

"Sir, you're going to need to move away now, we need to get her to the hospital," one of the paramedics told him.

"No," came a weak but determined voice.

Amethyst's eyelashes fluttered on her sooty cheeks before her eyes opened slowly, seeking his. "I don't lie," she told him. "At least not to anyone but myself," she clarified with a small smile.

"I'll have to remember that," he said with a small smile of his own.

Lifting a hand, Amethyst batted away the medic's to pull the oxygen mask down. "You better kiss me now."

"I don't need to be told twice." Brushing his lips across Amethyst's, Zeb felt himself relax a hair. She still looked awful, but he was sure that she was going to be okay.

"Amethyst, we need to take you to the hospital now," one of the medics said, sounding exasperated.

"Fine, fine, Doug." She rolled her eyes at the man. "But Zeb comes too."

"Fine, fine," Doug shot back at her, and she rolled her eyes again.

Seeing Amethyst as her usual sassy self, eased away a little more of his fears. Nothing could hold this woman down, not her cold-hearted parents, not a psychopath like Nikos, not a narcissistic murderer, not a fire, nothing at all.

Holding her hand, Zeb walked beside the stretcher as the EMTs maneuvered it into the ambulance, not only was this woman amazing, but she was his.

CHAPTER
Eleven

August 29th
11:20 A.M.

"How're you feeling?"

"Terrible," Amethyst replied because she knew that wasn't the answer Zeb was expecting. And because it was true. Her head ached, her lungs felt like they had inhaled half the fire at the house yesterday, and it was now burning inside her, but there was no way she was spending another night in that awful place.

He turned to look at her, his honey-colored eyes concerned. "Do you need to go back to the hospital?"

"Of course not, doesn't everyone hate the hospital? I was just telling you the truth, did you want me to lie to you?"

"No, of course not," he said, returning his gaze to the road. "What I want is for you to promise me that you are never ever going to put yourself in a dangerous position ever again."

"So, you want me to quit my job and give up all of the sports I like?" She knew that wasn't what he really meant, but she needed him to admit it because she didn't want this to be an issue that stood between them.

"No, not exactly. I just don't like the idea of you in danger. From anything."

"I'm not going to stop being a firefighter because I love it, it's the perfect job for me, and I enjoy a lot of the sports that I do, but I can promise you something. I can promise you that I have a newfound respect for life, and I have something to live for now, and I will be as careful as it is humanely possible to be." That was true. Realizing that she had been taunting death all these years, and then coming so close to actually dying had made her accept just how much she wanted to live.

"I'll take it," Zeb said, reaching over to hold her hand. "So, you have something to live for, huh?"

"I didn't say it was a tall, dark, and handsome cop," she teased.

"I just assumed." He winked at her.

"Oh, you did, did you, Mr. Cocky?"

"I did, my sassy princess," he teased back. "Now once we get to your place, I want you to stay off your feet, I have everything set up in the living room, blanket, pillows, a tray so you don't have to eat at the table, I want you to just rest, you need something, you just ask."

"Do you always fuss like this?" she asked with a bemused smile. It was cute seeing her tough cop boyfriend turn into a mushy puddle of goo.

"Only when the woman I love is nearly burned alive."

Amethyst sucked in a breath. "Did I hear you right? Did you just call me the woman you love?"

"Is it too soon?" he asked. "I know we never mentioned the L-word, but when you were missing, and I realized there was a chance I might not get you back, I knew that it was true. I love you, but I know you want to take things slow and if that's too soon for you we can just pretend that I didn't say it."

"How can I pretend you didn't tell me you love me?" she huffed. It felt too soon, they'd only been dating not quite a week, and she had been determined that she wasn't going to rush things the way her sisters had. She wanted to take things slow, let them develop naturally. Oh, who was she kidding? "I love you too," she said, why hold it back when it *did* feel natural to say it?

"That means we're in love," Zeb sang happily.

"Are you really singing that?" she asked with a giggle, then winced as she erupted into a coughing fit that reminded her just how lucky she was to be alive.

"See, I knew you should have stayed in the hospital another few days. Like the doctor told you," he added with a reprimanding tone.

"I'm going to recover so much quicker at home, where I can sleep in my own bed, and rest without doctors and nurses buzzing around me all the time," she countered once the coughing eased enough that she could speak.

"Are you always going to be this stubborn?"

"Yep," she agreed cheerfully. "Hey, you wouldn't love me if I changed into a whole different person."

"I suppose you're right," he grumbled, but he couldn't hide his smile.

He was happy.

She was happy.

They made each other happy, and she was glad that she wasn't going to be stubborn about keeping things moving slowly when being together made them both enjoy life so much more.

Wasn't that the whole point of love?

Loving someone was about the two of you being stronger together, better together, challenging each other to be the best person that they could be, and being there no matter what. Through thick and thin, good and bad and worse, and everything in between.

"Looks like the welcome wagon is here," he said as he pulled into her driveway where several other cars were already parked.

"Guess you'll have to wait until later to have your way with me."

Zeb burst out into a hearty laugh. "Have my way with you?"

"You don't want to have your way with me?" she asked, mock offended.

"Oh, I do, but I love the way you phrased it. And not until you're all better anyway," he added. "You have a concussion remember, and smoke inhalation, you're supposed to be taking it easy for the next week, and that means no sex."

"No sex?" She pouted. "So nearly dying in a fire isn't enough, I have to be punished as well?"

"Maybe we can do a little something," Zeb relented.

"You're a pushover." She grinned.

"When it comes to you, always."

"Curtis told me some stuff before he died," she said, abruptly changing the topic because thoughts of the man she had killed had never been far from her mind. She knew she had done the right thing by shooting him, the only thing she could have done that meant she and Zeb survived, but that didn't mean she felt good about it. "He told me about how his mom abused him."

"His mom said the opposite, that he was a narcissist who didn't care about anyone and that he was the abusive one in the house."

"Who do you think was telling the truth?"

"I think," he said, turning in his seat and taking both of her hands, brushing his thumb across the back of her knuckles. "That you did the right thing. It doesn't matter if Curtis was a victim of abuse, that doesn't give him a free pass to kill. You did what you had to do for us to live. Curtis made his choices, and he knew that it was going to end in his death. I know it's hard, but don't beat yourself up over this."

"You're right," she agreed, knowing that there would probably be a little self beating up about it, but that Zeb wouldn't let her be too harsh on herself.

"Wait while I come around with the umbrella," Zeb told her.

The rain had finally come. In the early hours of the morning a storm had hit, rain, wind, thunder, and lightning, it had woken her from a deep sleep, and she had lain awake for hours listening to it while Zeb slept in a chair beside her bed.

"Hold onto my arm so you don't slip," Zeb told her as he opened her door and held the umbrella so it would cover her as she got out.

"I do know how to walk you know, Mr. Fussy," she reminded him as she got out of the car, but despite her words, she did take hold of his arm.

Together they walked down the front path, it was nice to have someone beside her, someone who wanted to be beside her, someone who wanted to be beside her forever.

Her family rushed around her as soon as they stepped through the front door. There were hugs and kisses, and of course a glare from her little sister.

"You know I'm pretty mad at you for what you did," Sapphire told her.

"I know," she said, smiling at her spitfire of a sister. She was lucky to have so many people who loved her enough to be angry that she would trade her life for another. "I also know that you would have done the exact same thing."

"I would have had a plan though," Sapphire grumbled.

"Of course you would," she agreed, giving her sister a hug. When Sapphire held on tightly she knew how worried her sister had been. "Where's that little snuggle bunny of yours, I need baby cuddles."

"Brooke has him."

"Here you go," Brooke handed her the baby as she sunk down onto the couch, glad to be off her feet. She was tired, and although she hated to admit it, she would need to take things easy for the next few days. "I'm grounded," Brooke told her, dropping down beside her on the couch. "And I have to babysit Archie the next two Friday and Saturday nights."

"Congratulations," she told the girl, who grinned back at her.

Zeb sat on her other side and settled her against his chest, she leaned into him, staring down at the sleeping baby in her arms.

A week ago she would have argued until she was blue in the face that she wasn't lonely, and that she didn't want what her sisters had.

But that had been a lie.

She wanted it.

She wanted this.

She wanted a family of her own, a husband, maybe an itty bitty baby like Leo, maybe they'd even go all out and have a bunch of kids and dogs and cats and bunnies, and as many other pets as they could fill their house with.

As Zeb's lips touched a kiss to her temple, she sighed with contentment.

She'd have all of those things, it wasn't a matter of if just of when, she was already off to a good start, she had a man who loved her, everything else would come when the time was right.

As teenagers they were sold to human traffickers, now the Hatcher sisters have to rebuild their lives. To find out what happened to Emerald Hatcher continue with book five in this gripping romantic suspense series now!

Splintered Emerald (Broken Gems #5)

Also by Jane Blythe

Detective Parker Bell Series

A SECRET TO THE GRAVE

WINTER WONDERLAND

DEAD OR ALIVE

LITTLE GIRL LOST

FORGOTTEN

Count to Ten Series

ONE

TWO

THREE

FOUR

FIVE

SIX

BURNING SECRETS

SEVEN

EIGHT

NINE

TEN

Broken Gems Series

CRACKED SAPPHIRE

CRUSHED RUBY

FRACTURED DIAMOND

SHATTERED AMETHYST

SPLINTERED EMERALD

SALVAGING MARIGOLD

River's End Rescues Series

COCKY SAVIOR

SOME REGRETS ARE FOREVER

SOME FEARS CAN CONTROL YOU

SOME LIES WILL HAUNT YOU

SOME QUESTIONS HAVE NO ANSWERS

SOME TRUTH CAN BE DISTORTED

SOME TRUST CAN BE REBUILT

SOME MISTAKES ARE UNFORGIVABLE

Candella Sisters' Heroes Series

LITTLE DOLLS

LITTLE HEARTS

LITTLE BALLERINA

Storybook Murders Series

NURSERY RHYME KILLER

FAIRYTALE KILLER

FABLE KILLER

Saving SEALs Series

SAVING RYDER

SAVING ERIC

SAVING OWEN

SAVING LOGAN

SAVING GRAYSON

SAVING CHARLIE

Prey Security Series

PROTECTING EAGLE

PROTECTING RAVEN

PROTECTING FALCON

PROTECTING SPARROW

PROTECTING HAWK

PROTECTING DOVE

Prey Security: Alpha Team Series

DEADLY RISK

LETHAL RISK

EXTREME RISK

FATAL RISK

COVERT RISK

SAVAGE RISK

Prey Security: Artemis Team Series

IVORY'S FIGHT

PEARL'S FIGHT

LACEY'S FIGHT

OPAL'S FIGHT

Prey Security: Bravo Team Series

VICIOUS SCARS

RUTHLESS SCARS

Christmas Romantic Suspense Series

CHRISTMAS HOSTAGE

CHRISTMAS CAPTIVE

CHRISTMAS VICTIM

YULETIDE PROTECTOR

YULETIDE GUARD

YULETIDE HERO

HOLIDAY GRIEF

Conquering Fear Series (Co-written with Amanda Siegrist)

DROWNING IN YOU

OUT OF THE DARKNESS

CLOSING IN

About the Author

USA Today bestselling author Jane Blythe writes action-packed romantic suspense and military romance featuring protective heroes and heroines who are survivors. One of Jane's most popular series includes Prey Security, part of Susan Stoker's OPERATION ALPHA world! Writing in that world alongside authors such as Janie Crouch and Riley Edwards has been a blast, and she looks forward to bringing more books to this genre, both within and outside of Stoker's world. When Jane isn't binge-reading she's counting down to Christmas and adding to her 200+ teddy bear collection!

To connect and keep up to date please visit any of the following

www.ingramcontent.com/pod-product-compliance
Lightning Source LLC
Chambersburg PA
CBHW031945240626
47153CB00003B/863